To Max and Oliver

'Lost causes are the only causes worth fighting for'

— *The Wheel Spins*, Ethel Lina White

'Well, now that we have seen each other,' said the Unicorn, 'if you'll believe in me, I'll believe in you, is that a bargain?'

— *Through the Looking-Glass*, Lewis Carroll

Friday, 23rd November

1

'Cutting it fine, aren't you?'

The ticket collector waiting at the bottom of the ramp down to platform 1 at Euston was a short, tanned woman with greying hair and at least three decades of don't-mess-with-me experience in her eyes. She glanced at the ticket in Jenny Bowen's outstretched hand before waving her through. Jenny shot her a sarcastic smile in response and hurried past onto the platform, the wheels of her case bumping and rattling on the surface as she ran for the nearest door on the first carriage.

Old-fashioned swing doors, not sliding. The kind you have to manually open and close. One of the crew was walking briskly along the platform towards her, shutting the doors at the ends of each carriage. She made it just in time and pulled her case onto the train.

'Thank fuck,' she sighed, a combination of relief and exhaustion.

The guard slammed the door, giving her a pointed look as he did so. The last-minute detour to the storage unit had been a mistake that had almost cost her not only her transport, but her bed for the night as well.

She wiped the sheen of sweat from her forehead and took a moment to tuck the stray strands of her hair back into her ponytail. She let out a long breath and watched the platform outside begin to slide by; painfully slowly at first, and then gradually picking up speed. The squeal of the wheels echoed off the roof of the station and then quietened as they emerged into the open.

Looking down at the ticket again for the number of her berth, she realised she had a long walk to her carriage, at the front of the train. She grabbed the handle of her case and started along the corridor.

It was perhaps only two feet wide, most of the available room being taken up by the sleeping compartments on her left-hand side. Her case banged against the wall in the tight space as she walked. She passed through the join into an all-seated carriage, about half-full with passengers getting settled in, some eating hastily grabbed dinners from Burger King or Pret. Then it was the lounge car, which was occupied by a mix-ture of lone individuals and small groups. Some of them were on the couches, others seated at the tables sipping a civilised nightcap, or perhaps just attempting to knock themselves out for the journey. A line came to her from a half-forgotten song. *All kinds of people, ridin' the rails.* All of them were here until morning, come what may.

Jenny had booked the sleeper on a whim. She had never travelled overnight before, always taking the regular Virgin West Coast service to Glasgow where her dad would pick her up and drive the rest of the way, or occasionally flying to Inverness. But she had always been curious to find out what the night train was really like.

It had a romantic allure: a night on the rails. Going to sleep in one place, waking up in a completely different one. Her life seemed to be changing at such an alarming rate that it seemed like a sensible idea to deliberately slow down, take the time to decompress.

Her idealised preconceptions, hazily assembled from memories of old paperbacks and black-and-white Hollywood movies, had taken a hit after a conversation with Hannah from the finance department at Wedgwood & Hart, a law firm to which she provided freelance IT support. Hannah, a strikingly tall Californian with hair colour that seemed to change on a weekly basis, was the only person of her acquaintance with first-hand experience of the journey.

'It's like sleeping in a moving broom closet, honey. Don't do it.'

It hadn't deterred her. As a student, Jenny had once made the trip south to London on the overnight Megabus, not sleeping a wink as she tried to brace herself in a position that meant the large flatulent man sitting next to her would be less likely to topple over in his sleep and crush her. She shuddered at the memory. Compared to that, the sleeper would be the lap of luxury.

Reaching the end of the lounge car, she squeezed past an elderly couple standing in the aisle in a flutter of mutual apologies, and crossed into carriage F.

Ahead, she saw her path was blocked by a woman who was using her back to prop open the door to her compartment. *Room*, rather. The man at the ticket office had corrected her. They called them rooms now, like in a hotel. She supposed that made them guests, rather than passengers.

The woman wasn't large, actually the opposite, but the narrow space meant Jenny would have to wait for her to get out of the way before passing. She was very thin, perhaps in her early forties. Her skin was pale, and her washed-out blonde hair was hanging around her face. She wore jeans and scuffed white trainers and a faded blue long-sleeved t-shirt under a thin leather jacket. Not warm weather clothes, but perhaps she had been running, like Jenny, and had stuffed her overcoat

5

in the case. She was the only person Jenny had seen on the train who looked more dishevelled than herself. She looked harassed, swearing under her breath as she tried to push down the pull-handle of her suitcase. It kept catching, the case over-stuffed.

Jenny noticed something grey and crumpled lying on the floor between herself and the woman. She stepped forward, bent, and picked it up.

It was a stuffed toy; a grey rabbit. It hung limply in her hand. The stitching under one of the arms was coming away, and some of the stuffing protruded. She had seen similar rabbits in interior design magazines, propped up on bookshelves and positioned on pillows in idealised children's bedrooms.

'Excuse me, did you—' The woman flinched at the sound of Jenny's voice and looked up from fiddling with the handle of her case. There were dark shadows under her eyes. She looked like she hadn't slept for a month. 'Did you drop this?' Jenny finished, holding the rabbit out.

The woman's eyes were grey; as washed-out as her hair and her skin and her shirt. Up close, Jenny could see she was much younger than she had first thought, maybe just in her late twenties, but with eyes older than her years. She murmured a thank you, dropping her eyes from Jenny's.

The woman finished pushing her case through into the room and followed it inside, reaching behind her to close the door hurriedly. As it swung shut, Jenny saw a young girl, no more than six or seven years old, with long, shiny brown hair. She wore a blue denim dress over a black long-sleeved t-shirt. She was holding out her hand for the stuffed rabbit. The little girl's eyes – dark brown, almost black – met Jenny's for a second before the door clicked shut.

Jenny looked back down the corridor and saw the way ahead was still blocked. A tall man, over six feet, had appeared without her hearing his approach. He was turning the handle of the room next to the woman's. He wore a long, black raincoat. His light-coloured hair was shaved so close to his scalp that it was impossible to tell if it was blond or prematurely grey. She smiled politely. He seemed to study Jenny for a second before nodding acknowledgement and stepping inside.

She sighed and gripped the handle of her case again. All kinds of people ridin' the rails, and apparently none of them felt any more sociable than she did. She passed another door, found room number 9 at last, and opened the door.

Hannah from Wedgewood & Hart had been wrong. Jenny had seen broom cupboards far more spacious than this.

The room was a tight rectangle, about six and a half feet across by five feet deep. There were two bunks to the left of the doorway with a small, three-runged ladder for accessing the top bunk. The man at the ticket counter had told her that lone passengers travelling standard class had to share with another passenger of the same sex when the train was full, but looking at the bookings he hadn't thought that was likely. Unless her potential room-mate had been even later than she had been, it looked like he was correct. There was a small stainless-steel sink beneath the window, with a wooden flap that folded down to make a table. There was a free magazine on the bed and bottle of spring water. The cover of the magazine advertised the new, modern carriages coming next year: *CHANGE IS COMING*. She tossed it under the bed, thinking she had already had more than enough change for one year.

The window was open a couple of inches, the rattle of the tracks loud in the small space. Jenny had to tug hard to get it to close. Eventually it obliged with a squeak, and the track noise quietened as a long row of Edwardian terraces flashed by, their lighted windows affording fleeting glimpses into a dozen other lives.

She turned back to survey her accommodation. It would do. The last few weeks had taken a lot out of her. She didn't foresee any problems in falling asleep, even on the bijou bunk. Turning to glance in the mirror, she saw that there was a door in the wall, leading through to the adjoining cabin. Gently, she tested the handle, and was relieved to find it was locked.

She flinched at the sound of a sharp knock, then realised it had come from the other door. When she opened it, she saw one of the train staff was outside. Or 'hosts' as his nametag had it. He was dressed as smartly as the others she had seen: a deliberately old-fashioned style of jacket over a dark green waistcoat, matching tie and white shirt. The slight artificiality of the uniform reminded her a little of the train guards at Disneyland in Paris.

'Evening ma'am. Name?'

Jenny smiled at the formality. He pronounced it like charm, not like jam. Which was the royal way again? She was hopelessly behind on *The Crown*.

'Bowen,' she said.

The host looked down at the tablet device in his hand and tapped a stylus on the screen a couple of times. He told her they'd be arriving at Fort William at nine-fifty-seven tomorrow morning. She declined to book breakfast. Years of staying in hotels for work had taught her there was no hospitality-industry breakfast that could beat an extra twenty minutes in bed.

After closing the door again and checking it was locked, she changed into her pyjamas and brushed her teeth at the sink. She found the USB socket for phone charging, oddly positioned at head height, over the sink, and plugged her phone in. She switched the room light off and climbed up into the top bunk. It had been a long day.

Typical. Now she was lying down, she didn't feel tired at all. Instead her mind kept turning, working away at the upheavals of the autumn. Eric's infidelity: suspected for months, years if she was honest, finally confirmed by the text message the idiot had accidentally sent to her rather than his girlfriend. And then, when she was just about coping with the fallout of that and moving out of the flat, her dad's fatal stroke, completely unexpected, and more wrenching than she could have predicted.

She switched on the night light beside the bed and climbed down to dig out the book she had been reading. The new Dennis Lehane paperback. One of her favourite authors, but she was finding it next to impossible to focus on anything right now. She turned a few pages before realising she hadn't taken any of it in. She gave up, closed the book and switched the light off again.

She kept thinking of the funeral. The brutal finality of the polished oak coffin. *Very high-end*, the funeral director had assured her, as though closing a sale on a new BMW. It felt like the end of more than one life. A matter of months before, she had been confident that she was on track; that she was where she needed to be in life. Now she was single, between homes, and an orphan at the age of thirty-five.

The mattress was more comfortable than she had expected. After a few minutes, she realised that the gentle rocking of the carriage, the hum of the wheels on the track, the sound of the air rushing past outside, was all having an effect. She didn't fight it. Slipped slowly, gratefully into sleep.

Dim early morning light, and a stillness that felt strange.

It took her a few seconds to orientate herself. As always, the bad memories came to her before anything else. Eric's brutally intimate text message. Her father's coffin. And then she remembered where she was, and where she was going. Only that wasn't entirely correct. She had no real idea of *exactly* where

9

she was. The train wasn't moving. A scheduled stop? She knew the train had to make different connections during the night, stretching the journey out over the five hundred miles, splitting the carriages for different legs. She fumbled for her phone and checked the time. They weren't due into Fort William for ages. The sky was only just beginning to lighten, and she remembered the dawn arrived almost an hour later this far north.

Her mouth was parched, and she needed to use the bathroom, so she climbed down from the bunk and took a swig from the complimentary bottle of water, grimacing at the tinny room-temperature taste. She considered digging in her case for her slippers, decided she couldn't be bothered. The train was half-empty going by what she had seen, with any luck the toilet wouldn't be disgusting. She opened the door and blinked in the harsh fluorescent light of the passageway. She focused on the sign above the windows directing her to the toilets and turned.

And froze.

The door to the room two down from hers was ajar.

It was wedged open by the limp hand and wrist of a woman.

Saturday, 24th November

2

'Here.'

Jenny looked up at the plastic cup of water that was being held in front of her face. The voice was calm, but the hand holding it was trembling slightly. She shook her head.

'Come on, have a drink.'

She looked up at the face of the guard. Host. He reminded her a little of an older version of Eric. Blue eyes, scruffy hair. His accent was pure Lancaster, though. She shrugged and accepted the cup, sipping. At least it was cold, unlike the bottle of water in her room. Christ, that had been ten minutes ago, it seemed like ten years. Talk about waking up in a different place.

Everything had been a blur since the moment she had opened the door to the other room. Trying to rouse the woman, checking for a pulse, before turning and running; almost colliding with the staff member coming in the opposite direction at the entrance to the next carriage. She had led him back to the room.

Every time she closed her eyes she saw the face of the dead woman. She had fallen, or collapsed, with her back on the floor, her arm stretching out and propping the door open. Had she tried to get out, tried to summon help, when she realised she had taken too much?

Jenny hadn't seen many dead bodies in her time, only her grandmother, but she knew the woman was gone before she felt for a pulse. She tried not to look at the belt around the arm, the spent needle lying by the woman's right hand. The track marks. Her skin hadn't been all the way cold yet.

'Police are on their way,' the host said, adding a strained smile as an afterthought. Jenny supposed it was a comforting thought for him. Right now, he was in charge of the situation, like it or not. The sooner he could hand it over to someone else, the better. 'I'm Colin, by the way.'

Instinctively, her eyes moved to his nametag for confirmation. 'Jenny,' she said automatically.

She was thirstier than she had thought. She drained the water and held the empty cup in both hands. They were in a small room at the end of the adjoining carriage. It was about the same size as the sleeping rooms, but it just had a single seat instead of a bed, and a microwave and some stainless steel cupboards on the opposite wall. The door was open, so she could hear hushed voices and movement outside as the other hosts asked passengers to stay behind their own doors.

The sky was getting lighter. Through the window, she could see a stretch of open ground before a thick forest, a shroud of mist lingering above the ground, mountains on the horizon.

She started to speak and had to clear her throat first.

'Where are we?'

'About five miles south of Rannoch,' Colin answered immediately. On more confident territory now.

'Why are we stopped?' Jenny asked. 'I mean, we were stopped before I ... before ...'

'Scheduled,' he replied. 'We always stop here for a few minutes.' He consulted his watch. 'Longer today, now. The passengers will be starting to wonder.' He shook his head. 'What a waste, eh?'

Jenny nodded.

'What makes someone do that? Put that ... rubbish in their arm?' He looked somewhere between bewildered and angry.

'I don't know. A lot of things, I suppose. People do it,' she said, thinking about the desperate look in the woman's eyes last night.

He shook his head again. 'Silly girl.'

Girl. The word sparked a memory. The woman hadn't been alone last night. Jenny felt an almost physical jolt at the realisation that the little girl with the brown hair and the stuffed rabbit had lost her mother. But she hadn't been in the room with the body. Had she gone to get help?

'Is the little girl all right?' Jenny asked, the shock starting to settle into a dull ache in her stomach. 'I mean, someone else is with her, right?'

Colin's brow creased, and he studied Jenny's face, as though translating a foreign tongue.

'What?'

'The girl. The little girl who was travelling with her?'

Her question hung in the air for a long moment. Before he spoke the three words, Jenny knew exactly what he was going to say.

'What little girl?'

3

'Watch the potholes.' Detective Inspector Gregory Porter spoke absentmindedly as he finished tapping out an email on his phone.

Sergeant Mike Fletcher glanced over at his superior. He didn't know why he was bothering with that out here. It would only sit in his outbox for the next couple of hours.

'In case you hadn't noticed, boss, this road is about eighty per cent potholes.'

The road had seemed to narrow by half when they had covered a mile of it; the untamed hedges on either side encroaching onto the rutted surface. It was so narrow it would have been difficult for two cars to pass one another. Luckily no one else had any reason to be using it at this time of the morning.

'It's not too far from the bridge,' Mike said, glancing at the open road atlas on the dashboard, finding the spot where the railway line intersected with the road they were on.

'It better bloody not be,' Porter said. 'These are new boots.'

Mike saw it in the distance, a stone hump-backed bridge rising abruptly from the road. There was a wide spot just before the rise to allow one car to wait while another passed. Mike pulled into the space at the side of the road and got out. The air was bitingly cold outside after the heated interior. He

16

had noticed that ever since Afghanistan, the cold just seemed to get to him more. The sky was dark and overcast, but there was a dull glow on the crests of the mountains to the east, like someone had switched on a low-wattage bulb behind them.

Mike popped the boot and grabbed an overcoat, a torch, and a preliminary evidence pack, just in case the CSE was held up. He had been looking forward to an uneventful last hour of his shift, followed by the big breakfast at Curly's, a hot shower and bed. Those modest expectations had been dashed by the call from Bryden back at the station. Fatality aboard a train, with a location.

Mike was grateful for one thing. The location told him this likely wasn't a suicide on the tracks. A good few miles from the nearest station, probably at least as far from the nearest dwelling. Mike was fairly new to this posting, but he had already attended a couple of code 233s. He still had no idea what would drive somebody to jump in front of a train, but experience told him they didn't generally walk miles out of their way to do it.

It was out of the ordinary, though. Very early in the day for any kind of incident. There just weren't that many passenger trains heading north at this time in the morning. Thinking about it, he realised it had to be the sleeper. The overnight from London, due into Fort William around ten. Heart attack, probably. Some poor bastard popping his clogs in his sleep.

He and Porter had been assisting a driver who had broken down on a level crossing when the call came in. Looking at the time, he had briefly considered asking if there was anybody closer. Anybody not at the end of his shift. But he knew the answer; if Bryden had called them, it was because they were nearest. That was procedure. Nearest officer attends an incident, regardless of rank. That was because the clock was already ticking, and every second counted.

17

As Porter was getting out, his radio crackled. He sat back in the seat and gestured for Mike to go on ahead.

Mike walked to the crest of the bridge and looked north along the tracks towards Rannoch, then south. There it was. Perhaps a quarter of a mile distant, mostly obscured by trees and the curve in the track, was the front of the train, stopped on the rails. He strapped on the backpack, picked his way down the embankment and stepped onto the tracks.

When he had got within a hundred yards of the train, the door of the driver's cab opened and a guard got out wearing an orange hi-vis anorak, waving a hand at Mike. He was tall and broad, with a full head of grey hair.

'Morning.'

'I've had better,' Mike said. 'Sergeant Mike Fletcher.'

He didn't offer his hand, but took the guard's when he did.

'Bill Morley.' He was in his fifties, bald, Glasgow accent.

Mike glanced at his watch and noted the time. He turned back the way he had come and saw no sign of Porter. He pushed the button on his radio and called the time in to Bryden. Bryden acknowledged and told him the crime scene examiner was on their way.

'Clock's ticking,' the guard remarked, echoing Mike's exact thoughts a few minutes before. He knew the drill, then. 'After you.'

Mike nodded as he stepped up into the carriage. Accident, suicide, assault, heart attack; it was all the same to the clock. They had a ninety-minute window to process the scene and get the train moving again. A hold-up in one part of the system could have knock-on effects everywhere else, which meant somebody somewhere would lose money. Things came to a respectful pause for the dead, but only for a strictly defined time limit. Mike knew it wasn't exactly an ideal structure in which to carry out a police investigation, but from what he'd seen so far, it seemed to work. Maybe the clock focused minds, meant no one involved could forget it was game time. And at least it was a Saturday morning: fewer pissed-off commuters to worry about.

'Deceased is in F, another two down,' Morley said, in a tone that was professionally respectful, but not shocked or upset. The guy looked like a lifer, no doubt he saw worse a few times a year.

Mike had never been aboard a sleeper train, and though it shouldn't have surprised him, he found the narrow corridor running alongside the sleeping compartments a little tight. It accommodated his frame, but it made him want to walk sideways.

'Any idea what happened?' Mike said without looking back.

'Looks like an overdose.'

'Pills? Heroin?'

'Needle, so ...'

Mike nodded and slowed as they entered carriage F and he saw another guard, this one younger and female, standing outside one of the doors.

'Do you have a name?' he said.

'Oh, for the deceased? Yes, I suppose you'll need that,' Morley said, his footsteps stopping. Mike stopped and glanced back at him. Morley had produced a small tablet-size device about the size of a Kindle. He tapped the screen a few times.

'Sara Lee,' he said. 'Don't know if it's Sah-ra or Say-ra, there's no H.'

'Sara Lee like the cakes?'

It took Morley a second to get the reference and he shrugged. 'I suppose.'

Mike frowned. It didn't necessarily mean it was a fake name, but trains weren't like aeroplanes. You could pay cash and be whoever you wanted to be on the booking.

'Okay,' he said, addressing the female guard. 'Open it up, please.'

The body lay across the floor of the room, her left arm stretched out as though reaching for something. She was clad in white briefs and a vest top. One glance at the woman told him Morley was probably correct about the cause of death. It wasn't just the paraphernalia either, the thin belt tied around her upper arm, the needle loosely resting in the fingers of her right hand. It was there in the pale, almost translucent colour of her skin. The way Mike knew that if he wanted to, he could kneel down, tuck one arm underneath her torso, and lift her body off the floor without too much effort.

He knelt down in the cramped space and put two fingers against her neck, knowing it was a formality. She felt cold, but not all the way cold. He raised his eyes to scan the other contents of the room. There was a grey canvas backpack stuffed in the corner, nothing else that looked like it didn't belong.

'Are the compartments all this small?' he asked as he adjusted the position of his finger on the carotid.

'Rooms,' Morley said. 'We call them rooms now, it's a branding thing ...' He trailed off as Mike looked up at him. 'Sorry, yes, all the same.'

'You have a paramedic on board, anyone like that?'

'We're all first-aid trained,' Morley said. 'Lynne here checked for life signs.'

Mike looked up at the younger guard. Her eyes looked slightly red, though she was composed. She lacked Morley's years of desensitisation. 'Lynne ...?' he began.

'Lynne Sinclair.'

Mike committed the name to memory. 'Did you move the body, Lynne?'

She shook her head. 'Not really. I mean, her arm was poking

out the door,' she pointed down at the stretched-out arm, 'so we had to move that, but nothing else.'

'Her arm?'

'That's how the lady found her. The door was ajar because her hand was sticking out.'

Mike straightened up and stepped back into the corridor, examining the doorway. It opened inwards. Had she been trying to get help?

The sound of a familiar voice made him look back the way he had come. Porter was emerging from the next cabin. His paunch led the way, jutting out in defiance of the two buttons fastened on the jacket he wore underneath his overcoat.

'Sergeant Fletcher. Good to see you have the matter in hand. What have you got for me?'

Mike turned back to the room and took a couple of snaps of the body in situ on his phone. It was hard to get a good angle in the space. 'Name on the booking was Sara Lee, if you can believe that. Certainly looks like an OD.'

Mike actually felt the warmth of Porter's sigh on his neck as he moved in closer to get a good look. He turned and saw from the look on Porter's face that it was a sigh of irritation, rather than sadness at the human condition.

'Junkie. At least this won't take long. NHI, Sergeant.'

'NHI?' The letters rang a bell.

'No humans involved.'

Mike suppressed the urge to roll his eyes. He had learned a long time before his current career that open disrespect for superiors was never a good idea, even when those superiors richly deserved it. Instead he composed his features and turned back to the two guards on the other side of the doorway. The carriage was starting to feel a little crowded.

'Anybody speak to the deceased last night?'

Morley nodded. 'I checked her in myself.'

'How does that work?'

'We greet them when they come on board, show them to their room, take their breakfast order if they want it.'

'You do breakfast?' Porter's interest was suddenly piqued.

'Just a bacon roll. Tea or coffee. Or orange juice.'

'What does check-in involve?' Mike pressed.

'We check their tickets, make sure they get to the right room, tick them off the list.' He raised the tablet device to show the name. It was on a list with other names tagged against room numbers. From a cursory glance, Mike could see that the carriage had been about half-full.

'Can you give me a copy of this list? We'll need to speak to the other passengers.' One of the benefits to a situation like this. Potential witnesses stayed put, whether they liked it or not.

Porter folded his arms, in the manner of a senior mechanic inspecting a shoddy oil change by a green apprentice. 'A word, Sergeant Fletcher?'

They stepped to one side and the two train staffers moved a respectable distance down the carriage.

Porter lowered his voice. 'I don't think we need to go to too much trouble on this one, Sergeant. It's not exactly a head-scratcher. Let's get the departed attended to, and these people can depart for their own destinations.'

The ticking clock. Mike knew what Porter was thinking. If that response time averaged out below ninety minutes for the quarter, he would be left alone come reporting week. The Q3 average was currently a little over, so a quick resolution on this one would be in everyone's interests.

But on the other hand, Porter couldn't reprimand him for doing his job. Mike couldn't help enjoying the fact it wound the older man up too. Mike looked back at the staffers and raised his voice. 'We'll need to look at your CCTV, of course,' he said as he scanned the ceiling for the usual electronic eye.

Morley shook his head.

'What?' Mike asked.

'These carriages have been in service since the early eighties, Sergeant. Oldest rolling stock in Britain. No CCTV, no wifi, no air con.'

'Seriously?'

Morley gave a knowing smile, as though Mike was the hundredth cop he'd had to break this to. He probably was.

'Closest thing you'll find to a time machine. It'll be different next year, when they bring the new carriages online.'

'You'll have to forgive my young colleague,' Porter said with a smirk. 'He doesn't remember police work before there were *apps*.'

Porter's radio crackled. He gave his call sign and told them to go ahead. It was the crime scene examiners. Here already and boarding the train. He consulted his watch approvingly. A well-oiled machine.

Mike turned back to Lynne, the female guard, as he was speaking. 'You said a woman found her. Where is she?'

Morley answered for Lynne, angling his head in the opposite direction to the way they had come. 'We've got her down there, in the hosts' room. That's where we can get a break during the night, prep the breakfasts and so on.'

Mike ignored the way Porter's ears pricked up at the second mention of breakfast. Morley told Lynne to go and check on the witness.

'Anyone else see the body?' Mike asked him.

'Not that we know of. We asked the other passengers to stay put.'

Mike moved to step out into the corridor, but Porter put a hand on his arm. 'Tell you what, I'll deal with it. You help the techs out and I'll give you a shout if I need you.'

Mike started to object, then remembered his golden rule: choose your battles.

'Fine by me, boss.'

He heard footsteps approaching and turned to see Lynne. She looked a little more rattled than before.

'What's wrong?' Mike asked as she reached them.

'The lady who found the body earlier, Colin's been talking to her, and she ...'

'Yes?'

Lynne pointed at the doorway, reluctant to look directly into the room. 'She says she wasn't alone in there. The dead woman.'

'What?'

'She says there was a child with her.'

4

After the female host turned and headed back to tell the police, Jenny looked back at Colin, who was examining the screen of the tablet device she had seen earlier with a frown.

'Are you sure you saw a kid in that room?'

'Yes, absolutely sure.'

'It's just, there's only the one person checked in. Adult ticket.'

'Maybe she didn't have a ticket?'

Colin was shaking his head, but before he could answer, the door opened. A man in a grey suit stepped in, shooting them a wary look. He was in his mid-fifties, noticeably overweight, with ruddy cheeks and greying hair. Jenny knew he was a cop before he produced his warrant card and waved it perfunctorily at them.

'What's the story?' He directed the question abruptly at Colin, his tone reminding Jenny of one of the less-pleasant teachers at her school.

'The lady says the woman had a child in with her.'

'A girl,' Jenny said. 'Maybe six or seven.'

'So where is she?'

Colin opened his mouth to say something, but the officer had already turned to address someone in the corridor. Jenny couldn't see who it was from inside the room.

'Mike – go with Lynne here down to the bottom of the train, knock on all the doors. We'll take this end. We're looking for a girl, six or seven . . .' He turned to look expectantly at Jenny. It took her a second to realise he was waiting for a description. She took a second to gather her thoughts.

'Dark brown hair, blue denim dress, about this high,' she said, holding her hand at the girl's approximate height.

'Dark hair, three foot nine, blue dress. Got that?'

Jenny heard an acknowledgement and the sound of two sets of footsteps hurriedly retreating back the way they had come.

'You two, follow me.'

Colin explained that the train had six carriages in all, after it had split from the Aberdeen and Inverness services at Edinburgh. Jenny, Colin and the police officer who off-handedly introduced himself as Detective Inspector Porter walked through each of them, looking in vain for the girl with dark hair. Four sleeper carriages, one seated, one lounge car. There was no sign of her. No sign of anyone but the occasional bleary-eyed passengers they encountered making their way to the toilets at either end of each carriage. Jenny noticed that the urgency drained out of Porter's attitude as soon as Colin mentioned there had only been a single adult checked into the room.

They went through the same routine for each room. A knock on the door, sometimes followed by a passenger opening the door, sometimes by silence. When the room was down as empty on the list, Colin would use his key to unlock the door and confirm there was no one inside. Colin did most of the talking while DI Porter hung back, scrutinising each passenger's face in between glances at his watch. The same routine each time. A passenger has become unwell, we hope to be underway soon. We're looking for a child who may be missing. Blank looks, again and again. The advantage of the small rooms was that it was possible to see every occupant as soon as the doors were opened. There was nowhere for someone to hide, even a small child.

It took them twenty minutes to cover the whole of the train. No sign of the girl.

'Satisfied?' Porter asked her, not bothering to hide his irritation.

'What do you mean, satisfied?'

He glanced at his watch again. 'You were mistaken,' Porter said. He was opening his mouth to say something else when the radio clipped to his belt crackled. He held it to his mouth and acknowledged. Jenny heard a voice on the other end, and assumed it was the colleague Porter had directed to check the rest of the train.

'No sign. Staff say there wasn't a kid in the room.'

'That's my information too,' Porter said, glancing at Colin. He turned to look at Jenny, raising his eyebrows as if to say, 'Well?'

'Where could she have gone?' Jenny said, looking from Porter to Colin.

'I think you must have got mixed up,' Colin said gently. 'There's nowhere else to look. Unless she got out and walked.'

'Could she do that?'

'It was a joke,' Colin said, shaking his head. 'We need to open the doors, they're locked during travel.'

Porter's radio buzzed again. 'Go ahead.'

The same voice on the other end. 'I'll take a look outside.'

'No need, Sergeant. It's a misunderstanding.'

A pause. 'Are you sure?'

'False alarm.'

Porter clipped the radio back to his belt and gestured to the door to the host's station. 'Shall we?'

27

Jenny allowed herself to be crowded into the room, but turned to face Porter as soon as he followed her in. 'Listen, I know what I saw.'

Porter closed the door and leaned against it. 'You've had a traumatic experience, don't worry about it. I do need to take some details, starting with your name.'

'Jenny,' she said. 'Jenny Bowen. I really think—'

Porter held a hand up. 'Wait a minute.'

Jenny stopped talking, immediately feeling a flush of irritation at herself for obeying, as well as at Porter for ordering.

He turned to Colin.

'Why don't you rustle us up a couple of bacon rolls and coffees? The lady's had a shock.'

'I'm fine, thanks.'

'Milk and three,' Porter added, cutting across her. He turned to face her again, producing a black square-bound notepad and a pen. 'You can sit down if you want. I understand you were the—'

'There's a little girl missing, we need to find her.'

'The deceased was travelling alone, by all accounts. Only one person booked in. If you don't mind, I have to ask you some questions.'

'Shouldn't we . . .'

Porter didn't look up, just carried on as though she hadn't said anything. 'Take me through it from the start. What made you leave your room?'

'We need to keep looking,' Jenny said firmly. 'I told you, the woman had a child with her.'

Porter looked up. His expression and tone of voice said he thought he was talking to someone very slow-witted. 'But there was no child in that compartment.'

'No ticket,' she corrected. 'So what? I think this is a bit urgent, don't you?'

Porter seemed to consider it for a moment, and then put his notepad down. 'After you got checked in, did you do anything else last night?'

Jenny wondered why he was interested in her whereabouts all of a sudden. Surely he couldn't be suggesting she had something to do with what had happened?

'No. Yesterday was a very long day, I went straight to bed. Why?'

'Maybe a night cap before bed? A drink or two in the lounge car? To unwind. After your long day.'

So that was it. A nice easy way of discounting what she had seen. She spoke clearly and deliberately. 'No. I didn't have anything to drink other than water. I'm not making this up.'

'So if I ask the staff in the lounge car, they won't have seen you last night?'

'Do you want to breathalyse me, Officer?'

'Detective Inspector,' he corrected. They stared at each other for a few moments, the mutual dislike almost tangible.

His radio crackled again. This time it was a female voice. 'All clear for removal.'

He didn't take his eyes off Jenny. 'I'll be there in a second.'

'Good news,' he said in answer to Jenny's questioning look. 'We're clear to remove the body. That means we can get off this bloody train and do the rest of it somewhere else.'

5

Two hours later, Jenny was in the well-preserved Victorian waiting room at Rannoch Station. There was a tea room on the platform as well, although a sign on the door said it was closed for a family wedding. There were maps and placards along the wood-panelled walls of the waiting room outlining the history of the West Highland Line. A Robert Louis Stevenson quotation about the vast moor it crossed: '*A wearier-looking desert man never saw.*' One for the tourist board.

Rannoch was the next station on the line, and after the train started up again, Porter explained they could alight and take her full statement here. He handed her over to a younger PC waiting for them at the station, who introduced himself as Bryden. He had taken her statement about discovering the body, but only after she made him assure her that they were checking the CCTV at Euston to see if anyone matching the girl's description had boarded.

After he left, she had gone out onto the platform to have a look around. There were no other passengers. If there had been, they would have been waiting for a long time. Rannoch Station was a dozen miles from the nearest village, and PC Bryden had mentioned that only four trains stopped here a day. Rannoch Moor stretched out to the west, with a loch and the mountains in the distance. The single-track line stretched out in either direction, the iron rails quiet for hours at a time. It was unsettling. She had become so accustomed to the constant visual busyness of London that the fact nothing and no one was obstructing her view felt somehow unnatural. She was struck by how utterly the character of the landscape seemed to change with the movements of the clouds, which occasionally broke to let a shaft of sunlight through.

She went back into the waiting room and checked her phone. There was no signal at all: phone or internet. If the police somehow forgot about her, it would be a long wait. She had been left to stew for the better part of an hour when she heard a car pull up at the car park across the bridge. She had heard the engine getting louder for a couple of minutes now, because the silence was almost perfect.

The door of the waiting room opened and a man entered, late thirties, early forties by the look of him. In contrast to DI Porter, he looked in good shape. He was dressed in uniform, black stab-vest over a black t-shirt, white chevrons on his left shoulder. He had dark hair, greying very slightly at the temples. He was carrying a tablet and a sheet of paper. He was staring at the paper as he entered, then looked up and met her eyes.

'Ms. Bowen?'

'Jenny.' She had always been a first-name person, even before things had soured with *Mr* Bowen.

He offered his hand.

'Sergeant Mike Fletcher. Thank you for bearing with us. It's much appreciated.'

She remembered that Mike had been the name of the guy Porter had been ordering about on the train. She accepted the handshake. Firm, but not bone-crushing. His accent was one of those neutral ones, difficult to place. Like a newsreader.

31

'Anything?' she asked, as he sat down across from her.

He removed his hat and placed it on the table, shaking his head. 'You're absolutely sure you saw a child in the room? You couldn't have been mistaken?'

'I told your colleague. There was a stuffed toy on the floor, she must have dropped it. I handed it to the woman and when she went into the room, that's when I saw her.'

Sergeant Fletcher looked down at the sheet of paper again. 'Six or seven years old, dark hair, brown eyes, blue denim dress.'

'Yes, I saw her as clearly as I'm seeing you.' Jenny kept the irritation out of her voice with an effort of will. This was the fourth person she had given the story to in the last three hours.

Fletcher glanced down at the paper again and nodded slightly.

'They double checked the bookings, and I had them check again,' he said. 'There were only two children under sixteen aboard the train, according to the system. Both accounted for.'

'So they say.'

Fletcher put the paper down on the table and stared at it for a moment, as though it might be hiding some information from him. 'Not impossible that a child could have been travelling without a ticket though, I suppose.'

The comment caught Jenny off-guard. After the fruitless search, she had got the feeling patience was starting to wear thin. The police had enough on their plate with a sudden death on the train, without her throwing in an extra loose end. But the fact Sergeant Fletcher was even willing to consider the possibility she wasn't mistaken was reason for optimism. Cautious optimism.

Fletcher rubbed an ache out of his neck and sat down across the table from Jenny.

'Sometimes relatives board the train to see someone else off.

Could that have been what happened? She got off before it left Euston?'

Jenny shook her head. 'We were already moving before I saw them.'

'Another station then? Preston, Glasgow perhaps?'

'Why would she get off without her mother, though?'

'Are you sure the woman was her mother?'

Jenny shrugged. 'I mean I just ...' She didn't want to finish the sentence with the words, *Just assumed*. After verbally fencing with DI Porter earlier, she was wary of her words being turned against her.

Fletcher tapped a button to wake the tablet and turned the screen so she could see it. 'CCTV is a wonderful thing, usually. None on the train, unfortunately, because it's a relic. But there was on the platform.' He cued up a video and hit play. It showed a grainy colour view of the platform at Euston. There was a time stamp in the corner. As she watched, a familiar figure boarded, next to the camera. It took her a second to recognise herself.

Fletcher closed the window and played another clip. This one showed a different angle. Jenny squinted and recognised the hair and clothes of the woman she had seen, hurrying to the door on carriage F.

She was alone.

The time stamp said 21:11, a couple of minutes before Jenny herself had boarded.

She looked up at Fletcher. 'I know what I saw.'

He stared back at her. His green eyes were inscrutable. She remembered that he probably did this a dozen times a week. Listened to a story and had to decide whether to believe it.

'Then we have a mystery,' he said at last. 'The train arrived at Euston platform one at around eight o'clock, empty of course. The sleeper only makes one journey a day. The first passengers

33

boarded at ten past. The passengers boarding between eight-ten and nine-fifteen match the booked tickets. There are two under sixteens – a ten-year-old boy and a toddler. There's no one on the tape who could be the girl you saw.'

He had avoided saying, the girl you *think* you saw. Jenny was grateful for that, even if she didn't like the way the conversation was going.

'I suppose you've checked the other stops too?'

He nodded. 'A much quicker job, less than three minutes at each station. Hardly anyone gets off in the middle of the night; most passengers are on for the long haul. Eight passengers got off total ...'

'... none of them a little girl,' Jenny finished.

Fletcher looked back at her with an expression of mild sympathy.

'Do you know who she was, yet?' Jenny asked. 'The woman in the room, I mean.'

He didn't say anything for a moment, then looked down at the sheet of paper again. 'There was no ID on the body, which was a little odd, but her fingerprints were in the system. Her name was Emma Elizabeth Dawson.' He paused and looked at her to see if she recognised the name. When she showed no reaction, he continued. 'It wasn't the name she was travelling under.'

'Isn't that suspicious?'

'Unusual, perhaps,' he said after a moment. 'But it doesn't necessarily mean anything in itself.' He looked down at the paper. 'She was twenty-nine, grew up in Stockwell. Parents both deceased. No siblings. No children.'

'No children?'

He shook his head.

'So, what happened?' Jenny asked, adding, 'I mean, I can guess,' as the image of the body flashed before her eyes,

34

close-ups of the needle and the belt around her left arm.

'There will be a post-mortem,' Fletcher said. 'But she had a history of substance abuse.'

'She has a record?'

'Yes. That's why we had her prints. Nothing major, but she had had a few run-ins with our colleagues down south. The real history is all over her arms, old track marks.'

'No children,' Jenny repeated again.

'No.'

They sat in silence for a long moment.

'I don't know what you want me to say.'

Fletcher considered. 'I don't want you to say anything. I just wanted to talk to you and assure you we had looked into this. We've gone back to the other passengers to ask if they remember seeing a little girl. None of them do.'

Suddenly, she remembered there had been one other person in the corridor last night. She couldn't remember if he had been one of the people they spoke to when knocking doors. She didn't think so; he was fairly memorable.

'Did you speak to the man in the room next to them?'

Fletcher took a second to process the question. 'I didn't carry out all the interviews. Which man?'

She told him about the tall man in the black overcoat. He probably couldn't have seen the little girl from that angle, but . . .

Fletcher noted it down. 'You say he was in the room next to the woman?'

'Yeah. The one between me and her.'

'So that would make it . . . eight.' He noted down the number and circled it. 'I'll make sure we've spoken to him.' He didn't sound massively optimistic.

Jenny closed her eyes and rubbed the side of her head, where she could feel a migraine coming on. A long, traumatic few weeks of emotional upheaval followed by a night of uneasy sleep on the train, followed by the horror of the morning's discovery. She didn't doubt Fletcher was here in the capacity of Good Cop, but even so, she felt reassured that someone had been looking into it.

She thought about it from their point of view. Perhaps she couldn't really blame the police for being annoyed that she had introduced an additional complication by reporting a missing girl who seemed either to have vanished into thin air, or to never have existed at all.

Fletcher seemed to sense what she was thinking and moved the conversation on to a different tack.

'You're up here visiting friends?'

Fletcher had probably looked up her address. As far as the world was concerned, she still resided at the flat in Highbury. Jenny shook her head. 'No. My dad lives ... lived up here. He passed away a few weeks ago.'

'I'm sorry,' he said automatically.

'It's fine,' she responded, just as automatically. 'Massive stroke. Coming for a long time, he never had the healthiest lifestyle. So I'm back up here for a while, just until I can get things organised with the house.' Because there was no one else to get things organised, of course. She was an orphan now; the last of her line. Just like Emma Elizabeth Dawson.

'And then ... back home?'

'Yes. No ... It's complicated.'

Fletcher raised an eyebrow.

'I've recently separated from my husband. I've moved out, so actually it's worked out quite well.' She caught herself. 'I mean, not my dad dying of course.'

'I know.'

'I'm taking a kind of half-sabbatical from work.'

'Compassionate leave?'

She shook her head. 'I'm a keep-busy sort. And I can actually do most of the job from home, so I'll be checking in, in between everything else.'

'What do you do?'

'I'm a software dev. Freelance. I develop and manage systems, do some general support here and there.'

'Self-employed?'

She nodded. 'I like working on my own. Suits me.'

'And you can do that from home?'

'I can do it from anywhere. Anywhere there's an internet connection, anyway.'

He looked amused. 'That may be a bigger challenge than you think, in this neck of the woods.'

She returned the smile, wondering if this was her first genuine one in weeks.

'Sounds like you've had a rough time of it, the last while.'

Her smile vanished. 'What are you implying?'

He sighed. 'I'm not suggesting you're making this up, it's just ...'

'Just what?'

He sat back in his chair, looking annoyed with himself, and knitted his hands together around the back of his neck, looking up at the ceiling. 'I have an active caseload. We cover most of the Highlands, which is ten thousand square miles, fifty stations. Everything to do with the transport network is on us. I have a dead woman on a train who appears to have overdosed by accident or killed herself. I have my boss on my back about targets and paperwork and whatever else crosses his mind. And now you've given me a mystery. But without CCTV, without a corroborating witness ...'

'You can't do anything,' she finished.

Fletcher considered before answering. 'Not quite. I can make some calls. I'm waiting to hear if anyone's reported a girl of that age and description missing. I can promise to let you know if I turn anything up.'

'But I shouldn't hold my breath.'

He gave her a sympathetic look, not disagreeing.

'You look tired. I hear that train can be a rough night's sleep.'

She shrugged. 'It wasn't too bad. To be honest, it's more the rough few weeks beforehand.'

'I can imagine. We can't do anything else today, grateful as we are for your help. You said you were staying at your father's house?'

'It's outside Bridge of Dean, near Fort William. Can I get a train from here?'

'Sure, I think the next one's due in about ...' He consulted his watch. 'Eighteen months.' He dug in his pocket and pulled out a car key. 'I'll drive you. Least I can do.'

6

Fort William was only thirty miles or so from Rannoch as the crow flies, but eighty by the quickest road, which wound lazily east and then north around the Grampians. Fletcher drove fast. Slightly faster than Jenny, used to the glacial pace of city traffic, was comfortable with. The sky was thickly overcast, the clouds thinking of rain.

They made light conversation on the drive, not talking much about the tragedy that had brought the two of them into contact, or the circumstances which had brought Jenny here in the first place.

'Have you always lived around here?' she asked, flinching as a silver 4x4 flashed by in the opposite lane, seeming to come within inches of them.

He shook his head. 'Only for a few years.'

'Where are you from originally?'

He had to think about it. 'All over, you'd have to say. My dad moved around a lot for work. I was born in Oxford, moved to Edinburgh when I was eight, Germany for a while, America for a bit after that. Then the army for ten years.'

That explained the accent, or lack of one. Jenny had been told her own accent was similarly rootless. Understandable anywhere. A citizen of nowhere, in the modern parlance.

'So why here?'

He shrugged. 'I did ten years. Three tours in Afghanistan. After that, I just wanted to spend some time somewhere quiet and green. This fit the bill.'

Jenny looked out of her window and watched the country-side as it flashed past at sixty miles an hour: fields of brown cows, cleared patches of woodland with new markers staked for the next generation, white and orderly like war graves. Then straight ahead: sweeping hills, the cloud-draped peak of Ben Nevis looming in the distance. She could see the attraction. She might not have the motivation of having seen combat, but she understood the urge to find a quiet place to decompress for a while.

Fletcher guided the wheel around for a wide curve to the right and Jenny noticed a frayed blue-grey strip of fabric around his left wrist. She didn't say anything, but she thought it looked out of place with the picture she had been building of Sergeant Fletcher. A policeman and a soldier. Clean cut, comfortable in uniforms. The wrist band seemed a little ... hippyish? She turned to look out of her window again and watched the fenceposts at the side of the road whip past for a while, the trees and mountains in the background rolling past more sedately.

They turned off the A86 a few miles from Fort William and reached Bridge of Dean ten minutes later. The battered sign said it welcomed careful drivers. Fletcher slowed down to forty. They passed through the village and Jenny counted off the familiar landmarks: the old church, the swing park where the teenagers had hung out in her day and probably in this day too, the Spar at the end of the main street that had once been an ice cream parlour. Always the same feeling when she returned: familiarity, tinged with sadness that everything looked a little more shop worn and down-at-heel than she remembered.

'Just say when.'

Jenny told him to keep going. The house wasn't within the village itself, but about half a mile beyond the north edge of it.

They rounded the last bend in the road and Crossan Lodge came into view. A wide, two-storey farmhouse with white-washed walls and a steep shingle roof. The stables behind it had been converted to guest rooms. There was a red wooden porch with a pointed roof at the front door. Her parents had been running it as a guest house for years, but her dad had 'put it on hold' after her mum had died. It sat on twelve acres of ground, with a pine forest and the hills behind it. Jenny's most recent visit before the funeral had been last Christmas. There had been eighteen inches of snow on the ground, and the house looked like a greeting card.

It didn't look like one right now. As they approached the dark building under a slate-grey sky, it looked more like a haunted house: abandoned and unloved. The grass was in dire need of a cut, and her dad's black Ford Ranger was still parked on the drive outside, a hardened crust of mud on the sills.

'Is there anyone here for you?' Fletcher asked as the gravel crunched under the tyres of the car.

'No,' Jenny said. 'No one.'

To dispel the uncomfortable silence that followed, Jenny held out her hand. 'Thank you for the lift, Sergeant Fletcher.'

They shook hands again. 'Mike.'

She smiled, having guessed correctly that the sergeant was a first-name kind of guy too. It had been a long drive, but there hadn't ever really been a pause in conversation.

The smile faded as she thought about Emma Dawson again, wondering what she had been doing this time yesterday, oblivious of the fact she was living her last day. Why had she been travelling under a fake name? Mike might be able to dismiss it as merely 'unusual', but there had to be a reason for that, didn't there? Something else occurred to her then. The way he had said 'They checked the footage.' 'They', not 'I'.

'I just wondered. The video clips you showed me of the woman getting on the train. Did you find them personally?'

'Someone else did,' he said. Then added, 'They went through the whole evening though, like I said.'

'But you didn't personally watch it?'

He shook his head. 'I just got the edited highlights. But we saw the woman in room seven get on alone, so ...'

'Yeah,' Jenny agreed after a moment. 'I suppose you're right.'

7

Sergeant Fletcher – Mike – declined the offer of a coffee, saying he had to get back to the station. He gave her a wave as he turned in the driveway and headed back towards the road. She hoped he hadn't been offended by her question. The implication that he hadn't been thorough enough. But perhaps that was why she had asked it.

She turned the key in the lock and opened the door. Warm air drifted out, which meant the heating was on the timer, at least. She bent down to pick up the pile of mail that had accumulated since the funeral. A mixed assortment of bills and sympathy cards and garish flyers.

The familiar smell of the place greeted her. A unique combination of mustiness and paint. This had been her home for four years, from the age of thirteen. And for years after that, in fact. The fixed point to which she returned twice a year. She supposed it had never quite stopped being home. And now, it was the only home she had, for the time being at least.

The grandfather clock in the hall was still ticking away. She left her case beside it and dumped the mail on the breakfast bar in the kitchen before making a tour of the rooms of the house, just to check everything was all right. When she had last been here, in October, she had been too numb to feel much of anything, too busy to have time to think. Now, she flitted from room to room realising as if for the first time how big the house was. How big and how empty.

All she wanted to do was collapse on the bed in her old room, but she forced herself to unpack first. When she had finished, she went to the kitchen and made a pot of tea. Her dad had only drunk loose-leaf Jasmine, which would have to do. She noticed her phone had a missed call. Evidently the single bar of reception had decided to let a call through. Her heart sank when she saw the number. Eric. There was a voicemail.

She thought about leaving it until later and decided to get this out of the way too. At first the call wouldn't complete, so she headed out to the end of the back garden, where she usually got a better signal.

The message began with a clearing of a throat. 'Sorry to bother you. Listen, David and I were wondering if you might be available to sign the last batch of papers sometime this week?' David, their lawyer. Eric had swiftly signed him up for his side. 'We can Fed-Ex them to you, but you would need a witness. Also, I need to check what the Netflix passwo—'

Jenny rolled her eyes as she deleted the message. He could bloody well call her back.

The electric shower had been broken for the last year or so, so instead she ran a hot bath and lay back in the water, watching the steam circle in the air currents, listening to the novelty of the sound of nothing. No traffic, no sirens, no rumble of underground trains.

Perhaps everyone else was right. Perhaps the simplest explanation was the correct one: she had been mistaken. But how, though? Every other rational theory she could come up with still involved there being a little girl in that room, or at least on the train.

And hadn't she thought this about Eric, too? There had been

signs, before the text message. Nothing concrete, just little changes in his routine, changes in *him*. But she had allowed Eric to convince her it was all in her head. The few friends she had tentatively broached the subject with had been happy to give her pleasant reassurances. They had said they were a wonderful couple, they were sure there was nothing to worry about. They had been wrong.

Afterwards, she towelled off and went through to her old bedroom. It was a time capsule, depressingly datable by any amateur pop culture historian who might happen by. Posters of Radiohead and Weezer album covers. The big *Trainspotting* one-sheet. A corkboard of tickets: concerts and festivals and movies, each one necessitating a long trip from here.

She cast an eye over the bookcases along the wall, which charted her reading life up to the age of seventeen – *Narnia* and *Alice in Wonderland* through to Stephen King and Margaret Atwood. She remembered how PC Bryden had glanced at her battered paperback thriller back in the waiting room, the way it seemed like it answered a question. An over-imaginative witness. Read too many books.

She climbed into bed and closed her eyes.

Perhaps everyone else is right, she thought again, and this time it sounded hollower than before.

She told herself again that she was mistaken. The little girl was elsewhere, with someone else. Or there had been no little girl at all; just a figment of her overstretched imagination. She had never experienced hallucinations before, but if there was a time to start, then it would probably be now.

But then she remembered bending to pick up the grey rabbit. The soft feel of its fur on her fingers. That had been real.

It took her a long time to fall asleep.

Sunday, 25th November

8

'God, that sounds appalling.'

Meryl was so enthralled by Jenny's story that she had forgotten everything else. She realised she had been stirring her latte for over a minute, tapped the spoon on the rim of the cup and laid it down, taking a sip. They were in a new place in Bridge of Dean called Bean Around the Block. It had been a chip shop last time Jenny looked, but in the intervening time had transformed into some kind of artisan coffee house. Wood flooring and circular tables had replaced chipped tiles and Formica lunch counters.

Meryl was exactly four months younger than Jenny, but they had been in separate years in school. They had been in Girl Guides together, and the school netball team, and were best friends until Jenny went to university. They had lost touch for a while after that, until Facebook arrived and brought everyone back into touch, whether they wanted to be or not. Being contactable to everyone was a mixed blessing as far as Jenny was concerned, but the revival of this friendship was one of the good things.

Meryl was an estate agent now. She looked great, as she always did. Jenny had told her so when they met outside, and Meryl had brushed off the compliment with her usual excuse:

it comes with the job. Presentation is everything.

She was dressed for a viewing later on, in a slim-fitting char-coal suit with a lemon-coloured blouse. Her straight blonde hair was pushed neatly back from her face with a hair band, and the glasses – new since the last time Jenny had seen her – had the odd effect of making her look more grown up, but without looking any older. In short, she looked a hell of a lot better than the parent of a four-month-old baby had any right to.

'So are you all right?' she prompted.

Jenny nodded. 'Yeah, I mean, nothing happened to me. It was just . . .'

'A shame,' Meryl said when she didn't finish.

'Yes.'

'Still, at least you got to meet a hot man in uniform.'

Jenny frowned at her over the lip of her mug, taking a care-ful sip of the scorching Americano. 'I didn't say he was hot.'

'You didn't need to,' Meryl retorted. 'You had that look.'

Jenny gave a long sigh and shook her head.

'And you're coping okay with . . .' Meryl paused, uncharac-teristically short of words. 'You know?'

'Everything else?' Jenny nodded. 'Yes. So far so good.'

Meryl looked reassured. 'I knew you would be fine. You've always been . . .' She stopped and searched for the right word. 'Emotionally balanced?'

'Emotionally balanced?'

'Yeah. Like, in a good way. You're always on an even keel. You don't get too worked up about anything.'

'Thanks. I think.'

'And I suppose it could be worse. At least you don't have kids to worry about. Can you imagine? At least it's just you.'

'Just me,' Jenny said, giving her an exaggerated smile. Kids. She hadn't wanted them when he did, and then vice versa, and now that was another thing struck from the to-do list.

She was grateful when Meryl chose that moment to put her coffee down and open the folder she had lain on the red-and-white check table cloth. 'So, the house.'

Jenny couldn't help but be amused. She had no doubt that her friend's concern had been genuine, but she envied her ability to switch gears so efficiently. She was grateful for it today, in fact. She was looking forward to talking about something other than what had happened on the sleeper, or the fluctuating uncertainty of her life.

Meryl went through her evaluation of Crossan Lodge with practised ease. She thought that just by decluttering and giving every room a coat of paint and new carpets, Jenny could expect to see a decent return for the house. The garden would need attention too, of course, but Meryl knew a good local guy who would do the necessary for a few hundred quid.

'If you'd like to spend a bit more, he could do something quite nice. Maybe some decking, a reflecting pool. Chuck up a gazebo, perhaps?'

Jenny shook her head. 'Just the basics. We're not doing Grand Designs here.'

Meryl raised an eyebrow. 'Well, now you've brought up Kevin McCloud ...' She flipped over to a folded A3 sheet on which she had clustered some exterior shots of the house from the back garden along with some idealised catalogue pics of conservatories and expensive-looking deluxe summer houses.

Before she had got her mouth fully open, Jenny was shaking her head. 'Meryl, I said don't get carried away.'

Meryl's brow crumpled theatrically. 'You're no fun. And seriously, you should give it a bit more thought, investing a little extra time—'

'And money.'

'And money, yes. But it takes money to make money. You

could squeeze another fifty, maybe seventy K out of this with a few bold alterations, easy.'

'Well I appreciate your suggestions, but I'd rather just slap on a coat of paint, mow the lawn and get it on the market.' She took another sip of her coffee and stopped Meryl's next interjection with a stern look. 'Besides, I'm not exactly feeling like embarking on any ambitious ventures right now. Not until the divorce is finalised, anyway.'

'How's he been?'

Meryl had got on well with Eric on the three occasions they had met, and had been more upset than any of their other friends on hearing the news.

'Kind of a dick, to be quite honest.'

Meryl inclined her head sympathetically. 'Divorce, isn't it? Turns ordinary people into monsters. Nobody's fault, I suppose.'

Jenny had been staring out at the street, but that made her look back at her friend sharply. 'It's not "nobody's fault" that he was screwing someone else, Meryl.'

'Oh yeah, that.'

'That.'

She cleared her throat and snapped the folder shut. 'So no conservatory then, gotcha.'

Jenny sighed in mock irritation. Meryl's bulletproof self-confidence sometimes got her into trouble, but it was charming in its way.

They sorted out the rest of the arrangements and agreed that Jenny would give her a call in a couple of weeks to come and take the pictures.

As she was leaving, muttering something about her husband's inability to get the formula concentration right, she paused. 'You think they'll ever find out what happened? With the train thing, I mean.'

Jenny thought about explaining that 'they' had apparently done all they were going to. Instead, she just shrugged.

'Who knows?'

9

Porter was in a shitty mood today. Mike actively preferred this to his good-mood days. The barking at people and door slamming was better than the condescension. This particular shitty mood had been precipitated by an email requesting his presence at a strategic development day at Gartcosh.

He was standing by Mike's desk, reading the offending missive again on his phone, as though to make sure it wasn't all a terrible mistake. The office was housed in an ugly sixties concrete building that looked out on the water. It was one of those places where the view from inside out is the best thing about it. The squad was split across two floors, mostly open plan, but with two cubicle offices on the southwest corner of each floor.

'It's not having to go all the way to Glasgow I mind,' Porter muttered. 'It's the fact you then have to get to the arse end of nowhere from there.'

Mike suspected it wasn't anything of the sort. He noticed Porter was ill at ease whenever he left his own personal fiefdom and had to spend time with his peers.

'Look on the bright side, boss. Night in a hotel and all that.'

'A Travelodge. If I'm bloody lucky,' Porter said. Then he seemed to catch himself, as though realising that he had started

54

conversing with a subordinate like a human being. He cleared his throat and straightened his tie.

Mike sat back in his chair and looked out of the window. The sky was a cool cerulean blue. The first clear day in a few weeks. It reminded him of looking up at the sky in the hills outside Kandahar. Absent-mindedly, he began toying with the fabric bracelet on his left wrist. It was made of thin strands of ribbon entwined. Royal blue when he had bought it from the market stall, long since faded and dulled to a bluish grey.

He was thinking about Jenny Bowen's account of boarding the sleeper on Friday evening. It had stuck in his mind, so much so that he could almost picture it as though he had experienced it first-hand. A little girl with dark hair, brown eyes, the room door clicking shut.

'Did you get that report finished for me on the platform inspections at Aviemore and Kingussie?'

Porter had appeared again. Mike looked up and shook his head, resisting the normal human urge to affect an apologetic expression. 'No. You asked for them by Friday.'

'Well that was before I knew about this, wasn't it?' Porter snapped, holding up his phone. Mike just looked back at him, waiting for him to continue. Finally, he relented. 'This afternoon, all right?'

'The autopsy is due on Emma Dawson,' Mike said. 'I'm going to have a look at—'

'Dawson? The junkie?'

'The fatality on the sleeper, yes.'

Porter rolled his eyes. 'And what do you expect the autopsy to tell you?'

'I don't know, boss. I guess that's why we do autopsies.'

Mike knew immediately he'd crossed a line. Porter's eyes narrowed. He shot a glance around the office to see who else was listening to the conversation. Only PC Jennings and Emmy, the administrator. Both of them with sense enough to be staring intently at their monitors, pretending not to have heard Mike's comment.

Porter leaned in and lowered his voice. 'I'd like to speak to you in my office, Sergeant Fletcher.'

They travelled the six paces to Porter's office, a corner of the open plan squared off with a glass cubicle, and shut the door. Porter stayed standing, so Mike didn't take the seat opposite the desk.

'You give a superior that sort of cheek in the army, son?'

Mike bit back the urge to tell Porter that nobody ever called him 'son' in the army and considered his answer for a few seconds before speaking.

'I apologise if you thought I was speaking out of turn, that wasn't my intention.'

'And what exactly was your intention?'

'Just what I said. As you know, we have a couple of loose ends on that case, and—'

'"*We*" don't have any loose ends, Mike, we have a dead heroin addict, and a hundred things more important to deal with.'

Back to first name, rather than rank. That was mildly promising.

'What about the witness?' Mike asked.

Porter fixed a confused expression, play-acting.

'What witness?'

'Jennifer Bowen, the woman who said she saw a little girl with her.'

'She got mixed up. There never was a girl. You can't be a witness to something that never happened.'

'We can't be sure about that,' he said immediately. He realised he had raised his voice unconsciously. Porter flinched very slightly, and then narrowed his eyes. He was a little embarrassed now, and not happy about it.

'I'm sorry,' Mike continued. 'I just ... I don't think we should rule it out.'

'You checked it out. Exhaustively, as I seem to remember. There was no child of that age on the train when we searched it, and the records, the cameras, *all* the other witnesses ... suggest there never was.'

He had a point about that one. Sure, they were working without the benefit of CCTV on the train itself, but every other piece of evidence pointed to the explanation Porter had settled on, that there was no little girl. Confusion on the part of the witness, common and understandable.

Except that Porter only liked that explanation because it was easy and it allowed him not to have to devote any more time to thinking about it.

There was something about Bowen's certainty about the little girl. Not just her certainty, actually. She didn't at all seem like the sort of person who would 'get mixed up', or who would invent something like that.

Porter was still eyeing him cautiously, like a chained-up dog that had barked unexpectedly. 'You seem a little agitated about this, Mike. Anything I need to know about?'

Was he right about that? Mike shook his head quickly. Porter was very much on the list of people who would only ever be given the minimum information possible. A sly grin crept across Porter's mouth. 'She's easy on the eye. Is that it?'

'That's not it,' Mike said flatly.

Porter continued. 'I mean, that I could understand, at least. I've never really got a handle on you, Michael.' He glanced at the corner of the room, at the filing cabinet where he kept his files. 'We've talked before about your general demeanour. I was starting to think you were becoming more of a team player, but perhaps ...'

57

'Nothing to worry about, boss.' He shrugged in what he hoped was a conciliatory manner. 'I was just interested to see if anything came up on the autopsy. We wouldn't want to miss anything, is all I'm saying.'

Porter seemed to think about it. Sudden deaths aboard trains weren't all that common in the scheme of things, and he wouldn't want something coming back to bite him on a case that was at least technically more important than station inspections at Aviemore. Mike knew Porter had downgraded the case the moment he saw the needle, and had mentally closed it down when it became clear the deceased had no next of kin to kick up a stink. The simple fact of the matter was that they probably could do the bare minimum on this one and forget it. But Mike wanted to see if Porter would actually come out and say that.

He sighed and sat down. 'All right. Let me know if you're satisfied with the autopsy and we can close it off today. You can email me the station report tomorrow, I'll pick it up on the train down.'

'Sounds like a plan,' Mike said, turning to open the door again.

'And Mike?'

Mike turned back to him.

'Don't be such a smartass. There's always someone smarter than you.'

'That's certainly true,' he said.

And it was, but he still had to resist the urge to add that present company was excepted.

Monday, 26th November

10

Jenny thought about the girl in the blue dress a lot on Sunday, and when she woke up on Monday morning. But with each hour that passed, it grew easier to rationalise, to tell herself that there was no room for this entry on her long list of problems.

Besides, there was plenty to occupy her. A steady stream of tradesmen arriving to size up the work required to put the house on the market. Roofers, an electrician, a plumber and tiler to cost the main bathroom job. Jenny got to work giving the guest rooms a fresh coat of paint. She was surprised by the number of little jobs that needed doing. Dad had usually been on top of everything. She should have known something was wrong when she visited at Christmas and the shower had been out of action. Now that she had time to think about it, she realised he had gradually been letting go ever since Mum had died. The stroke had only put a punctuation mark on it.

She dropped the paint roller in the tray and sat down in the corner, feeling tears prick at the corner of her eyes for the first time since the funeral. It was a recurring theme, wasn't it? No room on the problem list. She had known it would have been good for Dad if she had made the effort to visit more often, but there hadn't been much room for him either.

She allowed herself a moment to wallow, and then got up and wiped her face. A long problem list, and sitting in the corner moping wasn't a good use of her time, no matter how you arranged that list. She went to the kitchen and heated a carton of leek and potato soup in the microwave while she added a few more repair jobs to the notepad.

She resolved to leave the garden alone for now. It was unlikely the house would be in any kind of shape to put on the market this side of the festive season, and besides, Meryl had assured her that after New Year was a better time to press go. Lots of new resolutions, lots of marital dissolutions.

And of course, that made her think of her own situation. She would have to find somewhere permanent to live once things were put in order here. An only child, she was the sole beneficiary of her parents' estate. She expected the house would sell quickly and for a decent price for the area. But that would hardly put a dent in the deposit on a half-decent place back in London. Eric owned the flat they had shared for the past five years, and she expected him to be no more generous in the division of assets than he was legally obliged to be.

She interspersed the decorating and minor DIY tasks with occasional email checks and calls to clients. As she had told Mike, she was technically on sabbatical, but the simple fact was that some things could be dealt with now rather than allowed to grow into bigger problems when she returned to work. The sort of quick and easy jobs she was grateful to attend to as a break from the painting.

She had almost forgotten about Emma Dawson and the little girl who might not have existed when her phone rang just after two o'clock. The number was withheld, so at least she knew it wasn't Eric. She picked it up and could hear a male voice asking for her, fading in and out. She yelled, 'Hang on a sec,' slipped her purple Converse shoes on, tucking the laces inside for speed, and hurried out to the bottom of the garden. She said hello all over again.

'That's better, I can hear you now. It's Sergeant Fletcher, we met on Saturday?'

'Of course,' Jenny said. *Sergeant Mike*, she thought, wondering why that mildly amused her. 'Has there been any news?'

'I just thought I would check in. The post-mortem was carried out on Emma Dawson. No great surprises, cause of death was a cardiac arrest brought on by an overdose of heroin.'

'Do they think ...' Jenny began. 'Can they tell if it was, you know ...?'

'Deliberate? As in suicide? I'm afraid we'll never know. She took a lethal dose – obviously – but that doesn't necessarily mean anything. Long-term users take lethal doses all the time. They have to, a smaller hit isn't enough after a while. The body builds up a resistance.'

Jenny said nothing, thinking about how small the woman's body had looked, even in the tight confines of the sleeper room.

'Jenny? Are you still there?'

'Yes, sorry. I was just thinking how sad it is.'

'There's another thing,' Mike said after a pause. 'The autopsy showed she never had any children.'

'You said that already.'

'There were no children in her file, no, but it's always good to have these things corroborated.'

'Of course,' Jenny said. Another nail in the coffin of her story, as far as the police were concerned.

Mike cleared his throat. 'The other thing I wanted to say was I made a few calls. Sometimes reports get held up, or get lost in the system.'

Jenny could tell where this was going from his tone of voice.

'But there's nothing about a girl like the one I saw being reported missing.'

'No. Which is a good thing, when you think about it, surely?'

'Of course.'

He cleared his throat again. 'We checked in with the guy in room ten.'

'I thought it was eight?'

'Eight was empty on that night,' he said. 'So I checked the other names. There was a lone male passenger in ten, I assume he's who you meant.'

She wasn't sure. 'Was he tall?'

'I spoke to him on the phone. A Mr Davies, lives with his wife in Corran. Sounded on the older side.'

'Oh.'

'But he didn't see anything. I asked if he remembered seeing the woman and he says he has a vague memory of her. I didn't know whether to believe him. He wanted to help, and the memory plays tricks.'

Jenny opened her mouth, and then closed it again. More than anything, she wanted to press him, to say she was sure the tall man had been in room 8, not 10. But she could hear the slight edge of hysteria in her own voice. And something worse in Fletcher's voice. Concern, for her. *The memory plays tricks.*

'All right,' she said finally. 'You were probably right. I might have imagined the whole thing, or got mixed up somehow.'

'Right,' Sergeant Mike said, and something in his voice told her he wasn't much more convinced than she was. But they had hit a dead end. Nowhere to go.

'Listen, I really appreciate you keeping me in the loop,' Jenny said. 'I'm sure you have a hundred more important things to do.'

'No problem at all. I'm just sorry you had to go through this. And if anything comes up ...'

'Thanks, Mike,' Jenny said.

After she hung up, she stood in the garden, the rainwater

on the long grass soaking the cuffs of her jeans, and stared at the screen of her phone. It had been a long drive from the little station at Rannoch, but she had enjoyed Mike Fletcher's company. She thought the feeling had been mutual. Part of her wondered if Sergeant Mike had gone beyond the call of duty because of that. But she didn't think that was the whole story.

Something was bothering him about all this too. He was curious.

Tuesday, 27th November

11

Jenny awoke with a start, with the sensation she was falling. The air was utterly still outside. The train had stopped again.

And then she remembered she wasn't on the train at all, she was at the house. The home that wasn't really home. She rolled over and checked the glowing digits on the white plastic 1980s alarm clock on the nightstand: *03:47*.

Immediately after that, she remembered the brown eyes of the little girl. She had been there, with the woman. And the tall man in room 8 had been there too. Jenny had seen three people in that carriage on Friday night. One of them was dead, and for all the world it looked like two of them had never existed. Two omissions from the official record now.

Perhaps everyone else is right.

It was raining outside. The raindrops battering noisily into the puddle at the side wall where the drainpipe was broken. She had been dreaming of a memory. Aged six, she had got lost in the big Marks and Spencer on Argyle Street, the Saturday before Christmas. Her mother always swore they had found her within a few minutes, but she remembered it being like an eternity, lost in a forest of grown-ups' legs, bustling past her, blocking her view. She had never quite forgotten the feeling of utter helplessness.

After forty minutes of tossing and turning, she gave up on trying to get back to sleep. The hell with 'everyone else'.

She went downstairs, wondering why the ticking of the grandfather clock in the hall always seemed louder at night. She sat on the couch next to the router where she got the best signal, opened her laptop and waited for the treacle-slow internet connection to kick in. It was like surfing the web back in the nineties.

She let her eyes adjust to the brightness of the screen, and got to work. She found the Metropolitan Police's missing persons page, knowing that she was probably wasting her time. If there was a matching child missing, Mike would have found it. She scrolled through the list of active missing persons cases, reading each sad summary of a person who had fallen through the cracks. A sixteen-year-old boy who had disappeared from a party. An unidentified elderly man seen falling in the Thames. A teenage girl last seen at a petrol station in Chingford. No one was looking for a girl of the right age, or even for Emma Dawson. She remembered the brief biography. Parents deceased, no siblings, no children.

If there was no one to miss you, could you really be missing?

A snippet about a man with mental health issues last sighted at a rehab clinic gave her an idea. She started to make a list of places to call in the morning, and then remembered she knew someone who might be able to make the task easier. She decided to give the living room another coat of brilliant white, knowing she couldn't do anything until nine, when Bradley's office opened.

She went through to the kitchen to make coffee. A sudden urge to listen to some music struck her. She didn't think the internet connection would be up to streaming, so she dug out some of her old CDs and put them on her father's sound system in the living room. Nothing too loud at this hour: Ryan

70

Adams, Elliot Smith, Julianna Hatfield. The singer-songwriters she liked to listen to on hung-over Sundays, or on long flights. With coffee brewing, the lamps on, some music, and a clear task to focus on, the world didn't seem quite as cold a place, if only for the moment.

By the time the sun was up and she was on her third cup of coffee, she had a good idea of what she needed to ask her contact about. She used the landline this time, having to look up the main number despite having worked with the organisation for years. It was a third sector support agency, which was a fancy way of saying they provided training and services to small voluntary organisations. The kind of places who might deal with the people who no one else missed.

Kirsty on reception checked Bradley's diary and said she could put her through. There was a pause and then Bradley's cheerful antipodean voice piped in. 'Good morning!'

'Morning, Bradley, how's things?'

He let out an exaggerated sigh and Jenny could picture him sitting back in his swivel chair, pushing his blond surfer hair out of his eyes while he looked back out of the window of the office in Hackney.

'You know. Same shit, different day. We're missing you. New IT guy's useless.'

'That's nice of you to say.'

'So, what can I do for you?'

'Do you still run that database with all the small charities?'

'Charo? I'm afraid so.'

'I was looking for the search form on your website but it seems to have—'

'Yeah the API was screwed up, we took it offline last month temporarily.'

'Temporarily?'

He sounded a little sheepish. 'Well, you're the first person who's noticed.'

'Any idea when it will be back online?'

'I'll get it done this arvo. If you're looking for something in particular I can just look it up on the back end for you.'

'Thank you.' Jenny told him what she wanted.

Her next call was to the UK Missing Persons Unit. They took down the information she had, and said they would check the database to see if it matched any of their cases. When she asked if it was possible for her to report a child missing, the operator sounded unsure.

'It's a difficult one. If you don't actually know the subject, or have a name ...' After a long pause, she fell back on what sounded like the standard line. 'In the first instance, any concerns about a missing person should be reported to your local police force.'

'Thanks,' Jenny said. 'Maybe I'll try that.' Local police force. Did she have one of those at the moment? She guessed the Met would be the people to speak to.

A couple of minutes later, her laptop dinged with an email from Bradley. A list of charities dealing with missing people, substance abuse, anything else Jenny could think of that might be relevant. Addresses, phone numbers, emails. Bradley had sent everything in a .csv file. Jenny printed it out in the downstairs study and sat down with the sheets of paper, making notes beside each record.

She called round the missing persons charities first; the easier job, and the one which required no subterfuge. She explained that she had seen the woman and the little girl and had been concerned about them. Had anyone reported either or both of them missing?

She struck out with all of them, though a couple promised to look into it and call her back. Emma Dawson wasn't in

72

anyone's system; but that was the easy part. With the little girl, she ran up against the same problem every time: no name, nothing but a description that could fit thousands of children. She moved on to the drug and alcohol support services and the rehab clinics, which would require a little more finesse.

In the long hours before dawn, she had considered a number of different angles, from posing as a journalist, to pretending to be a concerned relative. In the end she decided it was better to stick as close to the truth as possible. She described the woman and the girl, this time making sure to mention she had noticed the woman might have been an addict. She said the little girl had left her stuffed bunny behind, and she was hoping to re-unite them. Did the pair sound familiar?

The responses ranged from the cagey and non-committal, to outright refusal to discuss. She left her mobile number with the ones who would accept it, suspecting that the voices at the other end of the line were only humouring her, and that the number would be going in the bin as soon as they hung up, if it was even written down in the first place.

She looked down at the list. She had crossed off two thirds of the options from Bradley's list, and was no further forward.

She tapped the pen on the desk and thought about what to do next.

She thought about Sergeant Fletcher. Sergeant Mike. She thought he was open to looking into this further. Part of her wanted to call him, talk things through. But from what he had said yesterday, it would be difficult for him to stay involved without something more concrete. He had nothing to offer his superiors by way of an excuse for investing time and resources on an open-and-shut case.

Hers was the only voice suggesting there was more to investigate, and she knew it was a potentially unreliable voice at that. From the point of view of the police, the fact she had reported seeing a little girl who didn't appear to exist, and then a man who didn't either, didn't help her case. How could she explain that the second thing was what had reinforced her belief in the first? She knew she had seen the man in the coat go into the room between her and the dead woman, as surely as she could remember the feel of the soft fur on the stuffed rabbit.

If there was no trace of the man, perhaps that explained why there was no trace of the little girl. What if he had taken her somewhere? And then a darker thought. What if something worse had happened?

She looked down at the printouts, flat on the desk. The crossed-off numbers, and the handful left to call. The woman and the girl had begun their journey in London. She was sure Mike would have been thorough. If he said that no girl of that description had been reported missing, she believed him. But they weren't ghosts. Someone had to have remembered them. Someone must be missing them.

Her phone buzzed loudly on the surface of the desk and Jenny looked up with a start, hoping to see an 020 number. Her heart sank when she saw the name flash up. She hesitated before picking up.

'Hello Eric.'

'Hi Jennifer. How are you?'

He had always called her by her full name, despite everyone from her parents to the bank using Jenny. For years she had found it sweet.

'Fine,' she said.

'Listen, I know it's a bit of a pain, but I've spoken to David again.'

'Oh yeah, the papers,' Jenny said, remembering the voice-mail she had deleted the other day.

'He says I can sign here and we can get them to you, but you'll need a witness at your end to . . .'

'Why don't I just come down and we'll do it in person?' The words were out before she had thought about it.

There was a taken-aback pause of a few seconds. 'Are you sure? I mean it's—'

'I'm coming down anyway. For a work thing.'

'Really?'

'Yes, really. What reason would I have to lie?'

Eric cleared his throat, and she took a small measure of satisfaction from his discomfort at the mention of lying.

She considered quickly. The electrician was coming back tomorrow morning. She could let him in, show him the job, then drive down to Glasgow. She could get a flight or a train from there and she would have a day in town to make some enquiries.

'I'll be there on Thursday. Say, six o'clock. I hope that suits.'

'Of course, I'll let David know. He can come to the flat.'

'No,' she said, feeling a little queasy at the prospect. 'We can meet at a coffee shop or something. Let me know where and I'll be there. And fire through a copy to my solicitor first.'

'Sure, sure,' he said quickly. 'Jennifer, I just want you to know that I really appreciate how—'

'I have to go, I'll see you on Thursday.'

She hung up and bit her bottom lip as she stared at the phone screen. She got a physical ache in her stomach whenever she talked to him now. It wasn't an emotional thing, not exactly. It was the way she had felt for a week or two after being involved in a car crash years ago. An appropriate enough comparison, perhaps.

The phone rang a second time and she saw with relief that it wasn't Eric calling back. Another mobile number. She answered it. It was the bathroom guy. With no small measure of gratitude, she turned her mind away from everything else and focused on whether the subway tiles in the main bathroom should have a matt or a gloss finish.

75

12

Mike Fletcher had had a tough morning. An argument between two fans of rival football teams in the normally sedate Corrour Station Inn had turned violent, escalating into what the barman Mike spoke to had described, not without a hint of pride, as 'a proper old school brawl'.

He and Bryden had been nearest the scene, and got there quickly, but it still looked like someone had swung a wrecking ball through the place. The two men at the heart of the incident had been handed over to the local cops at Fort William, and were currently in a cell along with two other men and a woman who had got embroiled. The injuries were relatively minor. The worst was a long cut on one of the men's cheeks where the woman had thrown a bottle of IPA at him. Cuts and bruises for the participants, a heavy clean-up job for the bar staff, and for Sergeant Fletcher, lots and lots of paperwork.

He had been thinking again about what Jenny Bowen had asked him the other day. About whether he had watched the whole tape himself. He hadn't seen Bryden since Saturday, so after the fight was the first time he remembered to ask him about it.

'Of course, the whole tape,' Bryden said.

'Real time, or fast forward?'

Bryden snorted in amusement. 'What do you think? We knew what we were looking for. I'm not going to sit and stare at a still life of a platform for two hours. More to the point, I don't think Porter would call that a good use of my time.'

Mike didn't say anything.

'What?' Bryden asked. 'We got what we needed, didn't we? Everyone accounted for. Same number of passengers on the list as on the tape.'

'Everyone accounted for,' Mike repeated. 'Yeah, I just wondered. You remember if you saw a tall man get on the Emma Dawson carriage? Black raincoat?'

'Don't remember. Maybe? I was just looking for Dawson and a little girl who turned out to be imaginary. The numbers matched the passenger list though. You can go through it again if you really want to.'

'I might do that.'

'Witness confusion. Always makes you wonder, right?'

Mike left Bryden at the station and headed back into the office. After the autopsy results had come in, he had taken the time to go back over Emma Dawson's file. Something about it was niggling him. As he had told Jenny Bowen, Dawson had a history. In trouble from her mid-teens. Shoplifting and underage drinking busts at first, a series of drug and petty fraud offences trailed her into her twenties, all leading to a stint in HMP Holloway just before its closure. The addresses on the file told their own story; a different one for almost every conviction.

But the last few entries in the file were more promising. Her exit report from Holloway said she had made good progress in her addiction recovery programme. Her probation officer had given her a glowing report eight months later. Everything on the record up until Saturday morning suggested she had beaten her problems; that she was one of the rare glints of sunlight in a system that all too often failed to make things better, when it wasn't actively making things worse. He realised what it was that was bothering him: the last address on the file didn't quite fit with the rest. 17 Magnolia Lane. Not a flat number. The street name sounded like a new-build estate, rather than a B&B or a council facility. He looked it up and saw he was right. The street was part of a relatively recent development in Surrey – not extremely affluent, but a world apart from some of her other addresses.

So what had gone wrong?

When he got back to his desk, there was a green Post-it on his screen. It had a name – either Bob or Rob – and what looked like a mobile number, scrawled in Emmy's notoriously hard-to-read handwriting.

There was no one else in the office who might be able to decipher it, so Mike squinted at the note until he felt he could make a reasonable guess at the individual digits. He logged into his machine and then dialled what he hoped was the number. It was answered after four rings by a male voice. The 'Hello' was delivered with the usual suspicious tone people adopted on seeing a withheld number.

'Good afternoon, this is Sergeant Michael Fletcher from British Transport Police. I had a message to call . . .' He hesitated and looked at the name again. 'Bob? On this number.'

'Bill.'

'Bill, right.' He glanced at the note again. *Really?* 'Am I speaking to Bill?'

'Yes, it's Bill Morley, from the sleeper. We met the other day when—'

He remembered the man instantly. The 'clock's ticking' guy. 'Of course, sorry. Go ahead.'

'I don't know if you remember, but one of the other passengers said there was someone else there.'

'A girl,' Mike said, the bar fight immediately evaporating from his mind.

'No,' Morley said. 'I mean, yes, I remember we all got worked up about that before we figured out it was a misunderstanding. I was talking about the other room. You called back to ask if there was a passenger in the next room.'

Mike looked around his desk for the notepaper he had sketched a diagram of the carriage on and slid it in front of him to check the layout. 'That's correct. The deceased was found in room seven, the witness we spoke to was in nine, and she thought there was someone in eight as well.'

'Yeah. Only when we checked the log ...'

'The room was unoccupied,' Mike said.

'That's what we thought, yes.'

Mike fought back the urge to rush him to get to the point. 'Go on.'

'Like we said, door was locked, bed was made up, there was nothing on the system. And there were no other male passengers matching that description.'

'Which you know, because everyone gets checked in.'

'Right. But the thing is, we were only allowed to get that carriage back into service today. So it wasn't until this morning that we could get in to get it organised for tonight's run. Anyway, one of the cleaning guys, he found something in room eight.'

'Something?' Mike was staring down at the schematic, unconsciously drawing invisible circles with his finger around the box representing room 8 on the carriage.

'Yeah. A little plastic cover for a hypodermic needle. He recognised it because his wife is diabetic. Normally he wouldn't have paid it much attention, but because of what happened, *how* it happened I mean ...' Morley tailed off. Mike realised suddenly that he sounded a little embarrassed, like he had started to regret wasting Mike's time with this.

'You did the right thing contacting us,' he said quickly.

'Oh, okay,' Morley said, perking up a little.

'Where exactly did he find it?'

'There's a small electrical hatch on the floor under the bunks. It was trapped in the groove around it, probably rolled into it and got trapped.'

'Is there any way that could have got from room seven to eight accidentally? A gap under the dividing walls or something?'

'No, there's no gap.'

'What about the cleaner? Could they have brought it in from cleaning room seven?' He didn't think there was any way the CSE would have missed it, not in a space that small, but it was worth asking.

'No, the cleaner was going in the other direction, he hadn't got to seven yet.'

'It could have been there already, though. From a previous passenger, perhaps?'

'I suppose. The room had been turned over since the last run, though. Besides,' he added, 'it's a bit of a coincidence, isn't it?'

Mike agreed entirely, but he didn't say so out loud. He noted down the key points. He remembered that the room had an adjoining door to the next room. If it was unlocked, or someone was able to unlock it, they could pass through without going out into the corridor.

'All right, thanks for this. Hang on to the needle cap and we'll get someone down there to pick it up. If you could get me the names of everyone who's occupied that room this month, that would be great. Contact details would be even better, if you have them.'

Morley said he would see what he could do, and hung up.

Mike looked down at his diagram. The box with a number 8 in the centre. The room for the man who didn't exist. He knew what Porter would say – once again, this didn't prove anything. That was why he wasn't going to tell him anything. A needle cap would be too thin to take usable prints from, but there was a slim chance there might be DNA that could be matched to a future suspect.

'Suspect'. Maybe he was getting ahead of himself. No evidence anyone was in that room on that night, and this didn't really change that.

That was the problem, he realised. If Jenny Bowen had been right, and there were two passengers on that train who were unaccounted for, then someone had taken great care to ensure that there was a void where the evidence should be.

He glanced at the time in the corner of his computer screen. Twenty to two. He could make it to the station and back before Porter was due to call if he got a move on.

13

Anne Miller, the crime scene examiner from the Scientific Support Unit who had processed the scene, called him back on the way to Fort William. Without taking his eyes from the road he answered the call and put it on speaker. It was a short conversation. No, they definitely hadn't recovered the needle cap from the room where Emma Dawson's body had been discovered.

'Is that normal?'

'What's normal? It happens. It's like finding a Bic pen without a cap.'

Mike thought about saying he would think more carefully about carrying a hypodermic in his coat pocket than he would a pen, but he supposed an addict might be less fastidious. He turned onto Belford Road, which ran alongside the south side of the station, and slowed ahead of the turn into the car park.

'If I bring you a cap, can you tell me if it matches the needle?'

She was quiet for a second. 'Perhaps. You think it's important?'

'I don't know yet,' Mike said. 'I'll be in touch.'

He thanked Anne and let her hang up as he slowed and guided the car into a space that had just been vacated by a red Toyota, then crossed over to the station. There had been a station at Fort William since the Victorian era, but the present building was a nondescript concrete structure dating from the mid-seventies. Bill Morley met him at the entrance and escorted him to the train. The sleeper carriages were parked at platform 2 during the day.

The carriage was just as he remembered it, although it was easier to see the wear and tear in the remaining afternoon daylight. The worn carpeting, the scuffs in the siding, the newer signage looking out of place. It reminded him of an old hotel still being maintained for everyday use. The kind of place that's too expensive or too architecturally significant to tear down and replace, so it keeps being maintained, patched up, given a lick of paint.

Room 7 had been made up, and showed no trace that a person had died in it mere days before. The sleeper was a kind of hotel on wheels, so he guessed this was another thing they had in common. No place for sentimentality. The room had to be turned around for the next occupant.

Mike surveyed the room, picturing the position in which the body had lain, glancing at the made-up bed and the hospitality pack carefully placed on the pillow. Hotel rooms made bad crime scenes because of the high turnover. Too many fingerprints, too many hairs and fibres. He tried the handle on the adjoining door. It didn't budge.

'These are always locked during travel?'

'Always locked,' Morley agreed. 'Unless it's a group travelling together. They're locked unless we unlock them.' He stepped forward and produced a set of keys. They looked more like tools than door keys. He pushed one into the hole, twisted it, and unlocked the door, swinging it open into the next room.

'Always locked,' Mike repeated, almost to himself. 'Unless you have a key.' He reached out a hand and Morley gave him the set. He examined them close up. 'Wouldn't be difficult to get something that would do the job, would it? This is just an Allen key.'

Morley looked at the keys, as though he hadn't considered it. 'I suppose. Do you know many people who carry Allen keys with them just in case?'

Mike shook his head. 'No. You would have to expect to need one.'

Morley nodded, as though the question was settled.

Mike pulled the door closed again. It swung back quietly on oiled hinges and clicked shut. He opened it again, pulled it back and forward a couple of times to test it. 'Is there any way to tell if this door was opened on Friday night?'

Morley looked puzzled. 'It was locked.'

'Yes, but if someone unlocked it, then locked it again ...'

He shrugged. 'I don't know. It's not hi-tech stuff we're dealing with here. Like I said the other day, these carriages are probably older than you are.'

There it was again. An absence of evidence either way. Could it have happened? Sure. Did it happen? No way to know.

He opened the door once more and stepped into room 8. He crouched down and looked under the bed, saw the needle cap lying on the floor beside the small electrical hatch Morley had talked about. He got down on his hands and knees and managed to get his head under the bunk so he could examined the cap without touching it. The cleaner had been right about what it was. He took a small plastic evidence bag from his pocket, as well as a ballpoint pen, and nudged the cap into the bag using the pen, before sealing it.

'Did the cleaner touch it? Must have done, to get it out of the groove, I suppose.'

'He must have, yeah.'

It was academic. It was too small to worry about usable prints having been smudged. If there were any DNA traces on it, the cleaner could be quickly ruled out. If things ever got that far. Mike straightened up and examined the cap through the polythene. It wasn't nearly enough to convince Porter to take another look at the case; not by itself.

Had it even been here on Saturday morning? He didn't know. He hadn't been the one to check this room. Just like he hadn't been the one to personally check the CCTV.

When he stepped back onto the platform five minutes later, it had started raining again. He stood under the shelter and watched as the raindrops bounced in the puddles between the tracks while he thought about the room and the locked door. Without realising it, he was toying with the fabric bracelet again, circling it around his wrist with the thumb and forefinger of his right hand.

He took his phone out and called the BTP duty officer at Euston. He gave his badge number and said he was calling from Division 4.

'What can I do for you this afternoon, Sergeant?'

'Who do I speak to about the CCTV on platform one?'

Wednesday, 28th November

14

Jenny made solid progress on the house over Tuesday and Wednesday morning. She also managed to cross off most of the rest of the phone numbers on her list, although without finding anyone who remembered the woman or the little girl. But she had made one particular call that might save her all the effort: by carefully wording her enquiry, she had been able to arrange a meeting with a Met DI to discuss her concern about a missing person. If she could get them to look at the case from their side, perhaps they could come up with something.

There was a BA flight from Glasgow departing at ten past nine in the evening. Her dad's car wouldn't start when she had turned the key in the ignition the night before, and the local garage couldn't take a look until the weekend. Meryl apologised that she couldn't offer a lift, but said Jenny could borrow her husband's car and park it at the airport. The alternative was taking the train down to Glasgow, and quite apart from the fact it would take the best part of four hours, she didn't feel like getting on that particular form of transport again this soon.

She wondered if she had made the wrong decision when she hit the on-ramp for the Erskine Bridge and saw a line of motionless traffic as far as the eye could see. Roadworks, an accident maybe. She stole increasingly anxious glances at the clock on the dashboard, wondering why she always ended up running late. Eventually the traffic started to move, and she crawled the rest of the way to the airport, arriving less than fifty minutes before her flight was scheduled to depart. She parked and ran for the terminal, grateful she had checked in online. Security was reasonably quick, but she only just made it to the gate as the last few passengers were boarding. The attendant smiled without comment and checked her boarding pass before ushering her through into the cabin.

Just over an hour later, Jenny was switching off flight mode as she headed for arrivals at Heathrow. Her phone buzzed immediately with a voicemail notification.

'Hi Jenny, this is Mike Fletcher. Can you give me a call back when you get this?'

No 'Sergeant' this time. She stopped and hunted in her bag for a pen. She found an eyebrow pencil, played the message again, and scrawled down the number he had read out on the back of her boarding pass. Mike picked up on the second ring.

'I dropped in at your house this evening,' he said.

'Sorry, I'm down in London,' Jenny said, curious as to what would motivate a visit in person. 'Was it important?'

Mike was silent for a moment and she wondered if he was going to ask her why she was in London. But then he cleared his throat. 'Just routine, some follow-up questions.'

'Such as?'

'The man you saw, the one you thought was in room eight. Can you describe him again?'

So Mike didn't believe the man in room 8 had been a figment of her imagination either. There were now two of them against Everyone Else. Welcome to the club, Mike.

She kept the excitement out of her voice as she rattled off the description: over six feet, silvery close-cropped hair, long black overcoat. There was a pause and she could picture him scrawling notes on a pad.

'You're still investigating, then?' she asked carefully.

'We like to cross the Ts,' he said, his tone non-committal.

'I thought you said the autopsy showed no foul play. Case closed, right?'

There was a pause. Jenny stopped as she emerged into arrivals, her eyes scanning the signs for directions to the Tube.

'That's correct,' Mike continued. 'The autopsy didn't give us any reason to doubt this was anything other than what it appeared to be. On the face of it.'

She felt her lips curl into a grin. 'On the face of it,' she repeated.

'Look, officially, as far as my boss is concerned, this case is closed.'

'And unofficially?'

'I don't like closing a case when I still have questions about it. I want to know what happened to the girl you saw. And I'd also like to talk to this man who seems to have vanished into nowhere.'

The girl you saw, not *the girl you* think *you saw*. Jenny smiled. He believed her. She didn't know why, but he believed her. 'Thank you.'

Mike didn't reply to that. 'So you're back down south.'

'Divorce stuff, papers to sign.' She hesitated, then decided to trust him. 'But not just that.'

She told him about her idea to talk to rehab clinics, and local charities. She decided not to tell him about her appointment with the Met just yet. He listened without comment.

'Aren't you going to tell me I should be leaving this to the professionals?'

'I should, but like I said, as far as the professionals are concerned, this is over until we get a good reason to suspect otherwise. Let me know if you turn anything up.'

'I appreciate it.'

'One other thing: be careful.'

'I plan to be,' she said at once.

'I mean it. We discussed how there could be a simple, benign explanation for your disappearing girl, and I hope to hell there is. But if not, six-year-old kids don't disappear off the face of the Earth by themselves. If she was taken by someone – by this Nowhere Man perhaps – he knows what he's doing. And that means Emma Dawson's death may have been no accident.'

Jenny felt a shiver, but tried to keep her voice level. 'I'll be careful.'

She hung up and stared at the blank screen for a moment. There was no screen saver, ever since she'd deleted the picture of her and Eric in the Seychelles. Just a generic holding image where the picture was, waiting for something else to fill the void.

The Nowhere Man. She felt a shiver as she remembered the way he had studied her for a second, as though committing her face to memory.

She looked around her. Travellers walking purposefully back and forth, cases and bags and small children in tow. People sitting on the arrays of seats, reading magazines or eating snacks or simply staring into space. A phrase came to her, from the long summer she had spent in Paris after graduation. *La salle des pas perdus*, they called places like this, like the waiting area in the Gare du Nord. 'Room of the lost steps', or sometimes translated as 'the hall of lost causes'. As usual, the French were so much more romantic about functional spaces.

At first she had wondered if Mike was humouring her; or if his willingness to keep her in the loop was motivated by something other than professional concern. But she knew now he believed her, and this meant that neither of them had given up on this lost cause. Without any prior negotiation, they had become co-conspirators.

She put the phone back in her bag and followed the signs towards the Piccadilly Line.

As she walked, she scanned the crowd for tall men in long coats.

15

The Nowhere Man's name was Klenmore, and he was precisely on time for his appointment.

The receptionist who had shown him into the waiting room had indicated the four leather-upholstered chairs facing each other across a low, square coffee table. He ignored the chairs and stood by the window, looking down on the city.

He enjoyed gazing down from a height, watching the ants on the pavements scurry back and forth beneath the streetlights. He looked upwards to the neighbouring buildings, watched office workers pulling late shifts as the cleaners navigated around their cubicles.

He had looked down on many cities in many countries. Every city was unique. The building materials and street plans varied from country to country. Some were bomb-ravaged settlements in the Middle East, some were grey western sprawls like this one. But the people all looked the same from this height. All in a hurry to go somewhere.

So many of them. It was no wonder that some of them could be carefully snuffed out without anyone noticing.

He had carved something of a niche for himself over the years. Some people were paid handsomely to kill in as public a way as possible, to send a message. Some undertook to remove the evidence, to deal with an inconvenient body in a way that meant not even the merest trace would be found. Klenmore's speciality was beyond a skill; it was an art. His victims were left in plain sight, and yet they were almost never identified as victims.

He heard the door open behind him, but didn't turn. Instead, he shifted his focus to watch the reflection of the woman emerge from within. She had short dark hair, just reaching her neck and wore a grey suit. In the window reflection, her hair and the hollows of her eyes looked like blank space where the lights of the city were projected.

'Good evening.' She stopped a few feet behind him and watched him until he turned round. He didn't say anything. 'Coffee, tea?'

He moved his head slightly to the side to decline.

'Thought not. Step this way.'

The woman sat down behind her desk and took a long look at her monitor. Klenmore wondered idly if there was anything on the screen. He didn't care too much either way. He had nothing else to do tonight, and she would get to the important part soon. The assignment.

The woman turned and looked at him. They had met twice before, but she had never volunteered her name. Perhaps she sensed he wouldn't care. He would give her this much: she didn't seem to be rattled by him, the way some of her predecessors had been. He unnerved people, when he wasn't making the effort to go unnoticed by them. He wondered if she knew his reputation. The names they had for him.

'Things seemed to go smoothly in Amsterdam,' the woman said.

He didn't make any move to acknowledge the question. Things had gone as expected. He doubted whether the woman would describe his activities in such terms if she knew the full details. But then that was why he was employed. So that people like her didn't need to know the details.

She turned the monitor round to show him the screen. There was something on it after all: one of the standard files. A name. A picture. Data points: email addresses, phone numbers, an address. The name of a national newspaper.

'Journalist?'

The woman nodded. 'Strictly low-impact, this time. We don't need anything specific. Just pay him a visit, remove his laptop, devices, anything else that looks interesting.'

Klenmore stared at the screen, ignoring most of the details, absorbing what he needed. The address was a flat.

'Does he live alone?'

'Does it matter?'

When he didn't answer, the woman continued. 'Yes, he lives alone. Batchelor. Gay, apparently.' She sighed. 'Even ten years ago that would have been useful. Nobody cares any more.'

'Will I need to make a second visit?'

'We think a warning should do it in this case. If not, then yes, perhaps. He has a history of mild depression, it seems. He was on medication at one point.'

Klenmore pushed the chair back and got up to leave. He had everything he needed.

'I'll call you tomorrow at ten.'

Thursday, 29th November

16

It was a clear morning in London, and it felt ten degrees warmer than it had been in Bridge of Dean. Jenny had taken a room at a hotel on Russell Square. She had been momentarily taken aback when she checked the address of her appointment and realised that it was at Scotland Yard itself. She took the Piccadilly Line to Green Park, then changed for the Jubilee Line to Westminster. Jenny felt herself relax a little as she moved through the bustling crowds on Victoria Embankment. Back on familiar ground, where no one knows your name.

She passed through a security checkpoint and was escorted up to a smaller reception area on the fifth floor. There was a row of orange plastic chairs and a reception desk, in front of a window looking out on the rooftops; skylights and chimneys glinting in the bright morning sunshine. There was a set of double doors at the far side of the room, with a sensor panel for a security fob. A television fixed to the wall was tuned to BBC News, with the sound turned down. A reporter in the lobby of the House of Commons was moving his lips as headlines scrolled past on the ticker at the bottom. The uniformed officer on the desk looked at Jenny with the standard police suspicion as she tapped the keys in front of her and examined the screen. She was in her mid-twenties, and had strawberry blonde hair tied back tightly. She stared at the screen for a moment, no reaction registering on her face, and then turned back to Jenny.

'Have a seat, someone will come and get you in a minute.'

Jenny sat down on one of the plastic chairs, next to a small red-haired woman who was staring blankly at her phone as her thumb darted about the screen. Jenny looked up at the TV, where the feed was now coming from the studio. There was a map behind the newsreader showing the British Isles with a threatening-looking mass of swirls and arrows closing in from the northeast. Storm Catherine. They gave them male names sometimes too, these days. Somehow it always seemed to work out that the bad ones had girls' names, though.

'Jennifer Bowen?'

The accent had a slight hint of Belfast. Jenny looked up to see that a man had appeared, as if from nowhere. He was in his forties, with receding red hair and glasses, and was dressed in a dark suit with a blue tie. He held a dark green file folder in his left hand. His right was gesturing towards the set of double doors. His lips widened in a perfunctory smile. 'DI Robertson, come this way.'

Robertson ushered Jenny into a small office with a floor-to-ceiling window with blinds integrated between the two panes of glass. The sun was glaring through the blinds, so Robertson touched a button on the wall until they angled enough to cut the glare out. There were three chairs, slightly comfier-looking than those in reception, and a circular coffee table in the centre.

'Can I get you anything? Water?'

'I'm fine, thank you.'

Jenny sat down and DI Robertson took the seat opposite.

He opened the folder and laid it flat on the coffee table, examining the document on top of the slim pile. It looked like some sort of report.

He looked up. His eyes were a very pale green. Jenny felt

100

like she was being interrogated, and she hadn't spoken yet.

'There seems to have been a communication breakdown,' Robertson said.

'I'm not sure what you mean,' Jenny said, hearing a slight quiver in her voice and hoping it wasn't as evident to Robertson as it was to her.

'You contacted us about a missing person, last seen in London.'

'That's correct.'

'On the sleeper train out of Euston.'

'Yes.'

'You neglected to tell us all the facts.'

Jenny tried not to let the stab of anxiety register on her face. Caught out.

'We contacted our colleagues in Transport Police who investigated the death of Emma Dawson.'

Of course they had. 'Who did you speak to?' She hoped it was Mike. Or at least, not his boss.

Robertson glanced down at his report, but Jenny knew the answer before he spoke again. 'I had an illuminating conversation with Detective Inspector Porter a few minutes ago.'

Jenny internalised the '*Shit*' she wanted to say out loud, and her eyes dropped from Robertson's. 'Oh yes?'

'Yes. I take it you have an idea of what he said.'

Jenny took a moment. It would do her no good to go on the defensive. 'I understand that the police up there were focused on the death itself, naturally. I just wanted to—'

'If you had given us all of the information on the phone, I would never have agreed to this meeting. The case is being investigated by another force, and I am informed they have looked into your concerns. Thoroughly.'

'With all due respect ...'

Roberson held his hand up to silence Jenny as he flicked

through the sheets of paper. When he found the one he was looking for, he looked up.

'You said you had seen the deceased when you boarded the train, and there was a young girl in her room.' He glanced down. 'Approximately six years old, dark hair, brown eyes.'

'That's right.'

'They checked with the company. There were no children answering that description on board.'

'None with tickets, no.'

Robertson shook his head. 'I'm assured there was a thorough investigation. None of the train staff or the other passengers saw her, no ticket. DI Porter told me the CCTV at Euston shows Emma Dawson boarding alone. There isn't the slightest shred of evidence there ever was a little girl. The only reason anyone has had to invest any time on this . . .' He paused and looked up at her for effect '. . . is you.'

Jenny felt her face colour. Porter had been patronising, but this was something different. Accusatory. 'Why on earth would I make something like this up?'

'I don't know why you would make something like this up.'

Jenny opened her mouth. No words came to mind, at least none that wouldn't get her kicked out even faster.

Robertson continued. 'DI Porter mentioned you'd been bereaved recently,' he said. No sympathy in his voice. Jenny took a sharp intake of breath. She hadn't said anything at all about that to Porter, which meant it could only have come from Mike, which meant . . .

'That has nothing whatsoever to do with this,' Jenny said, straightening in her chair. 'And frankly, I don't like—'

'I don't particularly care if you like it or not, Ms Bowen. Perhaps if you had been more honest with us on the phone, you could have avoided wasting your time. Or anyone else's.'

By force of will, Jenny stopped herself from saying any of

the things she immediately wanted to. Instead, she stood up. 'I'm sorry to have inconvenienced you. I'll leave you to focus on something less difficult, shall I?'

Robertson didn't reply, just sat back in his chair and offered the same thin-lipped non-smile with which he had greeted Jenny.

Jenny kept her face completely composed all the way back out, through reception, and out onto the street. As soon as the door closed behind her, she let out a hissed curse that made a pair of passing tourists turn to look at her.

She got her phone out and hunted through call history for Mike Fletcher's number. It rang a half dozen times before cutting out. She left a message asking him to call her back, in a tone of voice that left no doubt as to her mood. When she hung up, she took a second to check her emails.

One of them was from an organisation called the Mary Wilkins Foundation. One of the domestic violence charities she had contacted.

Subject: Re: Can you help?

17

Mike was on late shift, three till eleven, but he decided to go in early to see if the CCTV from Euston had come in yet. He stopped at the bakery in the village on the way in and picked up a box of assorted doughnuts. He parked in his usual spot and walked in to the station. The second he entered the room, he could tell Porter wasn't happy from the look he gave him as soon as the door opened.

'Morning, boss,' he said, holding up the box. 'Doughnut?' He glanced around, hoping Emmy or one of the others would be about. There was no one else there. Porter didn't so much as glance at the doughnuts. Christ, it was serious.

'You have a message waiting, Mike. And the Met called for you, as well.'

The Met. What the hell had Jenny . . .? Mike hoped his face hadn't betrayed him. He spread his arms after a second, waiting for more. 'Yes?'

Porter crossed his arms and gave Mike the hard stare. He bit his bottom lip, as though deciding how to proceed.

'Jennifer Bowen.'

'The witness from the sleeper the other day?'

'That's the one. As you very well know. Any idea where she is right now?'

'Should I have?'

'Well that's the question, isn't it?'

'I don't quite follow.'

Porter left a pregnant pause. Mike held eye contact until he went on.

'She's in London. A DI Robertson from the Met called to ask about her earlier. She's been asking questions about a missing girl. She told them we were investigating, mentioned you by name.'

'Really?' Mike said, keeping his voice neutral.

'Yes. Really. I was under the impression we had finished our very thorough investigation the other day.'

'Come on, Greg,' Mike said. 'If she wants to look into this on her own time, what's to stop her? It's a free country.'

'Just *her* time, is it?'

Mike felt the hairs on the back of his neck stand to attention at the creepy little smirk that appeared on Porter's face. The bastard had something. No advantage in drawing this out.

'You said there was a message?'

Porter picked up the notepad beside him. Mike could see that there were a few words scrawled in ballpoint pen, one of them underlined a few times. Porter stared at it for much longer than he needed to.

'A Miss Tosin Akinyele called,' he read, mangling the pro-nunciation. 'From Euston.'

Mike put the box on the desk. Said nothing.

'Do you mind telling me why you're chasing up more CCTV footage when we already got what we needed?'

'I wasn't sure we did have all we needed.'

'Clearly. What are you playing at, Mike?'

'I just think we might have missed something on the Dawson case. I don't think it's as simple as it looked. Bryden didn't have the time to ...'

'Too late. It was *exactly* as simple as it looked, and we've concluded our investigation. Autopsy completed, nothing out of the ordinary. She's probably been cremated and scattered somewhere scenic by now.'

Mike considered how much easier it would be just to wash his hands of the whole thing. Let Porter keep believing there was nothing else to this case. But there was.

'I drove up to look at the sleeper at Fort William on Tuesday.'

Porter's eyes narrowed. Too late, Mike could see that he was making things worse.

'The cleaner crew found the cap from a hypo in the next room, the one where Jennifer Bowen said she saw a man.'

'A man who we subsequently established was as imaginary as the vanishing little girl,' Porter said. 'This woman is clearly a fantasist who's watched too many movies, and for some reason she has you wrapped around her little finger. You knew she was going to London, didn't you?'

'You don't think that's suspicious? A death from an over-dose, and the cap of the needle is found in the next room? A room she had no way of accessing?'

'The cap of *a* needle, perhaps. I clearly don't give you enough to do around here, if this is the kind of crap you occupy your-self with.'

'I gave it to Anne Miller in SSU. She says it isn't possible to say for certain, but there's a good chance the cap came from that needle.'

'You did what?' Porter shook his head. 'And you think that was a justifiable use of resources?'

Mike didn't reply. It hadn't taken Anne long to compare the needle to the cap, but he decided not to press on. Another good rule: when you're in a hole, stop digging.

Porter folded his arms. 'We discussed that you have some outstanding annual leave, Sergeant.'

Mike shook his head. 'I'll take it before Christmas. I've got a lot on this week and—'

'Yes, you do have a lot on,' Porter said, waving the notepad with the message from Tosin Akinyele. 'And this isn't part of it. If you can't focus on the day job, take a week off and come back refreshed.'

'I appreciate your concern, but I'm fine. I'll use it up before Christmas.'

Porter put the notepad down and crossed the office to Mike. Without breaking eye contact, he reached down and, with a practised motion, broke the seal on the box with his thumb, took one of the doughnuts and bit into it. He chewed and swallowed.

'No more contact with Jennifer Bowen, okay? Quite apart from anything else, taking an undue interest in an attractive witness is the sort of thing that gets you into trouble these days.'

'Oh, for God's sake—'

'If I were you, I wouldn't make this worse. Draw a line, Sergeant.'

Mike kept his mouth closed with effort. He nodded briefly, picked up the box and went back to his desk, tapping on his keyboard to wake the screen.

Porter took the remainder of his doughnut and walked over to his cubicle, shutting the door behind him. Mike watched out of the corner of his eye until he was sure Porter was engrossed in his newspaper.

Damn it. Why hadn't she told him she was going to see the Met? He knew bloody well why she hadn't told him: because she didn't want him to stop her.

He opened his emails and saw that there was an email from Tosin at Euston with a link to the footage he had requested. She had added a line asking him to give her a call. He checked his mobile to see if there was any message. There was no signal for most of the way between the house and the station, so he would frequently get messages popping up later, sometimes hours later.

There was a voicemail from Jenny Bowen.

18

The Mary Wilkins Foundation was one of the organisations that had promised to get back to Jenny the other day. The email was brief, acknowledging Jenny's query and asking her to call when convenient. It didn't have the feel of a form response, although Beth, the sender, didn't seem to want to say too much.

Jenny bought a green tea in the first coffee shop she could find, and sat in a booth at the back where there were fewer customers, away from the windows. She dialled the number in the email.

Beth answered on the third ring. She had a Birmingham accent, with a cold, clinical tone, even as she negotiated the usual pleasantries. Those concluded, she asked Jenny to elaborate on what she had said in the email. Jenny told her about the woman and the girl on the train. How the woman had been found dead the next day, and the authorities were satisfied that no one else had been with her on the train. Beth asked a few questions as she spoke. She made Jenny describe the pair twice. Jenny could tell she was making notes. Occasionally, Beth would ask a question that made Jenny suspect she was trying to catch her out. Confirming that Emma Dawson had had brown hair, when she had said blonde, things like that. Jenny pretended not to notice. Perhaps this was part of the job.

After Jenny had gone through everything, she sat in the coffee shop listening to the eighties power ballad on the coffee shop's sound system as Beth continued making notes, not bothering to provide a running commentary.

'Well? Are they on your radar?'

She heard the hint of a sigh. 'We have to be very cautious about providing sensitive information, I'm sure you understand.'

'What does that mean?' Jenny said.

'Thank you for getting in touch with us, we appreciate it,' Beth said, adopting a slightly more conciliatory tone. 'But I'm afraid ...'

'It's a yes, isn't it?' Jenny said. 'You wouldn't have any reason to be careful if this didn't ring a bell somewhere.'

'We may have a case that would fit some of the details you have provided today. I may be able to call you back when I have more information.'

'Fine,' Jenny said, and hung up.

She drank the rest of her tea and looked out at the cars crawling past on the street outside. She felt as though she had given everything up and received nothing in return. She wasn't holding her breath for a call back from Beth. She suspected that if her information proved useful, the Mary Wilkins Foundation would take it from here.

Would that be so bad, though? She had done her bit. More than her bit, actually. Perhaps Beth was completely right. This was none of her business, none of her concern. She had enough to be worrying about.

The phone rang again. Mike's number.

'Hi,' Mike said, his voice artificially airy. 'How's the Smoke?'

She kept her voice controlled. 'What did you tell Porter?'

He sighed. 'Why didn't you tell me what you were doing? I could have—'

'Could you? Or would you have told me the same thing, to keep my nose out?'

'That's not fair. You can't just go around trying every copper in the country until you get the answer you want.'

'The guy looked in two minds about whether to lock me up for wasting police time. Apparently Porter told them I was a basket case. Said I was struggling with a bereavement. Where would he have got that from, I wonder?'

'From the interview notes, I imagine, Jenny. We actually have to write this stuff down, you know.'

'That you think I'm a basket case?'

'No, anything the witness said, including information you volunteered. Any interpretation Porter chooses to put on that is not up to me.'

'Oh,' Jenny said.

'I'm sorry,' Mike said after a moment. 'If you had warned me, if I had been here to take the call ... Porter has a different style from me. Having said that, I don't imagine they would have gone with a radically different approach if they had spoken to me.'

'Why not?'

'Because I wouldn't have been able to give them anything more to go on. Just because I think there's something to this doesn't mean I can offer them any proof.'

She was silent for a moment, until Mike said her name, checking she was still there.

'Jenny, you can't just run your own freelance investigation. You could—'

'Thanks for all your help,' she said, interrupting him and hanging up.

Maybe he was right. Irritating, but right. It didn't mean she couldn't be pissed off at him for a while. She drummed her fingers on the table, looking out at the street and wondering how she was going to kill the next few hours until she had the joy of meeting her ex-husband. He had picked out an Italian restaurant in Soho and sent her the address. When her phone rang again, she was surprised to see it was the number she had just called: the Mary Wilkins Foundation.

'Hi, it's Beth again. I've spoken to someone who might be able to help you. Are you free to meet with her this afternoon?'

19

The address was on a quiet street of Victorian terraced town-houses, all built at the same time, some having weathered the years better than others. It was that strange London mix of multi-million-pound homes and flop hotels cramming in-experienced tourists into every box room. The Central Line was out of commission, so it took Jenny longer than she had planned to get there by a different route. It was almost half past three by the time she reached the street, the light already be-ginning to ebb out of the sky. She hurried along the pavement, checking the visible street numbers, which were few and far between, until she reached the one she was looking for.

Jenny opened the gate and walked up the path. Nothing outwardly suggested there was anything different about this house from its neighbours. But then, that was the whole point. She glanced down at the note on her phone where she had tapped out the address Beth had given her. The woman she was meeting was called Kate Lake.

There was an intercom on the door, probably the one sign that there was anything different about this address. Jenny buzzed it and waited. A few moments later, static hissed and a voice said.

'Hello?'

'I'm here to see Kate. My name is Jenny Bowen.'

'Just a minute.'

The sound clicked off. The door was solid wood, no glass. Perhaps it was reinforced, though again it looked unremarkable on the surface. She noticed a small camera tucked into the corner of the doorframe, and immediately looked away from it.

Briefly, she wondered why that impulse was so innate. To look away when being watched. At the end of the street she could see an uninterrupted stream of traffic on the main road. In the other direction she could hear the muted sounds of children playing in a back garden somewhere.

She heard the sound of an interior door open and close. Like an airlock. Then she heard three locks being disengaged on the door in front of her. It swung outwards towards her, not in like a normal household door. Security, or perhaps health and safety regulations due to multiple occupancy.

A heavy-set woman in her thirties stood in the doorway. Her hair was dark, and she wore jeans and a sweater. She peered out at Jenny from behind slightly tinted spectacles, her green eyes immediately checking the path and the pavement behind her were empty.

'Kate?' Jenny asked.

The woman held a hand out and shook Jenny's. 'Come on in.'

She led Jenny down a flight of stairs and ushered her into what had probably once been a servant's bedroom, but had now been converted into office space. Kate said she was going to make a cuppa and took Jenny's order before leaving her to look around the room.

It had a dull grey carpet that felt like it had no underlay, and she could see an ankle-height view of the pavement through the barred windows. There was just enough meagre daylight from outside for the lights to be off. The air smelled a little like a doctor's waiting room: a mix of bleach and coffee. An undertone of damp as well, now she was paying attention.

A door opened and Kate reappeared carrying two mismatched mugs of coffee. Jenny accepted hers, wincing at the heat, and put it down on the table.

'Just black?' Kate asked again.

'Perfect,' Jenny said.

'Sorry about all of the cloak and dagger stuff,' Kate said, 'but we have to be careful.'

'Of course. Do you ever have any trouble?'

'Occasionally someone finds one of the residents and comes round, but the local coppers are good at getting here when we need them. We had a guy a couple of months ago tried to pour petrol through the letterbox and set it on fire.'

'Jesus, what happened?'

'We've got a fire extinguisher in the hall, it was fine.' Kate waved away Jenny's expression of shock. 'It's not the first time.'

'Don't you have to move when your location is, you know . . .' She searched for the word. 'Compromised?'

She shook her head. 'It's the good thing about having a quick turnover. Different women all the time, with different men they're running from. These guys tend not to be the sharpest tools in the box, which is about the best thing you can say about them. Just because one dickhead works out where to find his girlfriend doesn't mean he bothers to tell all the other dickheads. We have to be conscious of the threat, but it's always a highly individual, specific threat. And like I said, the coppers know who to be on the lookout for, even if there isn't an official injunction.'

Jenny sipped from her mug. It was instant. She couldn't remember the last time she had drunk instant coffee. She hadn't particularly missed the experience.

115

'So tell me about the poor woman on the train,' Kate said after a moment. Her smile was kind, but her eyes retained that slightly suspicious look. It was probably impossible to entirely switch off. 'Why don't you go through it from the start?'

Jenny grimaced, wondering how many times this would make it. She had related the story so many times to so many different people that she was starting to question how much was really her memory and how much was rote repetition.

'I saw her as I was getting on the train. Last Friday night, the sleeper out of Euston. I almost didn't make it.'

And if she hadn't? Would that have been so bad? A budget hotel room and the price of another ticket, and she would never have known about any of this. She certainly wouldn't be sitting in this damp-smelling basement room, that was for sure.

'What did she look like?'

'She was about my height, quite skinny, blonde hair. Jeans, a light leather jacket. Maybe in her late twenties. She was moving her luggage into the room.'

Kate said nothing, her face unmoving. But Jenny thought she saw a flicker of recognition behind the rounded lenses. Just like that, she knew that she had found the right person.

'She looked young to have a kid of that age. She looked kind of ...' She hesitated, wondering how to put it.

'Like a junkie?' Kate finished.

'I don't mean ...'

Kate shook her head briefly to show she wasn't offended. 'What else?'

'The little girl,' she continued. 'I only saw her because I noticed they had dropped something.' She paused, knowing that Kate was hanging on her every word. 'A stuffed animal,' she continued, watching Kate.

'A rabbit,' Kate said finally.

'That's right. A grey one.'

Kate hesitated, and then said, 'Yes.'

'Who is she?'

'About this high,' Kate said, holding her hand just under four feet off the ground, and not looking directly at Jenny. 'Dark hair, brown eyes.' Her eyes found Jenny's, a question in them.

Jenny nodded. 'That was her. Who is she? The police said the woman's name was Emma Dawson.'

Kate took a deep breath. 'People don't always give us their real names here. We knew them as Em and Alice. They had been sent over by the Mary Wilkins people. Not an official referral, but if people come to us, we don't turn them away. Em told us she had left her boyfriend, that he was abusive.'

Jenny sensed a 'but'.

'You didn't believe her?'

Kate paused, as though considering the question for the first time. 'I don't have to believe, really. Whatever they're telling me, generally they have their reasons. I just have to know someone needs my help.'

Jenny smiled. 'You sound like my ex.'

'Is he a counsellor or something?'

'Christ, no,' Jenny said, taken aback by the idea. 'Accountant. He says he doesn't care if his clients are dodgy, he doesn't need to know. In fact it's better if he doesn't know, he says.'

'No, it's really not like that,' Kate said shortly. Jenny couldn't tell if it was deadpan humour or if she had actually offended the woman this time.

The buzzer sounded and Kate looked up sharply. She didn't move and a moment later Jenny heard the sound of someone climbing the stairs and the interior door opening and closing, and then the outer door opening and two female voices.

Kate took a drink of her coffee and looked back at Jenny. 'They came to us a few weeks ago. It must have been the last week of October, the Halloween decorations were up. We

117

had a room available, which isn't always the case. They kept themselves to themselves for a few days. No drama. No one came looking for them. They spoke only when spoken to. We offered them all of the usual help, Em said she just needed time to get things organised. I checked in on them whenever I could, but ... let's just say they were no hassle, and easy to leave alone. I did start to wonder, though ...'

'About what?'

'They didn't look all that much alike,' she said. 'For a mother and daughter, I mean. And that doesn't really mean anything, of course, but they didn't seem that much alike either. They seemed like they were getting to know each other.'

It tied in with what the autopsy had revealed, Jenny thought. Not the mother, maybe a family friend. Or a relative. So where was the mother, in that case?

'I wasn't concerned,' Kate continued. 'You could tell Em had had her problems, but she seemed clean.'

Jenny didn't doubt Kate would have a good instinct for these things. 'Did you talk much to Alice?'

'A few times. She was very polite for her age.'

'When was the last time you saw them?'

'You saw them last Friday? Perhaps a couple of days before. In fact yes, the Wednesday of that week, it was bin day.'

'Did they say anything to you?'

She shook her head. 'I ran into them when they were leaving with their stuff. I asked if everything was all right, but Em said it was fine, that they were going to stay with a relative.'

'She say where?'

'Up north somewhere, I think she said.'

North, that fit. 'How did she seem?'

She shrugged. 'Difficult to tell.'

Jenny sat back. 'What do you think happened?'

'I don't know, but if the little girl is missing ...' She turned her eyes to Jenny's. 'I want to help. I just don't know what else I can tell you.'

Jenny held her hand out and put it on top of Kate's, smiling. 'You have helped. More than you think.'

The street lights had switched on as Jenny left by the front door and turned right at the gate, heading back towards the station. Kate had confirmed what she knew. Her first instinct had been to get Kate to speak to the Met, but it would be much harder to get a second appointment. And again, there wasn't much else to go on. What to do next, then? Perhaps she should swallow her pride and speak to Mike again. He was a professional at this sort of thing, after all. Perhaps he would have some ideas now she finally had another person who could confirm Emma Dawson had been travelling with a little girl.

She wondered where Alice's real parents were. They had to be looking for her, surely. Did they know the person who had been posing as their child's mother? It felt like she had more questions than before. She was so caught up in her thoughts that she didn't hear the quiet, insistent voice at first.

'I said, hey!'

She turned round warily and saw a thin woman standing at the mouth of a passageway between two terraces. She was black, in her early twenties, with close-cropped hair and wearing a leather jacket.

'Are you speaking to me?' Jenny asked.

She glanced up and down the street before answering. 'You were just at the house.'

Jenny didn't say anything, waited for more.

'Asking about Em and Alice, right?'

Jenny nodded. 'Did you know them?'

The woman looked around before looking back at Jenny. 'Not here.'

119

20

Jenny carried the two cups back to the table and handed one to the woman, who said her name was Monica. They were in a coffee shop on the main road, five minutes' walk from the refuge. It was approaching full hipster: quirky blackboard messages, beards on all the male staff, and an extensive choice of bagels. Monica had picked a table at the very back of the shop, on a small mezzanine, next to the fire exit.

'You sure you don't want something to eat?'

Monica looked up sharply from stirring sugar into her coffee. 'I'm not homeless.'

'Oh I didn't mean like ...' Jenny said, faltering. 'I mean, the cakes looked nice.'

'So have one.'

'You know what? I'm fine too.'

Monica took the spoon out of her coffee and had a drink. 'You were asking about Em and Alice.'

'Did you know them?'

'She told me to keep an eye out, said someone might come by looking for her.'

'Someone ... you mean like the police?'

Monica shook her head. 'There were dangerous people looking for her.' She cast her eyes warily over Jenny's shoulder towards the door. 'People who wanted to hurt her, know what I mean?'

Jenny said nothing. From the first couple of minutes in her company, Monica had made her feel a little uneasy. She had the slight air of the person who sits next to you on the bus and wants to talk to you about the Deep State.

'What's your interest anyway?' Monica said, turning her eyes back to Jenny.

'I ... met her briefly the other night,' Jenny said, deciding she wanted to avoid going through the whole story if possible. 'After she left the refuge, it would have been. I was just a bit concerned about her and the little girl. About Alice.'

'Where did you see her?'

'They were getting on a train. Maybe going to Scotland.'

Monica nodded. 'She said she wanted to get out of London.'

'Why would anyone want to hurt her? Was it an ex, or ...'

'Not that simple.' Monica looked at the door again and took another drink of her coffee, as though deciding whether she should say any more. Jenny held her tongue, worried that the other woman would clam up if she pushed too hard.

'She told me the type of person to look out for. You're not it, don't worry. She said people might come by. One guy in particular she was really scared of. Tall, thin, light blond hair.'

Jenny felt a chill, but kept her expression neutral. The man on the train. She noticed Monica had a habit of staring right into her eyes, as though she wanted to make sure Jenny was really there. She didn't seem drunk or high at the moment. But it didn't seem like those states would be unfamiliar, either.

'Was he the boyfriend?' Jenny asked.

She shook her head, an amused expression on her face. 'Em said they wanted something she had. She said the guy had come looking for her at the last place.'

121

'They?' Jenny prompted. Monica just stared back at her. 'What did she have?'

The sound of rain spattering hard against the windows at the front of the coffee shop made them both turn to look out. The downpour had come out of nowhere. It had been clear half an hour before. Monica had a resigned look as she watched the water streak down the glass, probably wondering how long it would take to run back to the house.

She turned back and shrugged, and Jenny knew this line of questioning wouldn't get her any further.

'Can you tell me anything else about them?' Jenny said. 'I'm trying to get the police interested, but because nobody has reported them missing ...' Already, she was thinking about the reaction if she took Monica along with her to the police. They'd think Monica was nuts. Maybe she was.

Monica was thinking. 'She said she was waiting for someone to get back to her. Someone who might be able to help her out. I hoped when they left that her "someone" had come through for her.'

Jenny suddenly remembered that there was an important piece of information she had yet to share with Monica. The other woman must have seen it in her face.

'What? What is it?'

'Listen, the reason I'm trying to find out who the little girl was is ... well, there's no easy way to say this ...'

'What? Something happened to them?'

Jenny nodded. 'To Emma, yes. Em. She died. I'm very sorry.'

Monica looked away and blew her cheeks out as she absorbed the news. 'Wow.'

'It was ... the police think she overdosed. It was me who found her, on the train.' When Monica didn't say anything, she added: 'I'm sorry to be the one to have to tell you.'

'It's all right, I didn't know her that well, like I said. It's a shame, though. She had her problems, but she was clean now, I thought. I just feel bad for ... wait a second, where did Alice end up?'

'That's what I'm trying to find out,' Jenny said. 'The police say there's no evidence that there ever was a little girl. I'd almost started to believe it myself. This afternoon is the first time I've spoken to people who knew them. I was beginning to question my sanity. All I know is there's a six-year-old girl missing and—'

'Seven.'

'Sorry?'

Monica was staring back at her. 'She's seven. We had a party for her a couple of weeks ago. They had one of those big number candles, not seven little ones.'

Jenny gripped her pen. 'What day was it, exactly?'

21

Sunday, 11th November.

Jenny looked down at the last line of the notes she'd scribbled on her pad as the Tube train rattled to a stop at Hyde Park Corner.

Monica had had to think carefully about the exact day. She said they all tended to blend when you were in there. Sort of like when you're off on Christmas holidays, except less fun. Jenny had asked a few questions and Monica had snapped her fingers as it came to her. The television had been on, tuned to the news before somebody switched it over to CBeebies – they had a story about a big fire in Manchester. Jenny checked on her phone, dimly remembering the story. That had been Sunday the eleventh of November. An out-of-control blaze at a sheet insulation factory. She remembered the helicopter footage of the black cloud spreading across the blue sky. Did Monica think the eleventh was Alice's actual birthday? Sometimes people celebrate on a different day.

Monica had shaken her head. Of course it was her actual birthday. It wasn't like they needed to book a soft play in advance and invite dozens of other children. The party had just been a handful of people who were around. One of them had seen Alice with the bunny and had bought her a newer, less worn one. She had dutifully placed it beside the other one as she ate her Rainbow Cheerios, but Monica remembered thinking that there was no way the new model would be replacing the original in Alice's affections.

Jenny shuffled over on the seat to let two elderly women sit down as the doors closed and the train pulled off again.

Alice. Her name was Alice. It felt good to have confirmation that there really had been a little girl with the woman. She had a name, although it could be false, of course. But she knew exactly how old the girl was now. Which meant she had something almost as good as a real name: a date of birth.

If Alice had turned seven on that day, then her date of birth was 11/11/2011. Remembrance Day.

She remembered the other thing Monica had said. 'They wanted something she had.'

What did that mean? Drugs? Money? Could someone have taken Alice as some kind of punishment?

Before she could think too deeply about that, her phone buzzed in her pocket. It was a reminder for an upcoming reservation at a Soho restaurant. Eric. Shit. She was going to be late again.

22

'Sorry,' Jenny said as she reached the table. 'Meeting ran late.'

'Same as always,' Eric said, the familiar grin breaking out on his face.

He was waiting for her at a window seat, a whisky sour in front of him. The place was called Giordano and it was new. A small, bustling Italian joint with parquet flooring and a marble-topped bar lit by soft downlights. Eric looked annoyingly good, although Jenny took some satisfaction from the fact he'd clearly made an effort. The charcoal Ted Baker suit she had bought him last Christmas, over a shirt that looked new. He was clean shaven, his salt and pepper hair had been cut recently, and he seemed to have lost half a stone or so. The aftershave was new, too.

'Sorry you got caught in that,' he said, glancing at the downpour outside.

Jenny ran her fingers through her wet hair to sweep it into shape. 'It's fine. Did you bring the papers?'

Eric raised his eyebrows. 'Straight down to business. We need to wait for David to witness. I thought we could eat first. Apparently the veal is excellent.'

'Seriously?'

'I'm always serious about veal.'

'Eric ...' she began, rubbing her forehead.

'What?'

She leaned forward and lowered her voice. 'This is not a fucking date, okay? We're getting divorced.'

He grinned, the way she used to find charming. 'No reason we can't have a decent meal while we're at it, though.'

A waiter had appeared beside them silently, staring at Eric, his pen poised expectantly above his pad.

Eric turned his eyes to Jenny, questioning. She sighed. 'Fine.'

He glanced at the wine list. 'Glass of the Lagrein for my friend ... large?' He waited for Jenny's nod of assent, before continuing. 'A Peroni for me. And can we have another minute to look at the menu, please?'

'It's fine,' Jenny said, scanning the small and perfectly curated selection of dishes. 'I'll have the rigatoni Genovese, he'll have the veal.'

She folded the menu and handed it to the waiter, who vanished as silently as he had appeared. Another waiter passed by carrying two steaming plates of food and Jenny suddenly realised how hungry she was. She was still pissed off at Eric for acting like this was a friendly catch-up, but at least the food smelled great.

'So how was your meeting?' he asked.

'A little frustrating.'

The waiter placed a glass of red wine on the table and quickly departed again.

'I'm surprised they dragged you back down here so soon. Must have been important.'

Jenny made a non-committal grunt as she took a sip of the wine. Eric hadn't been so good at feigning interest in her work for the duration of their marriage. He really was on good behaviour. That made her suspicious.

'How's everything with the house?' he went on.

'Getting there. Should be ready to put it on the market after Christmas.'

'I would have come to the funeral, you know.'

'There was no need,' she said briskly.

Eric waved at someone over Jenny's shoulder and she turned to see David, their lawyer. Actually, just Eric's lawyer now. He avoided Jenny's gaze as he approached.

'Good to see you again?' he offered tentatively.

Jenny didn't return the pleasantry. She looked back to Eric. 'So. Let's get it over with.'

David looked down and reached into his briefcase. He produced a heavy-stock brown envelope. An expensive-looking one with a string catch. He pulled out a sheaf of papers. 'Here it is.'

She took the papers and leafed through them. Her own lawyer had given them the once-over, but she hadn't had time to examine them what with one thing and another.

'Nothing too onerous,' David said. 'Just dotting the Is and crossing the Ts.'

Jenny scanned the first couple of pages as Eric kept talking. She tuned his voice out, trying to focus on the words. Her brain was in exactly the wrong gear, she had to keep rereading every other sentence, not taking it in.

Eric's phone buzzed on the table and he looked down at it.

'Fuck. Excuse me a second.'

He got up and went to the door, standing to one side, just by the doorway.

'How have you been?' David asked.

She glanced back at him. 'It's fine, we can skip the uncomfortable small talk, David.'

He nodded, not without a measure of relief.

She looked back outside and saw Eric take out a pack of

cigarettes with his free hand and light one as he talked. All that wasted time trying to get him to quit. She shifted focus when something caught her eye on the other side of the street. A small figure in a yellow raincoat. A little girl, long dark hair protruding from her hood. She looked all by herself. And then a woman in a matching raincoat marched up to her, grabbed her hand and dragged her back into step with the rest of the family: a dad and two older boys. She bent down to remonstrate with the girl briefly. Too far away to hear the words or to lip-read, but the body language said it all.

Anyone could have taken you.

Alice. She had a name now. The name made her think of the books in her old bedroom. *Wonderland, Through the Looking-Glass*. Her editions had the original Tenniel illustrations that she had always found equally beautiful and frightening as a child. The Alice in the books had disappeared too, only her rabbit was white, not grey.

'You all right?'

Jenny looked up to see Eric staring at her with concern.

'Yeah, just thought I saw someone I knew. Why?'

'You looked . . . I don't know, worried.'

'Worry-free zone,' Jenny said, fixing a smile on her lips. 'Young, free and single. Thanks to you.'

Eric winced, and David became very interested in the positioning of the cutlery on the next table. Jenny dug in her handbag, looking for something to sign with. All she had was the eyebrow pencil she had used to write Mike's number down earlier. Probably not ideal for a legal document. Eric cleared his throat and produced an expensive-looking stainless steel fountain pen. She skimmed the rest of the pages, picked up the pen and signed next to the crosses. She handed the document over to David.

'That's that,' he said.

'Indeed.'

David hurried out of the restaurant. Two or three minutes passed, feeling like far longer. The food arrived. It looked delicious, but Jenny's appetite had evaporated. She looked outside again, at the spot the girl in the raincoat had been. Suddenly, she had a strange urge to tell Eric about what had happened on the sleeper. It had always been one of the things he had been good at, acting as a sounding board. Suggesting courses of action. But no. That wasn't who he was to her any more.

'Look,' Eric said after a minute. 'I didn't really get a chance to say—'

Jenny looked up at him and he almost flinched at the look in her eye.

'Say what? Sorry for imploding my entire life?'

He cleared his throat. 'I didn't plan for this, Jennifer.'

'Well that's good to hear. Who knows how much more damage you could have done if it hadn't been off the cuff.'

'There's no easy way to say this. Lucy and I are getting married. Next summer.'

Jenny took a large gulp of wine and set the glass back down on the table.

'How wonderful for you.'

'You want me to leave?'

'No,' Jenny said. 'Stay. Enjoy your veal.'

His phone rang again, buzzing on the table cloth. Eric reached for it, but not before she saw the picture of a blonde, pouting at the camera.

Eric stabbed at the screen with his thumb to cancel the call, then stuffed the phone back in his pocket.

Jenny said nothing, just raised her eyebrows.

*

130

Outside Jenny called up an Uber while Eric hovered uncertainly at the door. 'You're staying in Russell Square? We can share a cab if you—'

'I'm fine. Was that everything?'

'Was ...'

'The paperwork.'

'Oh. Yeah, yes, that was all they needed.'

He looked down at the pavement and she realised that he had actually wanted something else. Her blessing. *Fuck that*, she thought, grateful to have something in her control at last.

Her phone buzzed and she saw her car arrive, a white BMW. Driven by Ahmad, apparently.

'Excellent. Then I guess this is goodbye.'

'Jennifer, I—'

'Have a nice life, Eric. Try not to get as pissed at the wedding this time. The bride won't like it.'

She got in the back of the car and shut the door firmly. As Ahmad took off from the kerb, she saw Eric out of the corner of her eye standing in the rain, one hand slightly raised, his mouth open a little. He looked like a schoolboy following a reprimand. Once upon a time, she would have felt guilty about hurting his feelings.

23

Jenny took a long, hot shower when she got back to the hotel, standing under the powerful jet and cursing herself for thinking the two of them could meet without her wanting to stab him with a fork. Fucking hell. Divorce finalised and remarried within a few months, assuming things went to plan.

She got out, towelled off and donned a robe before opening her laptop, remembering that she had something else to focus on now. She took a bottle of beer out of the minibar and opened it. Two drinks in one night. Detective Inspector Porter would disapprove, presumably.

11th November 2011. The girl's birthday. *Alice's* birthday. She wondered how easy it would be to find information on births on a particular date.

The website of the General Register Office allowed you to purchase any birth certificate, but the search had too many mandatory fields. She didn't have a last name, never mind details of the parents or place of birth. Some googling turned up a range of websites offering to provide lists of births, deaths and marriages, but many of them only offered historic records for genealogy. After a few false starts, she found a free website that allowed her to search by a range of different criteria, with no mandatory search fields. She entered the details she was reasonably sure of, specified she was looking for a birth, rather than a marriage or death, and hit 'Find'.

Well over a thousand hits. The website informed her that Alice had been the 37th most popular girl's name of that year.

She tried to narrow it down by county. There were a couple of hundred Alices born in London that year, but none on November 11th. Nothing even a couple of days on either side, just in case Monica had been wrong about the date, no luck. She started running the query again for some of the surrounding areas.

Nothing in Buckinghamshire, or Hertfordshire. Nothing in Essex. And then she found an Alice born on the eleventh.

Alice Louise Parry. 11/11/11. She paid the £5 admin charge and downloaded a pdf scan of the birth certificate. This could be it, this really could be it. This Alice had been born on the eleventh at 5:17pm, at the Royal Surrey County Hospital. The mother's details: Hazel Parry, aged 32. No details of a father.

She opened another tab and googled *'Hazel Parry'* and *London*. Nothing promising on the first couple of pages of results, just LinkedIn pages and hits on 192.com.

She sighed and took a drink of the beer. She was reaching out to close the laptop when a stamp at the bottom of the birth certificate caught her eye.

AMENDED – 06/01/2012

Amended? What happened to the original version?

Five minutes later, she had the copy of the original birth certificate. Almost everything was the same. The date of birth, the hospital, the mother's details. Again, there were no details of the father. At least, not in the allocated space.

The surname was different.

Alice Louise Devlin.

Searching again. *Devlin, 'Hazel Parry', London.*

This time, she got a promising hit.

24

The motion-activated lights had gone off in every section of the open plan office except the one where Mike was working. Bryden was out at Bridge of Orchy, taking a witness statement about a series of incidents of vandalism to the station buildings, so he had the place entirely to himself. He had stayed on past the end of his shift so he could review the Euston footage without Porter catching him. Once he had finished, he was even more frustrated than before. With each new wrinkle, he had the sense that he was edging closer to a theory. But it was like trying to see something that wasn't there. Like trying to guess what a missing jigsaw puzzle piece depicted, with the only clue being the negative space where it wasn't.

He had asked the operator at Euston to send him the footage on the Friday night. When she asked if he knew they had already sent it, he said he was interested in the whole evening, not just the portion that showed Dawson apparently getting on board the train alone.

The idea had come to him when he had reviewed the footage of the woman boarding the train. It was grainy, low-res, but it was good enough to show that the woman in the footage was Dawson. Face clearly recognisable, same clothes, same small grey canvas backpack that had been found in the room. So what was wrong with the picture?

It was the backpack that made him realise. He looked back over the interview notes and found what he was looking for. Jenny had mentioned the woman had been struggling with a case when she saw her. It was unlikely she would have described the small backpack in the video as a case, nor that anyone would have any trouble manoeuvring it into one of the rooms. So the footage didn't just fail to show a little girl, or a tall man, it failed to show a suitcase as well.

He went back over the whole data file and watched it at normal speed, all the way from the train's arrival to the last carriage disappearing out of shot. Over an hour of mind-numbing tedium, trying not to let his attention wander. But it paid off. This time, he found something else.

There was a gap in the tape.

It hadn't been obvious reviewing it at high speed, as Bryden had done, and as he had done the first time. The recording had stopped and picked up again with no one moving through the shot. It appeared to be an unbroken feed, with only the digits in the corner hiccupping from 21:00:00 to 21:02:00. Bryden hadn't caught it because it seemed that all of the relevant footage was later on: 21:11:42, when Emma Dawson had boarded alone, and 21:14:11, when Jenny Bowen had rushed into the frame, only just beating the doors.

Tosin Akinyele, the security manager at Euston, had promised to send over the full footage from 6 p.m. that night. The reason she had called earlier, inadvertently tipping off Porter, was to warn him that there was not quite a complete record from six until midnight.

'I know,' Mike said as soon as he got hold of her. 'There's a gap in the tape.'

'We don't use tapes any more.'

'You know what I mean. Who could have accessed it?'

'We had a security patch installed, which means the cameras in that section of the station were offline for a couple of minutes.'

'Was that scheduled?' Mike asked.

'Not exactly,' Tosin replied. 'It was supposed to be overnight, at 2 a.m. when the station was closed. I asked IT why it happened early and they said it was a mismatch between time zones by the contractor.'

Mike didn't say anything for a minute. His head was spinning. This was the final straw. Everything else could just about be chalked up to coincidence, but this?

'Is there any way of recovering it?'

'No, the system was completely offline. Nothing was recorded, so there's nothing to recover for those two minutes.'

Mike didn't say anything, too busy thinking. When Tosin spoke again, it surprised him that he was still on the phone.

'I'm sorry, will the footage still be useful?'

'This is great, I really appreciate this, Tosin.'

He didn't ask why they hadn't mentioned the glitch before. They probably hadn't even noticed it until Mike asked for the whole evening. But now he knew there was a gap. A gap that could well have allowed two other passengers to board the train.

And something else. This wasn't a spur of the moment operation. If Jenny was right about the missing little girl, whoever was responsible knew exactly what they were doing.

He had to warn Jenny. All of a sudden it seemed like there could be repercussions to her poking around this case that were far more serious than raising Porter's ire.

As he reached for his phone, it rang.

25

'Hi it's me.' Jenny's voice.

'We need to talk,' they both said as one.

'You go first,' Jenny said after a second.

Mike paused, part of him wanting to know her news first, but then relented. 'Okay, a couple of inconsistencies have cropped up.'

'Inconsistencies?'

Mike told her about the needle cap in the next room, and the two-minute gap in the CCTV at Euston.

'That's it,' Jenny said. 'That's when they got on. The man in the black coat and the little girl. Do you think ... do you think he could have brought her on the train?'

'I have no idea. That's the problem, there's a two-minute gap when anything could have happened, or nothing could have happened.' He stopped. He hadn't considered that before, that the man and the woman could have known each other, that the girl arrived with him. 'You said you saw the woman first and then the tall man, the one we can't trace. Did you get the impression they were together?'

'No,' she said immediately. 'I didn't even notice he was there until she closed the door on her room.'

'The other thing,' Mike continued. 'Can you describe the case she was carrying?'

Jenny paused for a second. 'Blue, I think. One of those plastic hard shell ones. Yeah, light blue.'

'You're not talking about a backpack, this was a suitcase.'

'Yes, definitely a case. Like the size you would have to check in on a plane, quite large. She couldn't get the handle to slot in.'

'We never found a case. There was only a backpack in the cabin.'

'But I told Inspector Porter about it. The other guy I spoke to as well, at least I—'

'You did, it's in his notes. He didn't take down anything else about it, just the word "case". I didn't see it until I read back over the statement yesterday.'

There was a silence at the end of the line. It was impossible to read. Was she pissed off at Porter, or at him?

'I'm sorry, Jenny, we should have looked closer.'

'What are you sorry about? You did. You are.'

'Still . . .' He couldn't think of anything more to say. He had always known Porter was a lazy bastard, but he had really screwed up on this one. Several people had made mistakes, him included, but Porter had created an environment that made mistakes more likely. It was a lot easier for people like Bryden to miss things when they knew their boss didn't want to hear about any wrinkles. So many opportunities missed. What if it was too late now?

'Anyway, this is great,' Jenny continued. 'And I found something. I think I know who the little girl is.'

He was momentarily lost for words. *How?* 'Go on.'

Jenny explained in a rush. He had to ask her to slow down and back up more than once. It was like interviewing a witness to a car crash; someone so hyped up on adrenaline that they're

138

thinking and talking slightly out of sync with the rest of the world. After a minute she had laid it all out for him.

'Alice,' he repeated when she got to the name of the child she thought might be their little girl lost. He wrote it down on his pad and circled it. 'So the woman you talked to, she said they were on the run from someone? Ex-partner maybe?'

'I don't know. Maybe. She said Emma had "something they wanted". And she was worried about a tall man with short blond hair.'

Mike wrote a word on his pad as he listened, then scrawled a question mark.

Drugs?

'But with everything I've dug up, we know Emma Dawson wasn't her mum. And once I managed to get the date of birth, well, this is the only thing that fits.'

'What do you think?'

'What if Emma Dawson was kidnapping her? I had a look on the internet but I can't see anything about a child of that name. There's been no appeal, no media coverage.'

'There wouldn't necessarily have been,' Mike said. 'Not every missing child gets the full media treatment.'

He didn't know why the big cases every few years made such a big splash, when there were so many others that never seemed to catch the attention of the tabloids. There were a number of factors that helped, of course. Race, gender, social status of the family. But he suspected the truth was there were a limited number of slots available in the media, and once those slots got filled, everything else vanished like a pebble tossed into a deep pond.

'I've been looking for some more information on Hazel Parry, but there's nothing. I was wondering, do you have, like, a database you could check, now we have a name for Alice? I would go back to the Met, but ...'

'Yeah, I can check. There isn't a single national database, but with a name and a DOB there should be something logged somewhere if the parents are looking for her. Give me everything you've got.'

Mike took notes in his scrabbly handwriting as Jenny reeled through the information.

Alice Devlin / Parry
Hazel Parry
DOB 11/11/11
place of birth Surrey?
last seen ...

He asked her where she was staying and scribbled the name of the hotel down too, already having decided he would be making a trip south in the near future.

'I'll give the refuge a call too. You never know, your visit might have jogged something else loose.'

'Okay.' Something in the slight hesitation before she spoke told him there was something else.

'What is it?'

'I don't know for sure, but ... I found something else online. The only mention of a Hazel Parry that could be the one we want. A Hazel Parry is listed attending a conference representing a company called DDC. The founder is a guy called John Devlin.'

It took him a second to make the connection. 'The last name on the original birth certificate.'

'Right.'

Mike wrote the name down. He didn't think he had heard

of the man or the company, but that didn't necessarily mean anything. 'I'll check it out. This is very ... thorough.'

'Is that a compliment?'

'I suppose so. You weren't a journalist in a previous life, were you?'

'The way you said "journalist" definitely doesn't sound like a compliment.'

He started to smile, just as he realised that he was allowing himself to be swept away by Jenny's enthusiasm. He hadn't stopped to think about the implications of what she was doing. He cleared his throat.

'Look, what I said before. I'm still not sure about what you're doing here—'

'Mike, we're getting somewhere. You know we are, don't give me this—'

'I'm not telling you to stop,' he cut in. 'All I'm saying is I think we should be careful. It's starting to look like someone else could have been involved in Emma Dawson's death. And if someone killed her, they might not think twice about taking anyone else out of the picture. I think maybe you should come back here.'

'Okay, I'll think about it. Maybe tomorrow.'

'John Devlin,' he said, reading the name from his notes again. 'Leave it with me. Don't go rushing into anything rash until we know more. Not like the thing with the Met.'

'All right, that's a sensible suggestion. Duly noted.'

Before he could say anything else, she told him she had to go, and hung up.

He sat back in his chair and jotted down a quick series of tasks, running through them in order. First he looked up Alice Devlin on the missing persons databases he could access directly. Nothing at all. Nothing for Alice Parry either. He wasn't surprised. Next, he started looking into John Devlin.

He found very little about the man online, but a reasonable amount about his company. If it was the same John Devlin, of course.

He had more luck with Hazel Parry, if it was the same one. A Hazel Parry of Surrey, 39, had been killed in a car crash in April. Another accidental death. Mike felt a chill as he processed the brief two-paragraph news article. He logged on to the UK-wide database and accessed the collision report for the incident. Single car incident, lone driver, no witnesses. He scanned the rest of the report and felt a jolt when he got to the address of the deceased.

17 Magnolia Lane.

The Emma Dawson file was still on his desk. He tore it open, leafed through the sheets until he found the probation officer's report. Her last known address: 17 Magnolia Lane.

'Shit ...' he said out loud, sitting back in his chair and looking at the collision report on the screen while he tried to process this. Two accidental deaths. Two women. One address.

He made a call to a London number. It went to voicemail, as he had expected. He left a message for an old acquaintance. He wasn't sure exactly why this acquaintance had popped into his mind, but the hunch was strong.

His next call was to Porter. He was off duty, but fuck it.

'To what do I owe the pleasure?' Porter's voice was slightly slurred. A third-beer vibe.

'I was thinking about what you said. You're right, things have been piling up for me lately, I think taking those days would do me some good.'

Porter sighed. 'You know the procedure, you're supposed to give two days' notice for each day you take.'

Mike had pulled up a flight checker on his screen, entered tomorrow's date.

'I know, I know. Listen, I was thinking I could take a long

weekend? A couple of my mates have got a cheap last-minute deal to Barcelona, and we haven't caught up in a while ...'

The screen was showing flights to London. Glasgow and Inverness were about the same driving time away, but there were a lot more flights out of Glasgow. The earliest was 6:30 a.m. He could grab a couple of hours' sleep and drive down at 2 a.m., the roads would be empty.

'Spare me the details of your plans for a weekend of debauchery, Mike,' Porter said. He drew out the pause and then relented. 'All right. Only because we're quiet. But don't say I'm not good to you.'

Mike bit back the urge to tell him where to go. 'You're a saint, boss.'

Jenny's number went to voicemail when he called back. She had probably turned it off to get an undisturbed nights' sleep.

He could try again in the morning. Or he would see her in person.

Friday, 30th November

26

'*I think we should be careful.*'

She thought about Mike's words on the phone last night as the doors of the Victoria Line train sprang open and the tinny voice announced her stop over the speaker. If Mike had been worried Jenny would do something rash, he didn't say anything to betray it. He would have been right to be worried, which was why she hadn't switched her phone back on this morning. She promised herself she would call him the minute she got out. Better to ask forgiveness than permission, and all that.

Five minutes later, she stood across the road from her destination. The slight feeling of nausea in her stomach now she was committed had her wondering again if she should have taken Mike's advice to heart. She leaned against the side of a nearby bus shelter while she swapped her purple Converse for the new pair of smart black heels she had bought on the way, stuffing the trainers into her bag.

One King Place was on the South Bank, not far from the new US embassy that Donald Trump hated so much. It was a towering glass and steel edifice, twenty-five storeys tall but not conspicuously calling attention to itself like some of the other recent additions to the skyline. She looked up at the building.

In this neighbourhood, it didn't stick out, but it still felt more Manhattan than London. She took a deep breath and crossed when there was a break in traffic. The new shoes chafed, but she had learned a long time ago it was important to match the outfit to the meeting, and from the images on the website, she didn't think this place would be a jeans and t-shirt kind of operation.

She knew that instinct had been right as soon as she pushed through the revolving door into the gleaming atrium. Her footsteps seemed to echo impudently as she crossed the floor towards reception. The guy behind the desk looked like a male model. He raised his eyes to her and waited for her to speak.

'I have an appointment with Lucine Rinzler.'

He looked down at his screen, tapped on his keyboard and looked back up at her.

'Please take a seat.'

She sat down. She knew it probably wouldn't have done any harm to follow Mike's advice and wait until they had more information, but she wanted to keep moving on this.

With difficulty, she had dug up a little more information on John Devlin. The man whose last name was on the birth certificate. He was some kind of business magnate, specialising in big construction projects. There was a reasonable amount of information about his companies, but very little about the man himself. She had woken up before seven, trying the main number for DDC every ten minutes or so and getting the recorded out-of-hours message. When she hit redial at 8:31 a.m., the phone was promptly answered on the first ring by a female voice with an Australian accent.

Jenny heard the slight smirk in the reply when she asked if she could speak to John Devlin. She had expected that, of course.

'I'm afraid Mr Devlin is not available to take calls. May I ask what this is regarding?'

'Can you pass me through to his personal assistant? This is ... a rather personal matter.'

'If you would like to give me a message I can certainly pass it on, however ...'

She didn't need to finish the sentence. Jenny had paused, thought for a second, and told the person on the end of the phone to write down her number at the hotel. Then she had said she had some information about Alice Devlin. Ten minutes later, she was called back from a private number. Was she in London? Would she be free for a meeting with a Lucine Rinzler at ten o'clock?

So here she was. At ten precisely, she heard a soft ding from the elevator bank beyond the turnstiles and a young woman in a grey suit stepped out. She was wearing a white lanyard displaying an ID card in a plastic wallet, and was holding another lanyard, this one red.

'Ms Bowen?'

Jenny stood up and smiled as she approached. They shook hands. 'Are you Lucine?'

She shook her head. 'Ms Rinzler is upstairs, follow me.'

Jenny took the lanyard, which was printed with VISITOR in block letters. She glanced at her escort's lanyard and saw that her name was Julia Harrow. They rode up in the lift at dizzying speed. The doors were glass, and looked out on the central atrium as they rose up. They stopped at the eighteenth floor, and Julia took her along the corridor. One side looked out over the Thames. The other side was a glass wall, facing in on a series of offices. They passed open plan spaces and smaller rooms, some of which had the glass opaqued for privacy. At regular intervals were blown-up photographs of what Jenny assumed were John Devlin's construction projects. The man himself appeared in a few of them. They showed a man in his early sixties, with a full head of grey hair and a tanned

149

complexion. In every photograph, whether shaking hands with world leaders or standing proudly beside another edifice, he wore the same style of suit and the same wide smile.

They passed through a set of doors and into a corridor with more doors. These looked like conference rooms, rather than offices. The rooms all had names, set out on embossed plaques on the doors. Jenny glanced at some of the names as they passed. *King*, *Madison*, *Kowloon*, *Blacklaw*.

A door at the far end opened a little further ahead and another woman stepped out. This one was dressed in a black Dolce & Gabbana trouser suit over a lavender blouse. She had brown hair and dark eyebrows above a piercing stare.

Jenny sensed Julia fall back a step, deferentially. The woman nodded to Julia and she turned and walked back the way she had come without another word. She shook Jenny's hand. 'Lucine Rinzler. Thank you for coming.'

Rinzler showed Jenny into a medium-sized conference room, this one named *Yarra*. A suburb of Melbourne, she remembered. She had worked a summer in Australia while at uni. There was a long mahogany boardroom table and a floor to ceiling cabinet in the same wood, with an embedded screen. Jenny declined the offer of coffee or water and took a seat when Rinzler indicated she should sit down.

'Thank you for seeing me,' Jenny said. 'Will Mr Devlin be joining us?'

'No,' Rinzler said flatly. 'Mr Devlin is in Singapore this morning.'

'This morning,' Jenny repeated, trying on her best ice-breaking smile. 'That's at least a full day for most people.'

'Mr Devlin is not most people.'

Jenny dropped the smile. She could tell she could turn it on full beam for a month and not make a dent in Rinzler's arctic stare. 'You probably want to get straight to the point, right?'

Rinzler placed her hands on the desk. 'Before we go any further, you should know that we take a very dim view of people who try to use information they think may be valuable to leverage some kind of advantage for themselves.'

'Oh, that's not what ... I mean, I'm not trying to—'

'On the telephone this morning, you mentioned a name.'

Jenny felt her mouth go dry. For some reason she thought of her first job interview out of uni. All of a sudden, she wished she had accepted the offer of water.

'Alice Devlin,' she said. 'That's right.'

'And what do you have to tell me about Alice Devlin?' Rinzler said, holding eye contact. It felt like she hadn't blinked since they had been introduced. Jenny composed herself. She had no reason to feel like she was under interrogation. She straightened in her chair and put her own palms flat on the table, mirroring Rinzler's position.

'Let's get this out of the way first. I'm not here to embarrass your employer, and I don't want any money. I'm not interested in going to the newspapers or doing whatever it is you're worried about. I'm just concerned about the welfare of a little girl.'

Rinzler looked only mildly interested. It was likely an act. She had shown her real interest by requesting a meeting so quickly. 'Go on.'

Jenny told her about the sleeper train, seeing the little girl. The woman being found dead, and the child not being found at all. She explained how she had followed the trail back to London. She glossed over the details of the refuge, said she had got the girl's name from an acquaintance of Emma Dawson. When she had finished, she fixed a placid look on her face and sat back, waiting to see if her bluff would be called. When Rinzler said nothing, she spoke again.

'Hazel Parry worked here. The birth certificate said Devlin before it was changed. Was John Devlin the father?'

151

Rinzler blinked.

Jackpot. It was the same Alice. Jenny fought back the urge to grin.

'I'm not interested in the details. I know relationships are complicated. I just wanted to make sure that if the girl I saw was Alice, that I could find someone who would care enough to find out what's happened to her.'

'You seem unsure.'

'That's because I *am* unsure,' Jenny said with an exasperated smile. 'I told you why I called you – I think the girl's name is Alice, and based on her date of birth, I think this could be her. If you don't think it's Alice, I imagine it will be easy enough for you to check by contacting her mother.'

Rinzler didn't answer, just stared back at Jenny. She started wondering if it *wouldn't* be easy for her to check. But why? Merely an acrimonious relationship breakdown, or was there another reason?

'Describe the child you saw,' she said after a long moment.

'I guessed she was six or seven, like I said. She was wearing a blue dress over a black long-sleeved top. Looked like Boden, or maybe a good supermarket copy. She had long, brown hair down to about here.' She indicated the relative position on her chest.

'Eye colour?'

She couldn't forget that. 'Dark brown. Almost black.'

'Anything else?'

'No,' Jenny said after thinking for a moment. 'Just the soft toy I mentioned. I only saw her for a moment, but she was there.'

Rinzler seemed to think it over, holding Jenny's gaze for a good thirty seconds. The room was entirely silent. She heard the low murmur of office chatter through the wall. From the other direction she heard the engines of a low-altitude plane, probably taking off from City.

'I'd like you to sign this,' Rinzler said at last. She slid a thin stapled document across the desk, and then produced a pen.

Jenny looked down. It was a non-disclosure agreement.

'You were very perceptive in assuming we would be circumspect in speaking to someone about such a sensitive matter,' Rinzler said. 'When that person had essentially wandered in off the street.'

Jenny scanned the front cover and read through the other six pages quickly. It looked like a standard document. It made no reference to the specifics of why she was here. In essence, it committed her not to mention anything discussed with staff of DDC at a meeting on today's date. At the end was a series of dotted lines with names next to them. The lines with her name next to them had crosses in black pen next to them.

She looked down at the crosses. What was one more legal document? And yet . . .

'I'm not signing this.'

'Ms Bowen . . .'

'I'm not signing this until you give me a good reason.'

For the first time, Rinzler smiled. It was far more unnerving than her previous expression. 'Then we are at an impasse. Our legal advisors will not allow me to proceed without your signature on that piece of paper.'

Lawyers? How much prep had she done for this meeting in a couple of hours? What the hell was the story here?

Rinzler reached for the manila envelope again and slid it in front of herself. 'What if I could show you a photograph of Alice? That might at least tell us we're talking about the same person.' She paused and examined Jenny's face for a reaction. 'But you have to sign first.'

Jenny sighed. She knew she might be caving in a little too quickly, but she had to know what was in the envelope. A part of her hoped the photograph Rinzler had in that envelope would show a different little girl. But if it showed the *same* girl . . .

'Fine.'

Jenny scrawled her signature next to each of the crosses, mentally exempting Sergeant Mike Fletcher from the agreement as she did so, and slid the document back to Rinzler. Rinzler took her time, leafing through each page as though to check they hadn't changed in the last five minutes, and examining the signature carefully.

Wordlessly, she withdrew a five-by-ten-inch photograph from the envelope.

Jenny put her hand over her mouth to stifle a gasp.

It was her.

Even though she had expected this, even though she knew that what she had uncovered so far meant it was likely that she was on the right track, the picture of little Alice Devlin came as a shock. After days of everyone doubting what she had seen, here was confirmation at last.

The photograph showed Alice a little younger, perhaps a year ago, making her five or six in the picture. She was kneeling on a fluffy white rug, in front of a white background: clearly a photographer's studio. She was wearing a yellow dress, and there was a matching yellow band holding back her brown hair. She was unsmiling, a thoughtful look in her dark brown eyes.

Her hands were in her lap, cradling a stuffed grey rabbit.

27

'This is the most recent picture of Alice,' Rinzler said after a minute. She hadn't asked for verbal confirmation that the girl in the picture was the one Jenny had seen on the sleeper. Evidently the look on her face was confirmation enough.

'What happened?' Jenny asked, before she had consciously thought about saying anything.

Rinzler put a hand on top of the signed NDA. Whether to remind her interviewee about it, or reassure herself, Jenny wasn't sure.

'How much do you know, really?'

Jenny shrugged. She told the truth. 'Not much. I explained how I came to look into it. All I know is that she was on the train with a woman named Emma Dawson.'

The name didn't seem to register with Rinzler. But then, Jenny wasn't convinced anything would register on that face if you were to stab a hatpin into her foot.

'The child was the product of a brief relationship between Mr Devlin and Hazel Parry. When the fact of the product of this relationship came to light some time later, Mr Devlin was understandably concerned about the well-being of his daughter. Her mother had ... personal problems.'

'Such as?'

'She was an alcoholic and a pathological liar,' Rinzler said matter-of-factly. 'Mr Devlin became concerned that she might try to harm the child. He attempted to secure custody, but Parry made it difficult.'

It could be true, Jenny considered. Then again, she knew some wealthy individuals weren't above a bit of character assassination if it meant they got their own way.

'I suppose claims like that would complicate everything,' she said, non-committally.

Rinzler raised an eyebrow. 'They weren't just claims. Mr Devlin was proved entirely correct, sadly. The girl's mother was killed in a car accident earlier this year. She drove into a motorway flyover support. She was five times over the limit. Thank God Alice wasn't in the car with her.'

For the second time in five minutes, Jenny felt as though the rug had been pulled out from under her.

'Wait a second, you mean her mother . . .'

'Killed herself? I suppose that's a matter of conjecture. To all intents and purposes, that is what happened, yes. After her mother's death, Alice disappeared. The police believe she was taken, possibly by a friend of the mother.'

Jenny remembered the way the two of them on a train had seemed slightly off-kilter as a pairing, even before Mike had told her about the autopsy that showed she could not have been the girl's mother. Kate at the refuge had picked up on it too.

'Taken, as in . . . kidnapped?'

Rinzler gave a brief nod. 'The police were notified, but it was as though Alice had dropped off the face of the earth. We have all of the relevant agencies looking for her, of course, but they all say the same thing. With cases like this, it's all too easy for someone to disappear.'

'Why haven't I heard about this until now?' Jenny asked.

'What do you mean?'

'Well, this sounds pretty serious. If she was kidnapped months ago, why don't I know about it? Why hasn't it been in the newspapers? Television appeals, that kind of thing?'

Rinzler shook her head. 'Hundreds of children go missing every year. The media only picks up on a vanishingly small number of cases. Mr Devlin didn't think – and the police agreed with him – that it would be productive for Alice to become a cause célèbre.'

'I know all that. The sociologists have a name for it, they call it Missing White Girl Syndrome. As in, the media only cares when someone like that goes missing. But don't you see? She's exactly the sort of case that *would* attract attention. Why wouldn't you take advantage of that?' She looked around her at the expensive-looking office furniture and the spotless carpet. 'I mean, I'm sure Devlin would be able to scrape together a reward if—'

Rinzler's eyes flashed at the mention of money. 'How many of these high-profile cases have a happy ending, Miss Bowen? How many of them have *any* ending?'

Jenny thought about that. She had a point, unfortunately. The high-profile cases that sprung to mind ended, more often than not, with a body, or with nothing at all.

'These publicity campaigns are counterproductive,' Rinzler continued. 'They absorb vast resources which could be better directed elsewhere. They attract a deluge of crank calls. They warn the perpetrators that someone is looking for them. Mr Devlin is a businessman. He understands cost and benefit, and he chose to pursue Alice's safe return in the most effective way. And despite your misgivings, he decided that a few front pages in the tabloids was not the most effective way.'

Suddenly, this had changed from feeling like a job interview to feeling like a lecture. Rinzler was on the defensive about this.

'Okay, fine,' she said. 'I just wondered.'

Rinzler seemed to catch herself, and softened her tone. 'Anyway, we're very grateful to you for bringing us this information. There's someone I'd like you to speak to.'

'Who?'

'One of the specialists we have working on Alice's disappearance.'

'I already told you all I remember. Like I said, it was a brief moment. Hardly anything at all.'

'Some might say you seem to have gone to a lot of effort for "hardly anything at all".'

'You're right,' Jenny said. 'I was concerned. Sounds like I was right to be.'

Rinzler glanced at the screen of her phone. 'If you wouldn't mind waiting for a little longer, he will be here soon.' Something about the look in her eye unnerved Jenny. It reminded her of Dad when he had a tug on his fishing line.

She checked the time. 'Actually, I have another appointment in half an hour. I didn't realise the time. I can certainly leave my number and—'

'Please, he'll be here soon. Can't you call them, let them know you'll be a little late?'

Jenny stood up, grimacing. 'Sorry. It's not that kind of meeting.'

Rinzler stared back at her, the smile frozen on her face. She looked as though she was making a calculation.

'Of course,' she said finally. 'As I said, we're most grateful for this information, and ...' Her eyes slid to the document on the table.

'I understood what I signed. I can't say anything,' Jenny said, backing towards the door and then opening it.

'We'll be in touch soon, I hope that's all right,' Rinzler called after her.

Jenny forced herself to walk at a normal pace back to the lifts. All of a sudden she became very conscious of all the people behind the glass wall on her right hand side. She felt dozens of pairs of eyes burning into her, but every time she glanced into one of the offices, no one was paying her any attention. She glanced behind her and physically flinched as she saw that Lucine Rinzler had appeared at the door of the meeting room, and was standing in the corridor, wordlessly watching her leave.

All of a sudden, she needed to be anywhere but here.

28

The lift seemed to take an age to descend to the ground floor. It stopped once, on floor seven, and a burly security guard in a grey suit got in. He nodded acknowledgement, but not before his eyes had found the lanyard hanging around her neck and scanned it for the proper information. As the doors closed, she stepped back against the wall. The guard raised a bushy eyebrow, and then turned to look up at the display counting down the floors to zero. When the doors opened, she pushed past him and headed quickly for the turnstiles. She passed through them and was making for the revolving door in the glass wall when she heard a loud 'Excuse me', from behind her.

She flinched and turned round to see the security guard approaching her, his polished shoes clicking hard off the tiled floor as he quickened his pace to catch up with her. She opened her mouth to say something before she realised he was gesturing at her chest. She raised her hand and it closed around the visitors pass.

'I'm sorry,' she said, lifting it from around her neck. 'Running late.'

She turned round, made for the doors and held her breath until she was out on the pavement.

Why the hell hadn't she listened to Mike? Or even told him

where she was going? *Because he would have talked you out of it, that's why*, she reminded herself. She kept her head down and hurried back towards the Underground. As she put more and more distance between her and the building, her anxiety began to subside a little.

She stopped when she reached a busy junction and looked back at the Devlin building, the sunlight gleaming off the blue-tinted windows of the upper floors. Was she just being paranoid? Lucine Rinzler had made her uneasy from the moment she had walked into the conference room. Perhaps that was just the kind of world she lived in. Perhaps an intimidating air was a prerequisite. All the business with the NDA was probably standard practice for a big company, too. And yet Jenny's survival instinct had kicked in big time when Rinzler had asked her to wait, and hadn't seemed to want her to go. She had suddenly realised that no one other than Rinzler and the two other staff members she had encountered knew where she was.

What had she expected? Not this. She had hoped that she would be able to confirm that the little girl on the sleeper was indeed Alice Devlin, and she had done so. Beyond that? She didn't know. She supposed she thought that they would gratefully receive the information and act on it, perhaps put pressure on the police to look into it. Whatever else, she hadn't got the impression that Lucine Rinzler would be going to the police.

She took her phone out and switched it on, immediately calling Mike on the most recent number he had used.

'Hi, this is Mike, please leave a message.'

'Hey, it's Jenny, give me a call as soon as you can.'

A great bloody time for him to have his phone off. As she hung up, Jenny thought about the message. That was a personal greeting, definitely not a work one. Meaning he was definitely looking into this off the books.

As though in confirmation, her phone buzzed with the notification of three missed calls when it had been turned off, all from Mike.

She reached Vauxhall station and hurried down the stairs to the Underground, fumbling in her purse for her card. She tapped in at the barrier, descended the escalator, and quickened her pace when she heard the roar of an approaching train. She dashed onto the platform as the last passengers disembarked and just made it through the doors before they closed.

She found a seat and rested her head back against the window as the train pulled away, closing her eyes and letting her breathing return to normal. She hadn't slowed down since pushing through the doors of One King Place.

What the hell had that been about?

She had started out the day with hopes of making some progress on finding out who the little girl had been. Perhaps a part of her had been hoping to hand the problem over to someone else.

She opened her eyes and glanced up and down the car. She had always felt slightly uneasy on the deep lines. She didn't know if it was the smaller, more claustrophobic dimensions of the trains, or just the subconscious awareness of how far below ground they were. The car was two-thirds full, no one paying much attention to anyone else. A large man with a beard and outsize headphones caught her eye and they both looked away from each other instinctively.

She closed her eyes and massaged the lids with her thumb and forefinger. She hoped Mike would call her back soon. He could be calling her right now, of course, and she wouldn't know. For the next twenty minutes, she might as well be back in the Highlands as far as phone reception was concerned. What would she say to him when they spoke? The truth. That she had a very bad feeling about being in that room, in that building. Perhaps she should have started to worry earlier. She thought back to the conversation with Monica. *They wanted something she had*. Emma Dawson was worried about someone. Without thinking too much about it, Jenny had rationalised that as paranoia. A natural suspicion of the establishment. She had been so excited to make the breakthrough of finding a name for Alice that she hadn't thought things through.

Devlin was evidently a rich man. What if his wealth was the motive behind whatever had happened on the train? What if someone was trying to get at him through his child?

'Next stop, Pimlico.'

She opened her eyes at the sound of the announcer's voice. She happened to be facing down the carriage. As she opened her eyes the car swayed for a corner, the perspective shifting to show the passengers standing beyond the big man with the headphones.

And then it happened.

Her eyes locked with a man twenty feet along the car, staring right at her.

A tall man, with silvery, close-cropped hair, wearing a long black coat.

The ghost from the sleeper.

29

She saw immediate recognition in the man's eyes before he looked away.

He knew she had seen him.

'This is Pimlico. This train is for Walthamstow Central. The next stop is Victoria.'

Questions filled her mind. How long had he been following her? Had he been watching the Devlin building?

And then more pressing questions. What the hell could she do? No phone signal down here, for a start. The train pulled to a stop with a shudder and a screech of brakes and the doors opened. A few passengers shuffled off. She kept the tall man in the corner of her eye. He didn't seem to be looking directly at her. Was it her imagination, or had he moved closer to his nearest door? Some passengers started to get on. The car was busy, but not mobbed. She made up her mind.

As the door alarm sounded, she got up, not daring to look behind her. She darted through the doors as they closed. She glanced down the platform and saw that he had stepped out at the same moment she had. He was staring straight at her now, no pretence. He hadn't made a move towards her yet.

The train moved off, the rear lights glinting red against the tiles and the advertisements lining the walls. It disappeared into the tunnel, the roar echoing in its wake.

The alighting passengers were heading for the exit. A new batch of passengers was arriving for the next train, which was coming in three minutes according to the electronic update board. The man took a step back and stood against the wall, keeping her in full view. He was between her and the exit. *Shit*.

Stalemate. She could wait for the next train and get on, but he would do the same and they would be back to square one. Perhaps she should call his bluff and walk towards the exit. After all, what was he going to do with other people around?

She looked behind her. Wondering if there was another exit further up the platform. It didn't look like it. All the arrows were pointing in the direction of the man. It wasn't an inter-change station; there wasn't even another line to choose. She should have waited for Victoria.

She moved a little closer to the exit. Keeping the man in sight. He didn't move. She stopped about twenty feet from him. There were a few other passengers between them. A young woman with a baby strapped to her front in a Baby Bjorn car-rier. A group of tanned teenagers with backpacks and phones, American or European students, by the look of them.

He hadn't made a move since getting off the train, hadn't tried to approach her. Because there was no need, of course. She was backed into a corner. She cursed her luck in where she had been sitting on the train. If only their positions had been reversed.

The countdown on the message board changed from 1 MIN to APPROACHING. She heard the distant roar of the train in the tunnel, growing steadily louder.

Get on or stay here? As the train emerged alongside the platform, she decided she would get back on. It wouldn't make the stalemate any worse, and perhaps she would get lucky.

Perhaps there would be a police officer or a guard on the train. She tried to remember the last time she had seen a staff member from TfL on a train and couldn't.

The wheels screeched and the doors opened and a steady stream of passengers stepped off while those on the platform waited their turn. She took a step towards the nearest door, alongside a man in a suit.

The man took a step forward too, mirroring her action. The last passenger stepped off her car, but she hesitated. The guy in the suit glanced at her to see if she was getting on before pushing past. The other passengers got on. The tall man stood waiting. The door alarms began to sound, and as she was tensing to get on, a big, out-of-breath man wearing an olive-green puffer jacket emerged from the exit and collided with the tall man.

Jenny didn't stop to think about it. She turned away from the doors and ran for the exit, dimly aware of the tall man pushing the big guy out of the way in the corner of her eye.

She ran through the passageway and bolted up the escalator, pushing past a female tourist in a bobble hat who was standing on the left staring at her phone. She only dared to look behind her when she got to the top. He was at the bottom of the escalator, climbing quickly. The girl in the bobble hat had decided to start walking slowly and was blocking his way up.

There was a guard at the barriers, wide-built and tall. She ran straight towards him and put a hand on his shoulder. She had touched him harder than she had meant to, it was practically a hit. He whirled round.

'What's your prob—' He stopped when he saw the look on her face.

'Please, there's a man following me.'

The guard's eyes narrowed and he looked beyond her. 'What's he look like?'

Jenny turned, ready to point the tall man out when he reached the top of the escalator. The girl in the bobble hat appeared. Then an elderly couple. Then a fair-haired guy in his twenties. There was no sign of the tall man.

'He was following me up from the platform,' Jenny said as the two of them moved back towards the escalator.

'What did he look like?' he asked again.

'About your height, maybe taller. Short hair. Black coat.'

They reached the edge of the escalator. The man in the black coat wasn't anywhere on it.

The guard turned to her. 'What did he do?'

Jenny decided he didn't really need to know the background. 'He was staring at me on the train. When I got off, he got off. He tried to stop me leaving the platform.'

The guard unclipped his walkie talkie from the strap on his chest.

'This is Charlie, can you have a look on the platform ...' He put a hand on the walkie talkie and turned to Jenny. 'Which way were you going?'

'North.'

'The northbound platform. Tall guy in a black coat. He was hassling a lady here.'

There was an unintelligible murmur of static that sounded like it could be a voice. Charlie seemed to be able to understand it. 'He's checking the cameras. Did he say anything to you?' He peered back down the escalator again as he spoke. No sign of the man in the coat. From below, the sound of another train arriving drifted up.

Charlie's radio sputtered again and he pressed a button and told the person on the other end to go ahead. The sound didn't make any more sense to Jenny this time.

'Okay,' he said in acknowledgment. He looked back at Jenny. 'No sign of him. You sure it was a black coat?'

Jenny looked back down the escalator again, and then around the ticket area. Hundreds of people hustling back and forth, eyes dead ahead, tuning out the rest of the world.

'Thanks for your help,' she said. 'He must have got back on the train.'

Charlie nodded, clearly glad to be able to get back to what he was doing. 'Take care.'

He turned away and headed back towards the barriers, where someone was inserting a ticket over and over to no effect. Jenny thought about going back down and taking the Tube the rest of the way to her hotel, but she got chills at the thought of descending back down to where she had been cornered. Charlie's colleague hadn't seen the man on the cameras, but that didn't mean he wouldn't be there. This guy had a habit of not showing up on video. She turned away from the escalator and headed quickly towards the stairs ascending to street level, scanning the space as she walked, glancing at every face.

Five minutes later, in the back of the Uber she had summoned as soon as she picked up 4G, she got a text. It was from Mike.

Call me.

30

Klenmore remembered the woman with dark hair from the train, now. He recalled her getting on just after Emma Dawson, picking up the stuffed toy she had dropped. He hadn't paid her much attention; had only looked long enough to be sure she wasn't a member of the train staff. He didn't think she would remember him. Clearly, he had been wrong.

She had seen the girl, too. That was a big problem.

When she had reached the top of the escalator he knew he wouldn't be able to approach her without drawing attention. Instead, he had pushed back down and got on the next train. He got off at Victoria, exiting onto Vauxhall Bridge Road.

He wondered if the woman would still be with the security staff back at Pimlico, or if she had moved on already.

It didn't matter either way, he knew where she was going. He took his phone out and scanned through the scant details on the target. He would receive more soon, he knew. For the moment, he had a name: Jennifer Bowen, a phone number, and a hotel. There would be more information about her soon enough, but he didn't think he would need anything else.

He hailed a taxi that was approaching with its light on. The woman wouldn't risk going back into the Tube. If he was lucky he would be able to reach her destination before she did.

31

The eyes of the concierge didn't waver from Mike's as he held the phone to his ear. Mike could hear the muffled sound of the ringing. While he waited, he glanced around the foyer. It had art deco stylings, lots of chrome and dark wood. Two elderly American tourists waited behind him, the woman crouching to rub an ache out of her calf muscle. Mike had counted eight rings before the concierge shook his head and replaced the handset on the receiver.

'No answer I'm afraid, sir.'

'Do you know if she went out?'

The man consulted his watch. 'It's entirely possible, sir. Probable, even.' The corner of his mouth turned upward as he inclined his head apologetically. Mike wondered if it was a performance. Perhaps the clientele liked their staff mildly supercilious.

'Do you know if her room has been cleaned yet?'

A polite smile. 'I don't know that information off the top of my head, I'm afraid, sir. Are you a relative of Ms Bowen? Perhaps you could call her mobile.' Pointedly, he glanced beyond Mike at the two Americans.

Like he hadn't thought of that. Jenny still wasn't answering her phone, and he was starting to worry. He thought about taking out his warrant card, decided he really didn't want to risk that unless it was really necessary. The guy was almost certainly right, after all. She had gone out.

Probably chasing down another lead. He was opening his mouth to ask if he could leave a message when his phone buzzed in his pocket. He took it out, expecting to see Jenny's number. It wasn't her.

'Excuse me a second,' he told the concierge, who acknowledged with another of his smiles. Mike backed away from the desk and found a couch to the left of the revolving door.

'Hello?'

'Is this Mike?' Male voice. Impatient, a hard, official tone.

Out of habit, Mike's eyes scanned the foyer. 'Speaking.'

'I hear you've been asking questions about John Devlin.'

What he had been able to find out about Devlin by himself worried him. Rich and well-connected and, reading between the lines, not averse to resorting to extralegal methods to get his way. When he had hit one dead end too many, he had reached out to an acquaintance he thought might be able to help him. That acquaintance had implied he didn't know the half of it.

'Who is this?'

A pause, while the speaker thought about how to answer that. 'I'd rather not answer that. But you need to back off right now.'

Mike shifted position on the couch and gazed around the foyer, his hackles up. 'I appreciate the tip. You do know I'm about a hundred times more interested in the guy now than I was five minutes ago. Who are you?'

Another pause. 'You're a copper, aren't you, Mike? Tom Selzer told me you had been asking questions.'

Mike felt a tingle of anticipation. 'Then I know who you are. Or at least who you work for. Tom said he might know someone who could—'

171

'This is for your own good. Stay away from Devlin, you don't want to get involved.'

Mike took his time responding. 'All right, you've made your point. But you're going to have to give me a good reason to back off. And then I'm going to give you a good reason for me not to.'

A long pause. 'And what reason would that be?'

'What if there's a way we can help each other?'

32

Traffic was slow as the black Nissan crossed back over the Thames on Waterloo Bridge and skirted Covent Garden, but Jenny felt more secure in the closed environment of the car. She glanced at her phone and was surprised to see that since she had been picked up at Pimlico, twenty-five minutes had passed in what felt like the blink of an eye. After she had surfaced from the Underground, she got five new notifications of missed calls, all from Mike. She would call him as soon as she reached the hotel. She didn't want to speak to him with the Uber driver listening in. They were less than a mile from her destination when the line of traffic ceased its snail-like place and seized up completely.

'Oh dear,' the driver said philosophically.

'What's happening?'

He turned back to face her. He was young, with short blond hair and wispy eyebrows. His blue eyes looked bored behind his glasses.

'Accident, by the looks of it.' His eyes shifted focus to look beyond her, out of the back window. She turned round to see blue lights flashing further back in the traffic. 'Yep.' He glanced at the screen on his dashboard. 'You might want to hop out here, you know where you're going? This is going to be ages.'

'Thanks, it's not far,' Jenny said.

She got out onto the pavement and waved as the driver started trying to reverse back onto the side street, to a series of angry horns. It was dry for now, but the clouds above looked menacing.

The hotel was still almost half a mile away, but he was right, it would be much quicker on foot. A fast-walking teenager staring at his phone almost collided with her and she stepped to the side of the pavement, looking anxiously at the ceaseless flow of people around her. She remembered welcoming the familiarity of crowds only twenty-four hours before; now the parade of unsmiling faces made her uneasy. She took a moment, looking both ways, scanning the pavements for the man from the sleeper.

Her phone showed another two missed calls: clearly Mike had something to talk about. She called him back as she walked. She wondered if he would believe her. When he had warned her to be careful the previous night, she was pretty sure he hadn't had this in mind.

'Where are you?' he said, not bothering with a hello. There was an urgency in his voice Jenny hadn't heard before.

'Still in London, I'm heading back to the hotel. Listen—'

'Where exactly?'

She looked up at the shopfronts, saw the familiar red and blue roundel about a hundred yards along the street. 'Near Holborn Tube. There's a traffic jam, so I got out and walked.' She glanced behind her, the exposed feeling growing stronger. She was being paranoid, she told herself. She had lost him at Pimlico. He had no idea where she was.

'Listen, I need you to go straight to the hotel.'

'That's what I just said I'm doing, I—'

'I think you're in danger. Immediate danger.'

As he spoke, the urgency in his voice made Jenny glance behind her again.

The tall man in the coat was there. Thirty yards behind her and closing, weaving through the other pedestrians, looking straight at her. How on earth had he . . .

'Someone's following me, I'll call you back.'

'Jenny I'm—'

Whatever he was saying was lost as Jenny took the phone from her ear and gripped it in her hand as she started to run along the street. She could worry about how the man in the coat had managed to follow her later. She weaved between the people walking in either direction and past the ones who had stopped to try and get a better view of the accident. The road was jammed with stationary traffic.

She glanced backwards again, dimly aware that she couldn't hear Mike's voice on the phone any more. He had hung up. He couldn't do her any good now, she just had to focus on losing her pursuer. He had quickened his pace but wasn't running, and yet she hadn't widened the distance between them. He seemed to keep pace with her effortlessly. She stepped out into the road and squeezed between the radiator of a lorry and the rear bumper of a red Mini. The other lane was clear, blocked by the accident she could see up ahead at the junction.

A bus was stopped halfway across the road. She saw a figure lying on the ground with paramedics crouched beside it, the mangled frame of a bicycle lying five feet away.

She kept the stalled traffic on her left, passed another couple of cars and then a large Ford Transit. She glanced behind her to see if the tall man had followed her onto the road. No need for him to do so, of course, he could see her from the pavement. As she got halfway along the length of the van, she suddenly had a premonition of him stepping out from behind it, heading her off. She turned and ducked round the back of it, back onto the

175

pavement, just in time to see a black-shoed heel and the tail of a long black coat disappear around the front of the van.

She didn't have long, maybe three seconds before he rounded the front of the van and realised she had doubled back.

There was a café directly in front of her. She pushed through the door and ignored the waiter who saw her and approached the sign telling her to wait to be seated. She saw what she was looking for and headed for it. A green fire exit sign at the back by the toilets.

Another waiter, this one more senior looking, wearing a suit, stepped into her path.

'Excuse me, miss—'

She pushed past him.

'Sorry, I'm pregnant.'

The waiter opened his mouth and closed it. By the time he had gathered himself to say that wasn't a problem, Jenny was already at the corridor. She saw the door with the pushbar and charged it, hands out, smashing the door open so hard that it hit off something outside and rebounded.

She fell out into a narrow alley. Food smells drifting out from a dozen eateries. The smell of garbage from overflowing dumpsters, sweet and rotting. She tried to orient herself, and guessed that the alley ran roughly parallel to the main road. She ran past a kitchen porter smoking a cigarette and staring into space.

The alley ended in a T-junction with another narrow passage. She slowed down, deciding it had to be safer to turn left instead of right. Her head was turned in that direction, checking the route was clear.

That was when she felt the strong fingers close around her upper arm.

33

She screamed and lashed out with her free hand, clawing at the face of her assailant.

'Jenny!'

She looked at the face of the man who had grabbed her. With the civilian clothes – jeans and a dark blue jacket – it took her a second to recognise Sergeant Mike Fletcher.

'What the *fuck*—' she began, but he was already pulling her along the alley, away from the direction of the main road. 'Come on, this way.'

They reached the street on the other side and Mike stopped to look up and down the street. Taking advantage of the pause, Jenny took the opportunity to try again.

'What the fuck is happening, Mike? Why are you here?'

He didn't answer, eyes scanning the road. He spotted a black cab with its light on and flagged it down, it swerved into the side of the road.

'Mike!'

He glanced around them again. She realised she had forgotten all about her pursuer and looked back at the alley. She couldn't see down it from this angle; couldn't see if a tall man in a black coat was hurtling along it in pursuit.

He opened the door of the cab and the two of them crammed inside.

'Where to, mate?'

'Do you know the Radisson Blu on Great Russell Street?' The driver stuck a thumb up and pulled back out into traffic without another word.

Jenny took a deep breath and put a hand on Mike's forearm. He had been looking out at the street, but turned round to face her.

'Okay, what the hell is happening?'

'I saw the guy in the coat following you. Nice move with the van, by the way. Who is he?'

She raised her eyebrows. 'Maybe start a little earlier in the story? Like, why are you not five hundred miles away? How did you find me?'

'I went to your hotel, I'd been trying to call you all morning. I was a couple of minutes away when you told me you were at Holburn. You didn't give me a chance to tell you where I was, so I just headed in that direction and saw you running.'

'Sounds like everyone and his dog is able to find me,' she said. 'Not that I'm complaining, in your case.'

Mike glanced out of the rear window, his green eyes scanning the pavements. He turned back to face her. 'You remember I was going to make a couple of calls, find out more about John Devlin?'

'I remember.'

'I found out more. Nothing good. You went to the DDC offices, didn't you?'

She didn't answer.

'I told you to wait.'

'I'm sorry, I didn't realise you were my mum.'

'For fuck's sake, Jenny, these people are dangerous. When

178

I realised what you were getting yourself into, I got the next flight down.'

Mike glanced at the driver, who seemed to be taking an interest in their conversation. He lowered his voice. 'We've got to get somewhere safe.'

'My hotel's back that way.'

'Forget about it.'

'How the hell are they going to know which hotel I'm staying in?'

'I don't know. Maybe they won't. Or maybe you made your appointment with them from the hotel phone; or they can get one of their security people to check bookings in every hotel within a mile radius of where their man lost you. Or maybe they have another way to do it. Better safe than sorry, we can hole up at the Radisson.'

She realised he was right. They knew exactly where she was staying: she had given them the phone number. That must have been why the tall man was on the street on the approach to the hotel. He had probably done the same thing she had: taken a cab towards the hotel on Russell Square, probably using the same route, then got out when the traffic jammed up. She hadn't even thought about taking a more circuitous route.

Mike glanced back at the driver, who was focusing on a right turn against traffic.

'All right,' she said. 'We can catch up properly when we get there.'

34

Klenmore emerged onto the street just in time to see the woman being bundled into the back of a cab by a man with dark hair and a navy-blue jacket. They were two hundred yards away. He broke into a run as the taxi pulled away from the kerb, trying to focus on the number plate, losing it behind a silver SUV that had rushed up behind the taxi as it pulled out.

He scanned the street for any other cabs with their lights on. But the traffic was moving smoothly and soon their cab was out of sight.

Who was the man? He had been rather enjoying his prey's futile attempts to lose him. There had been no real risk of her succeeding. The arrival of an unexpected ally was a reminder of the dangers of overconfidence.

He gave a last look in the direction the taxi had gone and turned to walk in the opposite direction.

Ten minutes later, he reached the hotel on Russell Square. The call had come from there, but there had been no way to identify a room number.

The staff member at reception smiled at him. He returned the smile but bypassed the desk. You only get one chance to get what you want at front of house, and if things don't go to plan, there are phones and security cameras to compound the mistake.

He passed the desk without breaking stride and quickened his pace to reach the lift before its doors closed, squeezing into the small cubicle with three overweight tourists with suitcases, who greeted his invasion with a weary look. He hit the button for the first floor, prompting an audible sigh, and got out when the doors opened. He scanned the corridor in both directions. The carpet was noticeably worn, in contrast to the more maintained look of reception. There was no one on this floor, just a long line of doors in either direction. He could see that the corridor continued round the corner. At least twenty rooms on this floor, seven floors above ground according to the buttons in the lift. A hundred and forty rooms, give or take.

He followed the signs to the stairs and climbed up to the second floor, finding what he was looking for almost immediately. There was a service cart outside the second door from the stairwell, the door propped open. He approached the cart, keeping close to the wall and making sure he trod lightly on the carpet. The cart was piled high with clean towels. In the shelves underneath there were small bottles of cosmetics and individually wrapped tea bags and biscuits and toilet paper. There was a clipboard secured to the side with a strap.

He took the clipboard and was pleased to see that the document on top was a computer printout, meaning the likelihood of the kind of detail he wanted was higher. Bingo. The sheet was laid out in a grid, with a blank column on the far right where some boxes had been ticked by the cleaner in blue ballpoint pen, and some had been greyed out. The columns showed rooms and guest names and checkout dates and times.

Klenmore heard a gasp and looked up to see the cleaner had appeared in the doorway. She was slim, with pale blonde hair. She had a hand over her mouth as she wondered what to do about the strange man interfering with her cart.

'It is not allowed,' she said, with a strong Eastern European accent. She reminded Klenmore a little of a whore he had frequented in Bosnia, back when things were interesting over there.

'I work for the hotel. Your manager didn't tell you I was coming?' He frowned and tapped the pad sharply. 'Inspections.'

She looked unsure. He continued looking down at the sheet. He found the name. Bowen. 618. Checkout date tomorrow.

Klenmore replaced the clipboard and put a hand on the door frame. The woman flinched backwards. He leaned into the room, blocking off the doorway. He heard the breath catch in her throat as he inspected the room within. She had nearly finished. The bed was neatly made up, the accoutrements on the desk were neatly arranged, the tea and coffee station had been restocked.

After a moment, he stepped back out into the corridor.

'Excellent, well done,' he said. He reached into his pocket and produced a twenty-pound note. He held it towards her. 'Bonus.' As she reached for the note, he pulled it back. 'But don't tell anyone.' He put a finger to his lips.

The woman hurriedly took the twenty. Klenmore turned and headed for the stairs.

35

The Radisson was a refurbished Edwardian building on Great Russell Street, near the British Museum. Mike went in first and got them a twin room. It turned out to be a suite, with a separate living room and a huge bathroom. Jenny flopped down on the couch. Mike went to the window. He was looking down at the street below.

'I didn't say thank you.'

Mike spoke without turning away from the window. 'Looked like you were doing okay. Apart from getting yourself into that situation in the first place, I mean.'

'Okay, time to explain,' Jenny said. 'What happened after we spoke last night?'

Mike moved away from the window and sat down on the chair opposite Jenny. 'I did some checking into John Devlin. I found the stuff you were talking about. But I found out a lot more as well.'

'Like what?'

'I'd never heard of the guy. You hear about all these shadowy Russian oligarchs owning huge chunks of London, but we have our own home-grown dodgy characters as well.'

Mike got up and opened the minibar, taking out a glass

bottle of sparkling water and offering it to Jenny. When she declined, he spun the top off and took a drink.

'That's probably going to cost you a fiver, you know.'

He ignored her and continued.

'Devlin flies below the radar because it makes it easier to conduct business out of the public eye. He's not a Branson or a Murdoch or a Trump; nobody knows who he is. And yet he's worth more than ninety-five per cent of the guys who make the *Sunday Times* Rich List. His biggest interest is construction. His projects always get approval. Sometimes that's because the right person takes a bribe, and sometimes if the wrong person is standing in his way, they end up floating in a reservoir.' He picked up his tablet and woke the screen. 'This guy was the deciding vote on a planning committee that was going to block a hotel resort in a nature reserve in Colorado.' He showed Jenny a news article on his tablet. The headline read *Local Councilman Found Dead*.

Jenny scanned the article. 'It says there were no suspicious circumstances.'

Mike nodded. 'Newspaper code for a suicide. I dug up some more accounts that implied there were nothing but suspicious circumstances, but the local cops came under a lot of pressure from above to sweep it under the rug.' Mike opened his mouth to say something else, and then reconsidered. 'Your turn. Why don't you tell me about what happened today?'

Fair enough, Jenny thought. 'I called them this morning. I wasn't expecting much. I just hoped I could get someone to confirm if the Alice Devlin on the birth certificate was the Alice I saw on the train, and the one the people at the refuge knew. I didn't think it could do any harm. And then someone called me back straight away and asked me if I could come in for a meeting.'

She saw Mike's pained expression and gave an irritated sigh.

'I know, okay? Don't say it. I shouldn't have rushed in there like that. I just never thought ...'

'Did you meet him? Devlin?'

She shook her head. 'A woman called Lucine Rinzler. She was kind of like Mary Poppins crossed with Nurse Ratched.'

'Intimidating?'

'You can say that again. She treated it like an interrogation. Made me sign a non-disclosure agreement before she would tell me anything. She asked me to go through everything.'

'Did you?'

'The important parts: the sleeper, finding Emma Dawson dead, the little girl going missing. I left out how I found out her first name and her birthday. After I signed the NDA she showed me a picture of Alice. It was her.'

'Did she tell you anything else?'

Jenny thought back. 'Not really. She said the mother was dangerous, unsuitable. I took it with a pinch of salt. She said she was killed in an ac—' Before she could finish the word, her eyes were drawn to the news article on Mike's tablet. The smiling face of the councilman from Colorado. No suspicious circumstances. 'Shit, you don't think—'

'I definitely do think. She's telling the truth about Hazel Parry. About her dying in a car crash, anyway. Look at these.'

He handed her two printouts. One was a report on the accident that had killed Hazel Parry. The other was some kind of evaluation form. The subject was Emma Dawson.

'What am I looking for?'

'Look at the addresses.'

Her eyes widened. 'Shit, they lived in the same fucking *house*.'

Mike nodded. 'Last night I called in a few favours, used a few connections. Half an hour ago, I got a call from a guy who wants me to back off, because Devlin is under investigation.'

Jenny felt suddenly dizzy. She must have looked pale, because Mike held out the bottle of water. She took it and had a long gulp from it. The bubbles tickled her throat on the way down.

'Fucking hell.'

'What happened after you IDd Alice from the photograph?'

'She didn't want me to leave. She said there was somebody coming who they wanted me to speak to. I don't know, maybe I had just had a little more time to get suspicious of the whole thing, or maybe it was just the way her whole manner changed. All of a sudden she was too nice. Like she was trying to close a deal. I just knew I should get out of there.' Jenny closed her eyes. How easy it would have been to bow to the pressure, to stay in that room. What would be happening to her now? How would they have made sure she didn't have any other valuable information?

'You did the right thing. The man in the coat, did he follow you from the building?'

'I suppose he must have. He's the Nowhere Man we talked about.'

It took Mike a second to make the connection with their conversation yesterday. 'The man from the sleeper?'

'The very same. I only noticed him on the Tube. I thought I had lost him at Pimlico but then when I got out at the traffic jam, he was behind me again.' She stopped and thought about how quickly he had picked up her trail. 'He's working for Devlin, right? Has to be.'

'Could be,' he said. 'Or maybe he works for one of Devlin's enemies.'

'So what do we do now?'

'I don't know,' Mike said. 'But either way, I have a bad feeling Devlin and his people know a lot more about what happened to Alice, and Emma Dawson, than they're letting on.'

36

Jenny moved to the window and peered down at the street, watching the pedestrians and the cars pass this way and that. She wondered if *he* was down there somewhere, looking for her.

Mike said, 'How much did you tell them about yourself?'

'Just my name.'

'Where you live?'

She thought about it, then shook her head. 'I'm not even sure of that right now, so how could I tell them?'

'All right, then the smart play is we head back north and hope they decide you're not worth the trouble. Do you have someone you can stay with for a few nights?'

'Maybe,' she said, wondering if Meryl would mind if she crashed on her couch. 'But what about Alice? I'm not going anywhere until we know where she was taken.'

Mike sat back. 'Somehow I thought you might say that. We need to buy time to find out where she is.'

'You're the police. We can walk right in there and—'

'And what?'

Jenny stopped. What indeed? What could she really prove? She had felt uneasy at a meeting with Devlin's representative, and then a man had followed her on the Tube. A man she had seen before, but could not identify by name. There was nothing concrete to prove the two events were connected. Worse, there was nothing to prove his daughter Alice was the girl Jenny had seen on the train. And just because Devlin was shady didn't mean he directly had something to do with Alice being spirited away.

'Listen,' Mike said. 'About that. With all of the excitement earlier, I didn't get a chance to tell you something.'

'What?'

'I'm not here in an official capacity. I'm on leave.'

'What?'

He shook his head. 'Porter isn't interested in this case. As far as he's concerned it's closed. He made that pretty clear to you, didn't he?'

She nodded. That was an understatement. 'But he's not the be-all and end-all, surely.'

'Up there, yes he is. And I know you think I haven't exactly helped. But I tried to push for more time to look into it. Porter fobbed me off at first, then he started to get pissed off. He seems to think I'm only interested in what you're saying because I'm interested in you.'

Jenny looked up sharply.

'Oh, don't worry, I'm not. Not at all,' Mike said. 'Look, I'm the only single guy on the squad. They assume I have an active social life.'

'Well, thank you for being so certain about the impossibility of being interested in me,' Jenny said.

'I didn't mean—'

'Kidding,' Jenny said, forcing a smile.

He returned the smile apologetically. 'Anyway, I had some leave built up. We're quiet at the moment, and when I found out more about Devlin ...'

'So you're here as what ... a normal person?'

'Essentially, yes.'

'That's not a lot of help,' she said. 'Can't you do *anything*? That guy basically tried to kidnap me. He probably did kidnap Alice.'

'And we have zero proof of either of those things. We don't even know what his name is. You know what that means?'

'That we're screwed?'

'I was going to say, we need to know more. We need to find out who he is.'

She thought about the way the tall man had glanced at her on the train that first night. And then the way his eyes had looked on the Tube. Like a shark, zeroing in on its prey.

'The way I see it,' Mike continued, 'There are two possibilities: either he's working for Devlin, or he's working for someone dangerous enough to go after Devlin's family. And I'm not sure which scenario worries me more.'

37

They decided they had to find out everything they could about John Devlin, anything that might give them a clue to his relationship to the man on the sleeper, anything that might suggest what could have happened to Alice.

It wasn't easy. She spent time hunting down mentions of Devlin online, without much more success than she had had the other night. For such a high-net-worth individual, she was astonished there wasn't more. DDC kept a surprisingly low profile; just a slick but stripped-down website with a phone number, no social media.

Compared to its owner, it was practically attention-seeking. She could find very little about Devlin online. A few mentions in news articles, the occasional photograph shaking hands with a politician at a charity dinner or a foreign dignitary at the opening ceremony of another building. The most recent photograph she could find was five years old. He looked much like he had done in the picture in his building. Tall, well-built, his grey hair expensively trimmed. He looked a little like a more ordinary-looking Robert Redford in late middle age.

The world was run by people like this, she mused. Not the ones who did publicity, or headed up the brands everyone has heard of, but the men who made their fortunes under the radar, using any means.

She found a magazine profile from the early 80s. The pages of the original magazine had been scanned and uploaded years before, though still long after the article had been published, going by the creasing and yellowing evident on the scan. She blew the image up on her screen, wishing she had a desktop to work with, or a printer. The profile was reasonably in-depth, over four pages with pictures of the exterior of the then-under-construction Devlin East Coast headquarters in New York City, with a few of Devlin himself touring the site wearing a suit and a hardhat.

There was a smattering of biography throughout the piece, amounting to perhaps two or three short paragraphs, but still more than Jenny had been able to turn up elsewhere.

Devlin had been born in 1952, to a British diplomat and his wife in India. His family had been moderately wealthy, but Devlin had taken that advantage and run with it, establishing a construction company in the mid-seventies before expanding to build skyscrapers and stadiums in countries across the globe. At the time of the piece, he was estimated to be worth $2.6 billion, though Jenny knew estimates like that were pulled out of thin air, as often as not. He was married to his first wife at the time of the article, and from one of the few other articles Jenny had found, she knew there had been a second marriage in the late 90s.

The journalist did the usual thing of painting a picture of his subject in between quotes from the interview; talking about how guarded and enigmatic he was. Jenny could have guessed that from the quotes, anyway. He was always on-message, always managed to bring the conversation back to the subject of the new building. The only line that revealed anything of his personality was an aside about modern architecture.

Despite the clean lines of the new building, Devlin admits to a hankering for a more classic style.

'I'm more of a traditionalist in my own tastes,' he says, as we take a moment to admire the view over Midtown from the 61st floor. 'Someday I'll retire, and it won't be to a place like this. It'll be an old Victorian place in London, or some stately pile somewhere. Something that was there a hundred years before we were born. But of course, everything becomes classic if it's around long enough, doesn't it? I hope this place will be here a century after we're gone.'

It's an interesting moment. It's the only time in the interview when Devlin looks truly animated, at the thought of making his mark, leaving something for the future.

Jenny switched tabs to the Excel doc where she had been building up a timeline of Devlin's life, pulling together all the meagre pieces of information she had found. Two ex-wives. No children, at least not officially. A deliberate choice, perhaps. No time for a family with his business commitments.

Devlin's first wife had died years before. For the second, all she could find was a first name: Selina. No maiden name; nothing to show what had happened to her after she was with Devlin. If she was still alive, perhaps she might be able to tell them something.

She heard Mike's footsteps in the adjoining room and looked up to see him pulling his jacket on.

'Any joy?' she asked.

Mike raised his eyebrows noncommittally. 'Perhaps. I talked to my contact again.'

'The guy you spoke to last night? I thought you said that was a dead end?'

'He's agreed to give us fifteen minutes. I think I piqued his curiosity when I told him exactly what we were investigating.'

'Where?'

'I don't know yet. He's going to call me back with a place in a couple of hours. In the meantime, there's something I need to take care of. I'll be back in an hour.'

'Where are you going?'

'I'll be back in an hour.'

'Okay,' Jenny said, closing the laptop. 'I'm coming with you.'

'Absolutely not.'

She folded her arms and stared back at him until he shook his head and relented.

'Fine.'

38

Mike called for a cab and gave the driver an address in Lewisham. On the drive, Jenny stared out of the window and thought about the wives.

Devlin's first wife was born Eva Mills. There was a picture of them at the wedding, cutting the cake. Eva was an icy blonde with chiselled cheekbones. She could have played the female lead in a Hitchcock film. She had died of breast cancer not long after her divorce. Reading between the lines of the obituary, Jenny got the idea she had been quietly offloaded by Devlin when she became ill. There was very little information about the second wife, Selina. Married in 1999, divorced in 2003. No trace of a maiden name, no information about what she was doing now. Had Devlin made her disappear too? Had she been a problem in need of solving?

Jenny looked up as they pulled up outside a pub called The Thirteen Bells. It was a two-storey building perched on the corner of two main roads, with grubby whitewashed walls and shutters over the windows. Only the pair of unkempt smokers standing outside the doorway gave any clue that it was still in business.

'You sure this is the right place, mate?' the cabbie said,

eyeing Jenny in the mirror. 'Can get a bit tasty in this neck of the woods, know what I mean?'

'I'm meeting a friend,' Mike said.

The cabbie raised an eyebrow as though it was their funeral, and read off the exorbitant fare from the meter. Mike handed over some notes and they got out onto the pavement. As he did, the sleeve of his jacket pulled back and she saw the blue-grey fabric strip that she had seen on the first day she met him. The one that seemed out of place.

'Why do you wear that?' she asked, pointing to it as he shut the door on the cab.

He glanced down at it as though remembering he was wearing it for the first time. 'A keepsake,' he said. 'Or a memento, I guess.'

'I thought those were the same things.'

Mike shrugged and looked away. Conversation over, apparently.

Jenny glanced around the street. It was far less busy than the city centre. There were only a few pedestrians. A guy in a hi-vis vest stood at the nearby bus stop staring at his phone. The cabbie was right, it didn't look like the most salubrious neighbourhood, but given her experience earlier, Jenny was more than happy to be away from the crowds.

'"Meeting a friend",' she repeated as the taxi pulled away from the kerb. 'Who is this? Some kind of supergrass?'

'I'd advise you not to say that when we get inside,' he said.

He pushed open the door and led the way into the dimly lit interior. There was only one window, so the lights were on inside. Jenny's nose was assaulted by an olfactory cocktail of stale beer, bleach, urine and smoke. Over a decade since the smoking ban had come into effect, but probably a great deal longer since this joint had been properly aired out. It was a long room with a stained blue carpet underfoot. The bar was on the left side as they entered. A pool table at the back, in front of three doors marked 'Fillies' and 'Colts' and 'Private'. There were only half a dozen customers, most of them on stools at the bar, one of them lining up solo shots on the pool table. There was no music. A television above the bar was tuned to a football match.

'Nice place,' Jenny said under her breath.

If Mike heard the comment he gave no indication. He approached the bar and made eye contact with the person behind it: a short woman in her sixties with an unlit cigarette tucked behind her ear.

'What can I get you?'

'Is Jimmy about? He asked me to pop in.'

She gave the two of them a suspicious look-over and turned away from them, picking up a cheap-looking mobile phone from beside the gin. She lifted the phone to her ear and spoke quietly, then turned round and looked them up and down again.

'Yeah, that's him,' she said.

She hung up and waved a hand towards the back of the room. 'Door on the right, go on up.'

Mike led the way, past the drinkers on their stools, past the solo pool player, to the back of the room. He pushed on the door marked 'Private'. It opened on a narrow stairway, the steps uncarpeted concrete. They climbed a single flight to a door at the top. Mike glanced back at Jenny. 'None of this happened, okay?'

She kept following, wondering what the hell she was getting herself into now.

He knocked twice and turned the handle.

The door swung open on a small room with a window looking out on the street, the view mostly obscured by venetian blinds. There was a much stronger smell of smoke in here. There was a man sitting behind an old desk strewn with receipts and paperwork and folded-up racing magazines. There was an overflowing ashtray on the desk, a cigarette tucked into one of the notches on the edge and burning away.

The man behind the desk could have been any age from his forties to his seventies, but the shape he was in was less open to question. He was at least eighteen stone, had grey-black hair that was retreating fast from his forehead but streaming down to his shoulders around the back. His complexion was ruddy, with gin blossoms on his cheeks. He wore a hooded green top with the word ATHLETIC printed across the chest.

'All right?' he said by way of greeting, eyeing both of them carefully.

'Mo sent me,' Mike said. 'He said he'd call ahead with the specs.'

The fat man didn't acknowledge. 'You a copper, son?' He shifted his gaze to Jenny. 'How about you?'

Mike grinned, as if this was hilarious banter. 'If I was a pig, would Mo have sent me here?'

He shrugged and fixed Mike with a stare. 'His funeral if he did.' When Mike's gaze didn't waver, he broke into a wide grin. 'It's all right, sonny, just playing with you. He told me you were in the army with him. He give you a price?'

'Five hundred.'

'Seven.'

'Mo said he'd spoken to you. He said you'd said five.'

'Mo was mistaken.'

Jenny looked over at Mike. He seemed to be thinking it over. 'That's a shame,' he said finally. 'Sorry we got our wires crossed.'

He turned to go and had his hand on the handle when the man said, 'Wait.'

Mike turned round.

'Six hundred. Best I can do.'

'I have five-fifty on me.'

'There's a cash machine down the road.'

'And you probably have cheaper competitors down the road, too.'

He said nothing for a moment and then grinned again. He clearly enjoyed this dance. 'You drive a hard bargain.'

Mike took out a fold of fifty-pound notes and leafed through them, to show he was counting out five-fifty. He laid them on the desk. 'There you go,' he said.

The man picked up the sheaf of notes. He licked his thumb and expertly leafed through, although he had just watched Mike count them, and then nodded.

He reached behind the desk and unlocked a drawer. He took out a shoebox and put it on the desk in front of him.

Mike opened the shoebox and Jenny stifled a gasp. There was a gun in the box, a black pistol with a brown plastic grip. Mike took it out, examined both sides, peered down the barrel, then flicked a catch to eject the magazine. It was empty. He looked up at the man behind the desk expectantly.

'Marie at the bar will give you a box of ammunition. Wouldn't be a very good idea for me to sit around handing people loaded guns, would it? They might get ideas about not having to pay.'

'Perish the thought,' Mike said.

'Nice doing business,' he said, tapping the sheaf of notes square on the table.

Jenny didn't say anything until they were outside. Mike was reaching into his jacket for his phone. She glanced around them and pushed him into a side street between two rows of shops.

'What the hell was that?' she hissed.

'That was me making sure we have some protection.'

'Protection? This isn't the Wild West! What kind of policeman are you?'

'Apparently, not a very good one.'

She closed her eyes and rubbed her eyelids, feeling like she had a sudden tension headache. 'You really think this is a good idea?'

'What do you think? How scared were you this morning, when that guy was following you?'

She said nothing.

'I already told you, I'm not here. Right now, I'm not a police officer.'

Jenny sighed. 'This is all moving a little too fast for me, that's all. I didn't expect any of this when I woke up this morning.'

'You started this,' he reminded her. 'And somebody had to. No one would have known that anything was wrong if you hadn't been on that sleeper train, and if you hadn't stuck to your guns.'

Jenny gave him a wary look. 'You didn't have to believe me, and bloody encourage me. And speaking of guns ...' Her eyes went to the backpack hanging over Mike's shoulder by one strap. It was in there, along with a box of ammunition, supplied by Marie downstairs as promised. 'You know how to use that?'

'Wouldn't have been much use in Helmand if I didn't, would I? Look, I don't want to have to use it, and if we keep clear of your friend from this morning, we won't need to look at it again.'

'But?'

'But if we end up with our backs to the wall, I'd rather have a gun than not. All right?'

Before she could answer that, Mike's phone rang. He answered with a hello and listened, staring out at the cars passing by on the street. He checked his watch. 'Works for me, I can be there in half an hour?'

199

'Your contact?' Jenny asked as he hung up.

'That's right. Which means I have to be a police officer again for a while.'

39

The black Lexus rounded the corner five minutes after Klenmore had pressed send on the message.

The driver was a young man, probably in his twenties, with reddish-brown hair and dark glasses, wearing a white shirt and a blue tie. He looked at Klenmore just long enough to acknowledge that this was his pickup and pulled up to the kerb, engine running. Klenmore heard the soft click as the central locking disengaged on the rear door on the passenger side. He got into the back seat and closed the door behind him. The driver didn't say anything, didn't ask for a destination. He knew all of that already, and he knew not to speak unless he was spoken to.

Klenmore leafed through the notebook he had taken from Bowen's hotel room. It was the only thing of potential interest that had been left in the room. There was a suitcase with two changes of clothes, but nothing else. She had kept her phone and any other devices on her person, unfortunately.

From the notes, it looked as though she had been calling around various charities and council departments. He could guess what she had been looking for. Or rather, who. Perhaps some of the numbers could be useful later.

Why was she so tenacious? She had no connection to the woman or the girl, so what reason could she have for putting herself in harm's way like this? But perhaps she didn't realise just how much harm she could come to.

The driver's compartment was behind a glass screen. Klenmore pressed the white noise button and dialled one of the four numbers saved to this phone.

It was answered immediately.

'What's your progress?'

'She has someone helping her,' Klenmore said, then described the man he had seen Bowen getting into the cab with. 'He knew not to go back to the hotel.'

There was a long pause. 'What is she doing?'

Klenmore assumed the question was rhetorical. It wasn't his business to decide why anyone did anything. Stopping them doing things was more his purview.

'We have the details from the DVLA and HMRC,' the woman continued. 'I've sent you a copy.'

As she spoke, Klenmore felt his phone buzz with the email. He read it over. This was good. All sorts of useful information: date of birth, employment records. A home address: a flat in Highbury.

'Current residence?' Klenmore asked, a little sceptically.

'As far as I can see, yes. Why wouldn't it be?'

'She was going to Scotland last week. When she came back to London, she stayed in a hotel.'

'I see,' the woman said. 'Well, that's the address we have.' The rest was unspoken: *everything else is up to you.*

'All right.'

'I'll be making a report tonight.'

'It'll be over by then,' Klenmore said. 'Put me through to transportation.'

There was no acknowledgement. Just a pause, and then he heard a click and a ring tone. He rather liked the new woman's manner. No words wasted. Implication always clear.

'Transportation.'

'I need an alert on a traveller. All London departures.' The only one worth a damn would be airports, of course, but it was worth casting a wide net. The woman had used her real name at the hotel, after all.

He heard keys tapping. 'Name?'

He glanced down at the record on his phone. 'Jennifer Laura Bowen, white female, DOB nine three eighty-three.'

More tapping.

'That's in the system.'

Klenmore hung up and drummed his fingers on his knee. He didn't think Bowen would be at the flat in Highbury, but perhaps someone else would. He turned the white noise off and flicked the switch to the intercom. The driver spoke without taking his eyes from the road.

'Good afternoon, sir, everything all right?'

'Change of destination,' he said.

40

Jenny fastened her seatbelt in the black cab and sat back, looking out of the window as they headed north again. She felt her anxiety begin to rise as the crowds grew thicker on the pavements. She knew it was irrational. The man in the black coat was out there somewhere, but there was a good argument that a city of ten million people was the best place to hide. The sky was getting crowded too, thick storm clouds blocking out the last of the autumn daylight.

As they crossed the river again, she saw the dome of St Paul's, rising above the more modern additions to the skyline. She wondered if any of the new buildings would endure for as long, and that reminded her of the article she had found, the profile about Devlin's building in New York. She told Mike about it, and how something about it had stuck out to her: that he had had two marriages with no children.

'No children, just like Emma Dawson,' Mike mused.

She thought back to earlier, her speculation that Devlin had been too busy for a family. But perhaps that wasn't true. Business responsibilities didn't usually prevent a man from having children, if he wanted to. What if it wasn't his choice? And then there was the moment in that interview where he had talked about his buildings still being around a century from now. What if that desire to leave something for the future extended to more than just buildings?

'If Alice really is Devlin's child,' Jenny said after a minute, 'it's kind of weird.'

'How do you mean?'

'Well, he's pushing seventy. There were no children from either of the marriages, and then his first is from a fling with a subordinate? Maybe even a one-night stand?'

'Maybe Alice wasn't really his,' Mike said. 'Maybe Hazel Parry was trying to fool him, shake him down.'

'I don't think so. From what Rinzler said, Devlin was convinced it was the real deal. And it sounded like Parry kept it secret from him for a long time. Maybe until this year. That doesn't sound like a shakedown.'

Mike considered it. 'Can we talk to the ex-wives about this? Why there were never any children? It might answer some of these questions.'

She shook her head. 'One's dead, I haven't had any luck finding anything about the other one's whereabouts. Not even a last name.'

They reached the arranged meeting place a couple of minutes later: a branch of Pret on Islington High Street. A little less characterful than their last stop, Jenny was relieved to see. There was a man in a suit sitting at the back, a bottle of water in front of him. He looked up at them as they walked in. Mike raised a hand. Jenny let him go ahead while she bought them a couple of coffees. She stole glances between speaking to the server. Mike and the other man were shaking hands. The body language seemed to suggest a mutual wariness, and perhaps that this was the first time the two had met. In person, at least.

She brought the coffees over to the table at the back of the room. The man sitting with Mike was in his early twenties, with a grey suit, light pink shirt, sensible tie. Sort of blandly handsome, with light brown hair. He looked more like an IT manager in a council department than a police officer. As she soon discovered, there was a reason for that.

'This is Adamson, he and his colleagues have been looking into our mutual friend.' He turned to the man. 'This is Jenny. You two ought to get on, she ... does something with computers too.'

Jenny rolled her eyes. 'He's very technical. So you're what ... some kind of cybercrime guy?'

Adamson didn't speak. His eyes flitted to Mike.

'He does a lot of work with HOLMES,' Mike said. 'Making connections. What we're looking for.'

'"Holmes?"' Jenny repeated. 'As in Sherlock?'

Adamson's eyes slid to Mike, like he wasn't sure if she was winding him up.

'She's a civilian, she doesn't know any of this stuff.'

Adamson nodded understanding. 'HOLMES is the database we use to track major crimes across the UK.'

'Oh, like the NCIC database they have in America?'

Adamson's brow creased in irritation. 'How do you know about that?'

'Michael Connelly novels.'

Adamson sighed. 'Yes, like that. Murders, drug trafficking, serial killers, big-ticket fraud.'

'Has Sergeant Fl—'

'Mike,' he cut in. 'Unofficial, right?' he said, looking back at Adamson.

'Very unofficial,' he agreed.

'Has Mike told you why we're here?'

'The basics, yes. I'm afraid that, while what you were concerned about is relatively minor in the scheme of things, there's the potential to open a can of worms.'

'Minor?' Jenny repeated. She felt Mike's hand lightly on her

206

forearm and, with an effort, stopped talking. 'A missing child is minor?'

Adamson stared back at her, unapologetic. 'That's right, minor. The NCA has been looking into Devlin for quite a while. That's National Crime Agency. Like the FBI,' he added, eyeing Jenny with more than a hint of condescension. She didn't rise to the bait. 'A mutual acquaintance put Mike in touch with me earlier because he knew I was working the case. Mike said you don't think Hazel Parry's death was an accident.'

'We don't,' Jenny said. Adamson looked from her to Mike, who didn't say anything, so she kept talking. She explained how she had come back to London to find out what could have happened to the little girl on the sleeper. How her digging had turned up a lead to a woman and a child at a west London refuge. The date of birth that allowed her to link the girl she had seen with a name. The confirmation that the woman she had discovered dead on the train had not been the girl's mother.

'So you can see how we started to become a little suspicious,' she said. 'Two women dying suddenly, both connected to the same address, both connected to one little girl. A little girl who appears to be the sole heir to a billionaire.'

'A billionaire who is into some deeply shady stuff,' Adamson agreed. 'So, my next question is, what are you planning to do about it?'

There was an implied threat in the way he looked at Jenny and Mike. As if to say, he might help them if he could find an upside for himself, but only if they kept out of his investigation.

'We need to find out who has the girl,' Jenny said. 'And where she is now.'

'And how the hell do you propose doing that?' Adamson said. 'I don't recommend calling them up and asking, by the way.' He caught the slight glance that passed between them and looked astounded. 'You didn't actually call them up? Tell me you didn't fucking call them and ask.'

'It wasn't like that,' Mike began, and this time Jenny silenced him with a hand on his shoulder.

'I'm sorry, seeing as I'm just a civilian, it didn't occur to me that John Devlin was some big supervillain. So yes, when I worked out that the little girl I was looking for could be related to him, I got in touch. I thought he might be concerned enough to help.'

Adamson picked his phone up from the table and gripped it in one hand, like a rigid stress toy. 'What did you tell them?'

Jenny sighed. 'I told them I was concerned about a missing little girl named Alice Devlin and wondered if it was the same one. I finessed how I'd got the name. They asked me to come in. I got a bad feeling from the place when I got there.'

'Do you have any idea how lucky you are they didn't harm you?'

'I do, yes,' Jenny said coolly. 'They wanted to keep me there. I got the hell out of there, and the next thing I know there's a guy following me. The same guy who was on the sleeper. Don't worry, I won't be making a return visit.'

Adamson looked from Jenny to Mike, as if asking if he had known about this. Then he spoke through clenched teeth. 'Do you know how long we've been laying the groundwork on this case?'

'We don't know,' Mike said, 'and to be honest we don't really care. We're not particularly interested in corporate malfeasance. We're trying to find a missing child.'

Adamson rolled his eyes and then composed himself. 'I'm sorry. It's just, we really didn't need anyone blundering in to the situation at this point.'

'And yet here we are,' Mike said. 'Come on, we can help each other. It's too late for us to be uninvolved now.'

'For fuck's sake,' Adamson hissed under his breath. 'All right, I need you to tell me about this man who followed you.'

Jenny opened her mouth, but Mike held a hand up. 'This information is valuable to you,' he said.

'Maybe, maybe not. Tell me what you know.'

'And in return?' Jenny prompted.

Adamson's eyes flitted to Mike. 'We need to look at what you've got on Devlin's personal life,' Mike said. 'Any files, any ...'

Adamson was already shaking his head. 'Out of the question.'

Mike folded his arms. 'What happened to his daughter after Hazel Parry was killed? You can tell us that.'

'I can't,' Adamson said after a moment. 'Devlin's relationship with this woman wasn't on our radar, but it seems to check out. No mention of a kid, though.'

Rinzler had lied, then. They had never got the authorities involved with Alice's disappearance. Jenny wasn't surprised. She thought for a minute. What else was there?

'We're trying to find Devlin's other ex-wife. Selina,' Jenny said. 'She disappeared after the divorce. I hoped she might be able to help us if we could speak to her, even send her an email.'

Adamson tapped his fingers on the table for a moment before answering. 'I'll see what I can do. But first ...'

Jenny glanced at Mike. This was as good as they were going to get. She described the tall man to Adamson. His height, build, the silvery close-cropped hair. Adamson nodded when she had finished, as though she had given him another piece of the puzzle.

'Thank you.'

'Does that help you?'

He didn't answer that. 'Stay here.' He took a second phone from his pocket, a cheaper-looking model, and an e-cigarette from the other side. He went out to the pavement and tapped a number into his phone while he started puffing away on the e-cig.

'Interpersonal skills are clearly important in the NCA,' Jenny remarked as she watched him pace slowly outside.

'We don't need him for his charm,' Mike said.

'What do we do if he doesn't feel like helping us?'

'Then we find another approach,' Mike said.

A pair of twenty-something women in expensive coats entered the shop and Jenny saw Adamson come through the door behind them, tucking the e-cigarette back into his pocket. He took the same seat again.

'Well?' Mike said after a minute.

Adamson seemed to be considering something. 'I want a guarantee that you won't go anywhere near Devlin or his company directly. If he gets the slightest hint that we're close ..'

'Not a problem,' Mike said easily. Jenny didn't think he would have a problem breaking that promise.

'And you can't mention anything I've told you to this person.'

Jenny felt a surge of hope. Then he did have a way of contacting the surviving ex-wife.

'That's fine,' Jenny said. 'We don't even know if she'll be able to help us, it's just—'

'Thirdly,' Adamson said, cutting her off. 'If you turn up anything else on Devlin, no matter how inconsequential, I want you to tell me first. Okay?' He looked at both of them.

There was something a little different in his manner now. Jenny wondered if he was thinking that, with their unique approach, they might be able to get some information no one else could. Something that could allow an ambitious man to steal a march on his rivals.

'Naturally,' Mike said. 'You'll be the first person we call.'

Adamson's eyes flicked from Mike to Jenny again. Then he took out a pen. He started writing something on the back of the coffee receipt. Jenny had been expecting a phone number, or an email address, but what he was writing was spread over several lines.

'You're in luck,' he said as he slid the receipt across the table. 'She's local.'

There was an address, right here in London. And a name.

Selina Craddock.

41

Eric Bowen's face was ashen as he opened the door to the flat. He had had time to absorb the message Klenmore had given him over the intercom as Klenmore climbed the stairs to the first floor.

'What's happened?'

He was dressed in a robe and plaid pyjama bottoms. A day's growth of stubble on his face. A day off or a sick day, probably. Unfortunate for him.

'Is she okay?'

Klenmore peered over Bowen's shoulder. He could see a shallow hallway with doors leading off. A pine bookcase. A framed watercolour hanging on the wall.

'Is someone with you at the moment, Mr Bowen?'

He shook his head. 'No, my ...' He hesitated and searched for the words, still becoming accustomed to the new set-up. 'My partner is at a conference this weekend.'

Klenmore glanced back at the landing to make sure they were still alone. There were no cameras, but he disliked the peepholes on each door, staring out at him inscrutably. He didn't like not knowing if he was being observed, no matter how remote the chance.

'Can I come in?' Klenmore said.

Bowen's eyes narrowed slightly, and Klenmore could tell he knew something wasn't quite right, even if he couldn't put his finger on it. 'Sorry, do you have identification?' His eyes moved beyond Klenmore, to the empty space where one might expect a second police officer to be standing.

'Of course,' Klenmore said, patting his pocket. 'I'll be happy to go through all of that inside.' He glanced back at the landing again meaningfully, then lowered his voice. 'I'm afraid I have some bad news.'

Bowen's eyes closed and he pushed his hair back with the fingers of his right hand. 'Oh God.'

He let the door swing open and told Klenmore to come in.

'Just to confirm, you are Jennifer Bowen's husband?' he asked as Bowen showed him into the living room. It was pleasant, if unimaginative. Varnished floorboards, white walls, a Bose sound system and a television fixed to the wall that was large, but not vulgarly so. There were sliding glass doors leading out to a balcony with a view of the Emirates Stadium. A light fitting in the centre of the living-room ceiling which looked sturdy.

'Yes. No. I mean, we're getting divorced.' He looked back at Klenmore, his voice hardening. 'Now tell me what's happened.'

'There's been an accident. Jennifer was hit by a vehicle.'

Bowen sat down heavily. 'What? Where? I just saw her last night. Is she . . . ?'

'She's going to be all right,' Klenmore said, 'but I have some important questions.'

Bowen looked confused. 'Questions for me? What am I going to be able to tell you?'

'Does she have a workspace here? Laptops, phones, any devices?'

'Why would . . . ?' Bowen looked back up at him again, the

suspicion in his eyes less diluted now. 'I'd like to see the ID now, please.'

Klenmore took a step towards him before answering. 'I'm afraid that won't be possible.'

42

They got the Tube from Angel. Deep line again. Jenny made a point of sitting as near to a door as possible. She was torn between keeping her head down and surveying the other passengers to see if any one of them were paying too much attention. To distract herself, she asked Mike what they would do if the address was wrong, or if Selina Craddock wasn't at home. They decided the best course of action would be to leave a note asking her to call urgently, mentioning only that it was an important matter.

They changed at Kings Cross and took the Piccadilly line to Hyde Park Corner. That brought them two minutes' walk from the address Adamson had given them, in a nice street in Belgravia. But then, Jenny thought, there weren't really any not-nice streets in Belgravia. Even a studio flat would set you back half a million pounds here.

The address was a first-floor flat. A basement conversion was underway next door to Selina Craddock's building. There was a precariously stacked skip outside and they could feel the churn of heavy machinery through the soles of their shoes.

'Imagine paying all that money to live next to a building site,' Jenny remarked, as they climbed the steps to the front door. The new shoes had stopped hurting as much; she was giving them a good breaking-in today.

'I suppose they'll run out of basements sooner or later,' Mike said. 'That or they start digging deeper.'

The door was solid and painted black, with an ornamental knocker. Looking up at the building, Jenny guessed this had once been a townhouse that had been converted into four flats. There was a tasteful brass unit recessed into the wall beside the door with four engraved names and buttons next to them, and a small camera. Three of the buttons had full names next to them. The fourth, the button for the address they had been given, simply said 'S.C.'

Mike pressed the button and they waited.

Thirty seconds later, they heard the handset at the other end being picked up.

A female voice. 'Hello?'

'Good afternoon,' Mike said, an authoritative tone in his voice that was similar to the one he had used with the guy in the pub, but subtly different. 'Sergeant Mike Fletcher, British Transport Police. We'd like to speak to you briefly, Ms Craddock.'

As he spoke, he held up his warrant card to the camera. The two of them had discussed this on the journey. This was overstepping a line; and leaving a potential trail. If Mike was caught using his police credentials on an unofficial investigation, it could mean the end of his career. On balance, he had decided it was a gamble worth taking. Neither of them could think of another way to ensure Selina Craddock opened the door to them.

And would even this be enough, Jenny wondered as they listened to the silence on the other end of the line. What if she refused to let them in? What if she insisted on checking up on his credentials?

'What's this about?' the voice said.

'We'll explain in a minute, I'd rather not go into it on the street.'

There was another pause, and they exchanged a glance. Jenny wondered if Mike had made a tactical error in the calculated note of irritation he had injected into his voice.

But then the buzzer sounded and they heard the catch on the door disengage. Mike pushed the door open and motioned for Jenny to go first.

'Well done,' she said, relieved, as the door closed behind them.

Mike tucked his ID wallet back into his pocket. 'There's a way to get through every door, just takes experience.'

They climbed the carpeted stairs to the second floor, passing well-tended pot plants and tastefully framed watercolour prints hanging on the walls. When they reached the door of Selina Craddock's flat, it was already opening.

It stopped after travelling six inches. Jenny saw dark hair and blue eyes peering out at them from above a taut door chain.

'What's this about?' she asked again.

'Can we come in?' Mike said.

This time, he had to pass his ID under the chain to the woman for her to examine, which he did with a barely perceptible grimace. Jenny hoped she wouldn't be committing the name to memory.

A moment later, the door closed and she heard the chain rattle, and then it opened again.

Selina led them to a pair of couches arranged in front of the bay window that looked out on the treetops and the street below. The flat was austere, almost unlived in. There were whitewashed wood floors and white floor-to-ceiling bookcases, and a cello on a stand in a corner. The place looked as though it had been set-dressed. Or perhaps its occupant liked it that way.

'If you're here to talk to me about ...' She paused momentarily, as though having difficulty saying the name. 'My ex-husband, you should know that I can't talk about anything to do with our relationship.'

'Part of the settlement?' Mike asked. Jenny noted that he didn't point out she had jumped to the conclusion this was about her ex-husband.

She hesitated, as though unsure whether to confirm even that, before nodding.

'I haven't seen your identification,' she said, looking at Jenny pointedly.

'I'm not a police officer,' she said. 'My name is Jenny. Jenny Bowen.'

'Jenny is helping us with our enquiries,' Mike said.

Selina Craddock was in her late forties, Jenny guessed. She had dark hair, the cheekbones of a model, and long, thin fingers. Different from the first wife, but equally striking. Devlin seemed to collect beautiful things.

She was dressed casually, clearly not having expected visitors, in jeans, socks and a long-sleeved t-shirt. Whether it was the fact that the simple clothes were no doubt more expensive than the outfits either she or Mike were wearing, or something about Selina herself, she somehow managed to make both of them look underdressed for the occasion. She seemed to exude a sort of effortless grace.

'We're not here to pry into your personal affairs,' Mike said. 'But there's a possibility the matter does relate to Devlin, yes.'

Selina crossed her arms over herself. The gesture made it look like she was cold, though the flat was pleasantly warm.

She looked back at Mike. 'Have you ever been through a divorce?'

He shook his head. 'I can't say that I have.'

She turned to Jenny. Before she could repeat the question,

Jenny answered it. 'I'm going through one right now.'

'My commiserations,' Selina said. 'Then you'll know the process is unpleasant for everyone concerned.'

'You can say that again.'

'Two times, for me,' Selina said. 'The first one, I thought at the time was as unpleasant as it could get. The second one, I don't talk about. Not only because I'm legally prevented from doing so, but because I wouldn't even if that wasn't the case.'

She sat back on the couch, seeming to relax ever so slightly. 'British Transport Police,' she said. 'I haven't been on public transport in years, and I highly doubt my ex-husband has ever been.'

Mike opened his mouth to reply, and then thought better of it, perhaps because he had noticed Jenny had established the beginnings of a rapport with her. He looked over at her. She took up the baton.

'This is to do with something I witnessed. I was travelling on the sleeper train last Friday. London to Fort William.'

Selina nodded. 'I thought that sounded like a Scottish accent. Edinburgh?'

'Glasgow, originally,' Jenny said. 'But I've lived here for the last fifteen years or so.'

'I haven't been up there in many years. Some happy memories.' She started to smile and then stopped, perhaps remembering a not-so-happy one.

Jenny glanced at Mike, who was waiting for her to go on. 'Anyway, when I was getting on the train I noticed a woman and a little girl, just in passing. The next morning, I found the woman dead.'

Selina raised an eyebrow, but didn't say anything.

'It looked like a heroin overdose. That's when the police got involved, of course,' she said, gesturing at Mike.

'What happened to the little girl?'

'Well that's the question,' Jenny said. 'There was no sign of her. When I told the police, they said there was no record of a child being on the train. They checked the CCTV, the tickets, no trace of her.'

'Some sort of mistake on your part?' Selina asked.

Jenny shook her head. 'Everyone thought so at first. I started to wonder myself, but I couldn't let it go. I knew what I had seen. I started to look into it. I found out that the little girl was there all right, and that her name was Alice Devlin.'

Selina Craddock bristled at the name.

'How old?' she said after a moment.

'Seven years old.'

She considered this for a moment before speaking. 'I can't talk about anything between 18th November 1999 and 12th July 2003. You should know that.'

The dates of her marriage.

'We understand that,' Mike said. Jenny saw him take a moment to glance around the flat. Perhaps it was a conscious act, perhaps not. Either way she knew what he was thinking. This flat and whatever financial arrangement she had reached with Devlin would be in jeopardy were she to break the terms of the settlement. Jenny couldn't be sure, but she believed there was more to it than that. She wasn't just prevented from talking about her marriage, she was afraid to.

'We're working on some assumptions here,' Mike said. 'We realise you can't volunteer any information, but if we were to ask you some yes or no questions . . .?'

'I can't guarantee that I'll answer.'

'That's fine,' Mike said. 'Did you and Mr Devlin ever discuss having children?'

She paused. 'Yes.'

'Do you know if Devlin engaged in extra-marital affairs during your relationship?'

220

Selina bristled again. 'Is that relevant?'

'I apologise for the personal nature of these questions, we're just trying to establish—'

'This is skating very close to the line, Detective.'

'Did Mr Devlin have fertility problems?'

'I can't answer that.'

Mike stopped, unsure of where to go next.

'Do you?' Jenny asked.

Selina's eyes flashed to hers. Jenny didn't blink. When Selina didn't say anything, she softened her voice. 'There's a little girl out there somewhere. I just want to know she's safe.'

Selina shook her head. 'No. I have a daughter, she's twenty-two now.'

From before the marriage to Devlin, then.

Mike asked a few more questions, but every time it got too close to John Devlin, Selina closed up like a Venus flytrap. Eventually, he had exhausted his list of questions. They thanked her and she walked them back to the door.

'I do hope you find her,' she said as she opened the door. She turned to Jenny. 'You said you lived in Glasgow and then London, yes?'

Jenny nodded. 'A little time in the Highlands in between.'

'I thought I detected a little of that,' she said. 'A lovely part of the world. I spent some enjoyable summers near a place called Inverkiln. Do you know it?'

Jenny smiled. 'Never been there, but I've heard of it.'

She closed the door behind them. Jenny and Mike stood out in the hall, looking at each other. They moved away towards the stairs.

'That was a waste of time,' Mike said under his breath. He looked back at Jenny when she didn't speak. 'What?'

She wasn't sure what. Something about the way Selina

Craddock had spoken to her at the door had seemed important. Just polite small talk? Or something else.

'Inverkiln,' she said quietly.

'What about it?' Mike asked.

Before she could say anything else, her phone buzzed. She took it out and examined the screen. It wasn't a number she recognised. She answered with a tentative hello.

'Hi, is this Jenny?'

'Who's asking?'

'It's Monica. Em's friend? We spoke yesterday.'

'Of course,' Jenny said.

'I've got something you might be interested in having.'

43

Monica eyed Mike with suspicion. Jenny could see the same distrust in her eyes that the fat man in the upstairs room at the pub had exuded.

Mike sensed her discomfort and excused himself, saying he had to make a call.

'You got the police interested then,' Monica said as she watched him retreat to the entrance to the McDonalds where Jenny had agreed to meet her.

'So, you wanted to see me,' Jenny said, changing the subject from Mike's line of work.

'There was something I didn't tell you yesterday. I wasn't sure if . . .'

Jenny smiled. 'It's okay. Best not to assume you can trust anyone, right?'

Monica looked around, checking if anyone was watching, and then dug her hand into her pocket. She planted something down on the table. It was a cheap mobile phone.

Jenny took an involuntary breath. 'Is that—'

'Don't get too excited,' Monica said. 'It's out of charge, and I don't know the pin.'

'Where did you get it?'

'She left it in her room. I was keeping it for her.' She looked slightly defensive as she said that, as though waiting for Jenny to accuse her of stealing it.

'I just ... when you said she died, I thought someone should have it.' She cast a suspicious glance over at Mike.

'Thank you,' Jenny said.

Five minutes later, she stood outside with Mike as they watched Monica hop on a number 10 bus without a backward glance. It was just after six o'clock, but full dark already, and gusts of wind were starting to ruffle the awnings of nearby cafés.

Mike examined the phone. 'We can probably find someone who can unlock this. I know a guy who ...'

'Used the key combination hack to get past the pin on an Android?' Jenny finished. She shook her head. 'They closed that loophole with a security update a couple of years ago.'

'Oh,' Mike said, looking a little disappointed. 'So how can we do it?'

'You might find a guy in a phone repair shop who knows what he's doing,' Jenny said, 'but most likely you'll have to restore to factory settings, which means bye-bye data.' She felt a mild sense of satisfaction about finding herself on territory where she was the expert.

'So ...?'

'So luckily, we've already found someone who can unlock this.'

He looked confused for a moment and then grinned. 'That's right, you're a techy.'

'Some of my clients get me to manage everything that's more technologically advanced than a Rolodex, including their phone contracts. I've got a device that should open this up no problem. The only problem is, we need to pay a visit to the last place in the world I want to go.' She stopped and remembered her narrow escape from the Devlin building earlier in the day. 'Maybe the second last place.'

44

The rain was coming down much harder by the time they reached the flat, the reflections of the streetlights glistening in the road, distorted by the impact of a million raindrops. They took a cab for speed, but it still took longer than Jenny had expected to get there thanks to the conditions. She just hoped Eric would still be at work, or lingering for a Friday drink or two with his colleagues. It was a reasonably safe bet, going by experience.

The flat was in a building in a new development in Highbury. Only a two-bedroom, but generously sized for the location. They had gone for this one because it had been the best balance between their respective must-have lists. They both liked that it had a balcony: Jenny because she could sit outside and work on her laptop in the mornings, Eric because he enjoyed sinking a few beers outside on summer evenings. It had been just enough space for them for the moment, and they could always compromise and move further out when they got around to having children. That part hadn't gone to plan, of course.

Her fob still worked, which meant that Eric hadn't had building security deactivate it, which was good. Not that it was likely he would have got around to it even if it had crossed his mind, of course. The entrance hallway was deserted, and they took the stairs to the first floor. She really hoped his new girlfriend wasn't there.

When Jenny started to push her key into the lock, the door sprang open. She exchanged a glance with Mike.

'That's odd.'

She knocked loudly on the door. 'Eric? Hello?'

As they paused, waiting for a response, Jenny became aware of a regular creaking sound. Like someone gently listing in a rocking chair. They didn't own a rocking chair, and she doubted Eric would have rushed out to buy one in the last month. Something else behind it. The sound of the rain hammering down outside. Too loud; someone had left a window wide open.

She looked back at Mike. The look on his face suddenly made Jenny feel even more anxious.

'Hello?' she called again, then took a step across the threshold.

Mike put a hand on her arm. 'I'll go first.'

Mike cleared his throat. 'Police, anyone here?'

The door to the living room was ajar. The creaking noise was coming from within.

Mike quietly opened his backpack and took the gun out. He stepped across the threshold and raised the gun as his eyes evaluated the hallway. Jenny followed as he covered the length of the hall. He reached the living-room door a moment before Jenny. The look in his eyes told Jenny everything.

'Stay there,' he said, holding his hand up.

Jenny didn't even bother to refuse. As she took another step forward, he opened his mouth to protest, but then stepped out of her way.

Eric's body was hanging from a leather belt attached to the light fitting in the centre of the living room. The body swayed gently in the cold breeze from the open window. The belt creaked rhythmically every couple of seconds.

227

He was wearing pyjama bottoms, but naked from the waist up. His blue terrycloth bathrobe lay discarded on the floor. She started forward, wanting to hold his body up, cut him down, anything, but Mike put a gentle hand on her shoulder.

'It's too late.'

She knew that already. Just like she had known with Emma Dawson.

'Don't touch anything,' Mike said as he tucked the gun into his belt and looked around for something to stand on. He yanked the throw from the couch and covered his hand so he could grab a chair from around the small dining table. He dragged it over, stood on it and put a finger to Eric's throat. Jenny knew it was a formality. His face was bloated and red, his tongue jutting out. Mike shook his head, confirming a certainty, and stepped back down, pulling the chair back into its previous position and replacing the throw on the couch. He moved to the window and stepped outside. He looked over the edge of the balcony, careful not to touch the polished steel railing.

'Only a ten-foot drop. He left this way.'

It took Jenny a moment to process the words. Then the meaning of them hit her like a pile driver. 'Oh my God, this is my fault.'

Mike turned and gripped her by the shoulders. 'No. This is not your fault.'

She kept her eyes on his, not wanting to look back at ... 'Can you cut him down?'

He shook his head.

'Of course,' Jenny said quietly. There would need to be people taking forensic samples, looking for the evidence of foul play, all that sort of thing. 'Do you think they'll believe us?'

Mike considered. 'I'll make them believe. I hope. Either way, it's out of our hands now. We need to tell them everything.'

'But if we go to the police, what about Alice? We still don't know where he took her. Even if they believe us, Devlin will have a warning. What if he just … cuts his losses?'

Mike shook his head. 'We don't have a choice.' He glanced up at Eric's body. Jenny instinctively followed his gaze and looked away hurriedly. He put a hand on her shoulder and gently turned her away from the swaying body. 'The man who did this – he came here to get you. Maybe we can't help Alice now, but we can make sure you're safe.'

She didn't say anything. He was right. So how come she didn't care? Why did she want to block this out and keep going?

'Come on,' Mike said after a moment. 'Let's go outside and call the police.'

All of a sudden, Jenny felt hot, despite the temperature in the room. There seemed to be black borders on her vision.

She saw Mike mouth her name, but it sounded like the word was coming from far away.

45

He's dead.

It didn't seem real. Didn't seem possible, even though she had seen the irrefutable fact of it with her own eyes. Was still seeing it, in fact. Like she had looked at the sun and then closed her eyes, the afterimage of Eric's hanging body remained, impossible to shift.

Mike was saying something, but his voice sounded as though she was at the bottom of a swimming pool, and someone was trying to speak to her from the surface. Eventually, a word got through and she realised what he was asking her. She gestured absently at the top drawer in the office desk, and Mike rummaged in it. She nodded when he held up the small device, about the size and shape of a remote control.

Widow, she thought. *I'm a widow now*. But was she? Could you be a widow of an ex-husband? Perhaps there wasn't a word for this.

She felt Mike's hands gently on her shoulders, and she raised her eyes to look at him. The dull, echoing sounds resolved themselves into a question. A question that could only be answered with a lie.

'Yeah, I'm okay.'

He looked like he was going to say something, but then

shook his head and took her hand. Led her out of her home, away from her husband. Her not-any-more husband.

They went back down the stairs, through the entrance vestibule, and out onto the street. As they descended, it was like the pressure abated. The pounding in her temples lessened, the black patches at the edge of her vision seeped away. The fresh air started to bring everything back. All of a sudden, she needed to be sick. She turned from Mike and gripped the railing of the walkway outside, expecting a torrent of sick. But nothing came. She retched twice, and then turned back. She remembered she had barely eaten a thing all day. A blessing, perhaps.

'Are you okay?' Mike asked again.

'Better out here,' she said. She took in a long breath and let it out through her nose. In school, Meryl had suffered from panic attacks. She had held her hand through a few of them, and tried to mirror what she had seen work with her friend.

She looked beyond Mike to the street. Cars swept by on the road. A group of people stood at the bus stop, staring into space. A thin, bald man in a raincoat jogged by with a golden retriever on a lead. The world went on in stupid, oblivious normality.

'Call them,' she said, when she was sure the act of speaking would not bring on the urge to retch again. Mike held her gaze for a moment, and then nodded. She glanced back at the building, physically unable to raise her eyes to look at the balcony on the first floor that had been her home.

She wondered if the police would believe them, even with Mike to back her up. Once again, she knew with a dull certainty that there would be no hard evidence. She knew the person responsible was able to make a murder look like a suicide. He had done it before.

There was no CCTV inside the building. The suggestion had

been mooted in a residents' committee meeting a while ago and rejected. She wasn't sure about the street outside. It had never occurred to her to look until now. She glanced around as they moved away from the door. She couldn't see anything obvious.

No cameras. Again. She remembered reading a *New Yorker* article that said the UK had more security cameras per capita than anywhere else on Earth. And yet, everywhere it seemed there were gaps in the net. The older places, the forgotten nooks and crannies. The empty spaces between things. Like a quiet residential street. Like the sleeper. The tingling feeling of shock she had felt ever since entering the flat was settling into a dull, anxious ache in her stomach.

Mike already had his phone out. She heard the 999 call connect and Mike's voice asking for the police. She knew he was right, they didn't have a choice. But she knew that as soon as he told them what had happened, they would be taken away and interviewed for hours, and in the meantime Devlin and the man in the black coat would be making sure that no one ever found out what they had done with Alice.

She was thinking. Forcing herself to focus on the mission, rather than what they had just found in what had been her home. She couldn't think about that now.

Where in the world was Alice? Like the Alice in the story, it was as though she had fallen down the rabbit hole, or stepped through the looking-glass. Fallen into the gaps between things. The empty spaces. The train had stopped in the middle of nowhere and Alice and the tall man in the black coat had vanished into the night.

And now, for some reason, she was thinking about leaving another flat and walking out onto another street. The look on Selina Craddock's face as she bid them farewell at her door. The look that said she was telling them something, even though she couldn't tell them anything.

'Inverkiln,' Jenny said quietly.

'What?'

Jenny realised she had to make a decision – and she went with the only one she could deal with at the moment. Perhaps there was a way to stop the people who had done this. But they had to move now, and that meant she couldn't let Mike finish his call. She grabbed the phone off him, hearing the faint voice saying, 'Police, what's the nature of your emergency?' She stabbed at the screen to cancel the call.

'We can't go to the police,' she said. 'We need to go back, now.'

46

The two of them slid into opposite sides of a leather-upholstered booth at the back of the first pub they could find on Holloway Road. Jenny plugged the cheap mobile Monica had given them into the USB port at the table to let it charge. Mike had bought them both double whiskies. He necked his as soon as he sat down, and Jenny suddenly realised that, professional or not, he had been shaken by what had happened at the flat too. She left hers alone. Five minutes ago she would have welcomed the stiff drink, would have happily swigged from the bottle, but now she wanted to keep completely focused. She had to make sure this wasn't all for nothing.

'Inverkiln,' she repeated as Mike put the glass down on the table with a thunk.

'Okay,' he said cautiously. 'What the hell does Inverkiln mean?'

She expected the realisation to dawn on him quickly. Instead, he just looked even more confused. Worse than confused. He looked worried. About her. She forced herself to take a breath, talk slowly.

'It's a village. In the Highlands.'

'I know it's a village, but ...' He paused, remembering the

moment at the door of the flat. 'Selina Craddock thought you were from there.'

She shook her head. 'No, she said I had a little Highland in my voice. I didn't really pay much attention to it, I don't think there is, really, I wasn't there long enough. I thought she was just making conversation.'

'Okay, and?'

She took her laptop from her backpack and opened it on the table, moving her whisky to one side. 'We might need some of your official help, here, Mike.'

He put a hand over hers. 'You've just had a massive shock. You need to take a minute to—'

She snatched her hand away and shook her head. 'No. No minute. The people who killed Eric, they're the people who took Alice, and they can't be allowed to get away with this. We need to stop them, and we need to make them pay. We don't have time to waste.'

Mike thought about it as she booted up the laptop and finally motioned for her to go ahead. Perhaps he was only humouring her, but she would convince him.

'Inverkiln is maybe twenty miles from where the sleeper stopped that night,' he said. 'Do you think Selina Craddock meant Alice could be there?'

'I don't know. But she made a point of mentioning it. That means it could be important. If we can find some link between John Devlin and Inverkiln, maybe some land or a cottage or something ... Selina said she spent summers there.'

'Yeah, that would make sense,' Mike said. 'If Devlin has a place out there, perhaps that explains why it happened where it did.'

The screen of Emma Dawson's phone lit up. The charger had finally pumped enough juice into it to turn it on. Jenny took the code breaker out of her bag and connected it to the phone.

'I've seen our people use those gizmos,' Mike said. 'I thought they were only available to law enforcement.'

'You can arrest me afterwards, okay?' Jenny said, not looking up as she adjusted the settings. A couple of minutes later, they were into the phone.

Jenny tapped into the SMS inbox. There was one conversation, with 27 messages. A number listed against the name Kelly.

'Kelly,' Mike read out. 'Could be a male or a female. First name or last. Did Monica say anything about a Kelly?'

Jenny shook her head. She tapped on the conversation and scrolled through the individual messages.

Making arrangements to leave. This had to be the contact Monica had spoken about. The person who was going to help Emma and Alice escape London. They stretched over a period of around two weeks. Most of the messages were oblique, talking about making preparations and staying under the radar. The final message said:

Train leaves at 9:15, don't be late. See you in FW.

See you in FW. Fort William? Who was Kelly? Who was the mysterious ally Emma was communicating with?

A wave of realisation hit Jenny. There had been no Kelly. There had just been a way out dangled in front of a woman at her wits' end. A fiction that had led her to her death.

'It was a set-up,' she said quietly. 'The man in room eight, he didn't follow Em and Alice onto that train.'

'What do you mean?'

'He lured them onto it.'

47

'Are you okay?' Meryl said after a pause. 'You sound really . . .'

Jenny was getting sick of that question. She cleared her throat. 'Totally fine, think I'm coming down with a cold. How did you get on?'

Meryl was quiet for a second and Jenny wondered if she should have gone for a little more preliminary chitchat. Problem was, chitchat was the very last thing she felt like engaging in at this moment.

'Sorry, no joy,' she said after a minute. 'The agency has only sold three properties in Inverkiln over the last fifteen years. It's not exactly a hotspot. I had a look at the land register to see what else has been moving, and there's not much else. Certainly nothing high-end, like you were looking for.'

'And the name?'

'Devlin doesn't come up at all. Sorry.'

Jenny sighed. 'Okay, thanks anyway.'

'Jenny, what's this all about? Is this to do with the dead woman on the train?'

With an effort, Jenny managed to make her voice sound bright, cheerful. 'It's a very long story, and I promise I'll tell you soon.'

'Ooh, so it's need-to-know? Very mysterious.'

Jenny couldn't think of anything to say, and perhaps her friend detected something in her silence.

'It's nothing dangerous though,' Meryl said, her tone changing to concern again. 'Right?'

Before Jenny could muster a convincing denial, she heard the sound of a baby crying.

'Oh for *fuck's* . . . I put him down twenty minutes ago. I'll call you back later. Don't do anything silly, will you?'

'On my honour, I promise I will do my best,' Jenny recited.

'Oh, shut it. Talk to you later.'

Mike returned from the bar with two cups of coffee a minute later. She filled him in on the call with Meryl. 'I think you might be right,' Mike said. 'That she was trying to tell us something.'

Jenny checked the rest of the data on the phone Monica had given her. The text conversation was all there was. No apps installed, no social media. Emma had been using it as a burner; perhaps that was why she had discarded it.

She put the phone aside and opened a new tab on her laptop. She searched 'Inverkiln', clicking on the map to bring up the village. As she widened the focus to take in the surrounds, she saw the distance from her current location had been calculated: 497 miles. 8 hours, 52 minutes' drive. 156 hours walking. If this lead didn't die on the vine like all the others, they would need to get there in a hurry.

Mike came round the table and slid into her side of the booth so they could both see the screen. Jenny switched back to the map around Inverkiln. She widened the focus until they could see the railway line, twenty miles away. Mike tapped the button to switch from map to a satellite image and examined the screen thoughtfully. After a momentary blur, the screen redrew with a god's eye view image of empty country. Mostly flat green, only occasionally interrupted by the edge of a black loch or a deep green forest, looking like deep-pile carpet from above.

'Do you think she meant he had a place in Inverkiln itself? If not, it's a hell of a lot of ground to cover.' He traced his finger along the rail track. 'This is where the sleeper stopped. Next station is . . .' He started to scroll up.

'Rannoch,' Jenny said, remembering the deserted platform, the little Victorian waiting room where she had first met Mike. 'It's in the middle of nowhere.'

'It isn't really that close to Inverkiln,' Mike said, a hint of frustration in his voice. 'Twenty miles. Maybe he had a car waiting. Otherwise, why there?'

He stretched the touchscreen on the laptop to close in on the area of track. It cut across the contours of the land, a ruler-straight line against the topographical curves and variation in colour and shade. Something on the edge of the screen caught Jenny's eye as Mike zoomed in again.

'Wait, what was that?'

'What was what?'

Jenny used her finger to drag the map to the side. There was something else disturbing the green. Something in a large clearing in the middle of an area of dense woodland. The structure occupied most of the clearing, bounded by trees on three sides and a lake on the fourth.

She stretched her thumb and index finger to zoom in closer.

'A house,' Mike said under his breath.

'A big house.'

'It's not tagged,' he said. He switched back to the map view. The outline of the forest and the little road stayed in place, now represented as a map rather than satellite imagery, but the house vanished.

'What is it?'

Jenny switched back to satellite. The house reappeared. She hovered the pointer over it. A geocode appeared on the screen.

She wrote it down on the hotel notepad. A minute later, she had it.

'Blacklaw House,' she said, reading from the text on her screen. It was a short article on a website so old it could have qualified for historic renovation funding itself. Pink background, Times New Roman font, even a welcome message running cheerily across the top using the old Marquee HTML tags. Blacklaw House. Why did that name sound familiar?

There were two pictures of a building at the top of the page. One of them, in colour, showed a dilapidated Gothic revival country pile. Broken windows. Blackened smoke damage to one of the wings. A collapsed roof on the other. Turreted towers at both sides. The gardens in front of the building were overgrown and forbidding, like the forest of thorns around Sleeping Beauty's castle.

To the right of that picture, a much older black-and-white image, showing the same building in its early Victorian heyday. The windows and the roof were all intact. Topiary bushes flanked the entrance, guarded by ornate gates missing in the colour picture.

Below the pictures were captions: *1987, 1858*. What a difference a hundred and thirty years or so makes.

'Bloody hell, it's like the House of Usher,' Mike said, evidently looking at the picture on the right. 'You think he could have her stashed here?'

'Maybe this is what Selina wanted us to find,' Jenny said. 'We told her where the sleeper stopped. Maybe she knew he had a place near there.'

She switched tab and searched the name of the house. There were a few other Blacklaw Houses in other parts of the world, but there was frustratingly little on this one. And then she found it, near the bottom of the second page. A local newspaper article.

Historic Scotland in Negotiations to Save Forgotten Stately Home.

She clicked through. It was a very brief piece, just a couple of paragraphs. It mentioned the house had been built in 1820, designed by the architect James Robert Dunn, for the McAlpine family. Built on the grounds of an old priory of the same name. It had fallen into disrepair after the death of the last of the line in the 1960s, and been badly damaged by a fire in '69. It was threatened with demolition, but Historic Scotland were carrying out a feasibility study.

The Historic Scotland website had no mention of Blacklaw House. It wasn't one of their listed properties. But if they hadn't bought it, who had? It hadn't been demolished, going by the satellite images, which couldn't be that old, and in fact ...

She switched back and zoomed in as far as it would go. No Streetview out in the country. But she could get close enough on the satellite view to see that the roof on the north wing looked whole again. Difficult to tell from above, but the gardens didn't look as overgrown either. There was a giant circular skylight in the centre of the house, and a smaller oval-shaped one over the front entrance.

There were three cars in the wide, curving driveway.

'I can make a couple of calls,' Mike said. 'Find out who the owner is.'

'I can too,' Jenny said quietly, thinking of Meryl. She switched back to the pictures of the house. She looked at the colour one, the neglected heap with broken windows that seemed to stare back at her. She remembered where she had heard the name before. Or seen it, to be precise. One of the conference rooms at Devlin's building. All of them seemed to be named after places where he had properties. *Yarra. Kowloon. Madison.*

Blacklaw.

'This is it.'

48

'I checked the flights,' Jenny said, eyeing the clock on the screen which told her it had just gone eight o'clock. 'We won't make the last Edinburgh one, but there's Heathrow to Glasgow at ten-thirty.'

Mike was shaking his head. 'We can't.'

'Mike, this can't wait until tomorrow. Okay, we don't know if she's still there, but it's our only lead.'

'I mean we can't fly,' he said. 'Devlin's people can get to you anywhere. They got Emma. They got Eric. They almost got you.'

'He can't have people watching every flight, for God's sake.'

'He doesn't need to. All that needs to happen, what almost certainly *has* happened already, is someone needs to pick up the phone to some underpaid ticket desk worker at each of the airports. All they need to do is make a call if a Jennifer Bowen books onto any of their flights.'

'Shit,' Jenny said as she realised he was right. 'We can't even give fake names, we need photo ID.'

Mike glanced outside. The rain seemed to be gaining in intensity, rattling against the window pane. Even so, the pub was much busier than it had been when they had arrived. The foul weather didn't seem to have dissuaded the Friday night crowd.

'If this gets any worse, chances are flights will be grounded anyway.'

'I haven't rented a car in ten years, can you do that without ID?'

'You need a licence, but we'll use mine. Besides, that's a lot more ground for them to cover than a couple of calls to the airports. They wouldn't have a fixed point to wait for us, either.'

They packed up and squeezed through the teeming mass of drinkers until they reached the exit. The rain was coming down even harder now, pooling in the hidden dips in the road and on the pavements, turning the night-time streets into inverted mirrors for all the headlights and the streetlamps. Every other pedestrian carried an umbrella, others took shelter beneath the awnings of cafes, some just hunched their shoulders and quickened their pace.

Jenny and Mike stood outside under the pub's awning. A lone smoker in a skinny t-shirt grinned good-naturedly at them, not a care in the world. Mike was examining the screen of his phone.

'The Edinburgh flight is cancelled anyway. Glasgow delayed.' He looked at the traffic crawling past without much enthusiasm for a marathon drive through the storm. It would take them a lot longer than flying, and the last fifty miles on single-carriageway roads would be tortuously slow. There was no fast, direct route other than ...

Of course. Why hadn't she thought of it before now? Jenny looked south. 'I have another idea.'

They stopped on the way to Euston to buy suitable clothes and walking boots from an outdoor clothing store. Even if the storm had blown itself out by the time they got there, the approach to Blacklaw House would take them over some ground that was a lot rougher than B roads. Mike had maxed out his card on the clothes and the hotel earlier, so Jenny withdrew cash from an ATM to avoid using her credit card, wondering if they were being overly paranoid, or not paranoid enough. The man at the ticket desk at Euston told them they were in luck. Two adjoining rooms.

'I guess it's appropriate,' Mike said as they turned away from the desk. 'Taking the sleeper again.'

Jenny's phone buzzed with a text. It was from Meryl.

You were right! BH sold in 2001, cash buyer, DDC holdings. Have emailed the scan. That what you need?

2001. Two years before Devlin and Selina Craddock divorced, which meant she would certainly have known about the purchase. Jenny showed Mike the text before tapping out her reply.

Perfect. Owe you one. x

She slipped the phone back into her pocket and checked the giant bulletin board hanging over the concourse again. The sleeper was ready for boarding. Platform 1 again. Back to where it had all begun.

49

'Not exactly the Orient Express.'

Mike eyed the modest confines of the sleeper room with scepticism as Jenny opened the door and lifted her bags inside. Although the two rooms they had booked were nominally first class, the only difference from standard was that there was only one bed instead of bunks, and some lavender pillow spray.

'You want the tour?' Jenny asked.

'Good evening, can I have your names?'

Both of them turned to see one of the train hosts outside the door.

'Thornhill,' Mike said after a brief pause to remember the name they had booked under.

The host looked down at his tablet and clicked off two names. Roger and Eve Thornhill, rooms six and seven. Jenny had suggested that. *North by Northwest* was her favourite film.

'All the way to Fort William, yes?'

'That's right,' Mike said. They had thought it was safest to book through tickets. The number of passengers buying tickets to Rannoch would be small to non-existent. Even travelling under aliases, it didn't make any sense to draw attention to themselves.

'We should be getting in just before ten, what time would you like breakfast?'

'Late as possible, please,' Jenny said. They would be long gone by breakfast.

He sucked his teeth but made no comment, jotting another couple of marks on his tablet. Then squeezed past Mike and inserted a key in the lock of the adjoining door, pushing it open into Mike's room. Mike and Jenny exchanged a look, knowing that the man in room 8 must have done the same thing when he entered Em and Alice's cabin the previous week.

Mike thanked him and the host left them alone, letting the door to the corridor swing shut on its spring hinges. Mike moved the complimentary magazine and the towel and the lavender pillow spray and sat down on the bed. Jenny closed the lid of the sink so they could see out of the window again. Not that there was much to see on the platform at Euston, beyond the occasional passenger trundling a suitcase past.

'All right,' he said. 'We need to talk about what happens when we get to Blacklaw.'

Jenny folded her arms and looked down at him. In all of the excitement of making the breakthrough with Blacklaw House, they hadn't had much time to formulate a detailed plan. The good news was, they had all night to think about one now.

'Listen, I know you've been helping in a strictly unofficial capacity, but ...'

Mike was already shaking his head. 'We can't.'

'You didn't let me finish.'

'You were going to ask if I can get my colleagues to come along with us and knock on the door. First of all, I don't think Porter and his cronies are in the mood to do me any favours. Best case scenario, if we're right and Alice is there, they look terrible for not properly investigating a report of a missing child.'

'But surely if you talked to them, explained—'

'Explained what? That I'm carrying out my own unauthorised investigation? That I left the scene of a suspicious death?' He shook his head. 'And anyway, what do we have, really?'

'We have a trail that shows someone bought a ticket and told Emma to get on that train the night she was killed,' she said. 'We have a missing child with an estranged father who owns property a couple of miles from the spot where the woman she was with was killed. Those aren't coincidences, Mike.'

'I know they're not coincidences,' Mike said. 'But they're not evidence. Even if I was working this officially, you know what would happen if I tried to get a search warrant based on this?'

'The judge would laugh in your face?'

He looked amused at her phrasing. 'Something like that. Sure, I could try to knock on the door, ask some questions, but they would refuse to let me in and we would be back to square one. Worse than that, because we would have warned them.'

'Well, I don't see how you and I are going to get any better results than that.'

Mike opened up the laptop and navigated to the map they had taken a screenshot of.

He indicated the spot on the map a few miles south of Rannoch. 'This is where the sleeper stopped that night. This is where we think the killer got off, so this is where we'll get off.'

He trailed his finger from the tracks to the road that wound past. 'It's still a few miles to the house. Maybe he had a car waiting to take him to the house with Alice. We won't have anyone meeting us. At least I bloody hope not.'

'So we just follow the road?'

He shook his head. 'No. There's a gatehouse about a mile from the house, and it's fenced off on either side.' He indicated the spot on the map, and then dragged the screen a little to the left. 'But there's a trail across country here. It goes through the woods west of Blacklaw House. We take this and we approach from that way.'

'And then we just storm the castle? Save the princess?'

Mike smiled wryly. '*Then*, we take a good look at what we're dealing with. We suss out the security. Going by his other places, it's likely there'll be some. However, being as it's in the middle of nowhere, I'm hoping it won't be anything too elaborate. We see what we can see. Maybe we can even get inside somehow. If we're lucky, we find something that gives me a reason to get us through that door officially.'

'And if we're not?'

Mike said nothing for a moment. He reached under the bed and pulled out his backpack. As he reached in, it took Jenny a second to realise what he was doing. She had forgotten all about the gun.

He took it out and rested it on his knee. Without taking his eyes off her, he ejected the magazine, placing it on his other knee. He held the gun up side on, holding it at either end with two fingers of each hand. Like he was displaying an item at an auction.

'Have you used one of these before?'

Jenny shook her head. 'Not a real one. Air rifles, years ago.'

'It's very simple. An idiot could do it. Thousands of idiots do do it, every year.'

With practised hands, he let the gun slip into the palm of his right hand. He clicked a catch with his thumb. 'Safety off.' Clicked it the other way. 'Safety on.'

He turned and pointed it in the direction of the window, setting the catch to the off position again.

'Point it at the stomach of your target, squeeze the trigger.'

As he spoke he squeezed the trigger and the hammer snapped down on an empty chamber with a loud snap that made her flinch.

248

'Nothing to it.' He turned it round and handed it to her. It felt lighter than she had expected, although she supposed that was because he had taken the bullets out. She mirrored his actions. Safety on. Safety off. Point. Squeeze. Snap.

'Perfect,' he said. She handed it back. He flicked the safety to the on position. He slid the magazine back into the butt, and it connected with a quiet click. He put the gun back into his bag and sat back on the bed. He rubbed his temples.

All of a sudden he looked ten years older. He looked like Jenny felt. He glanced at his watch. 'We should try to get some rest.'

'You're right, but I don't think I'll sleep a wink if I try right now,' Jenny said. 'How about I buy you a drink?'

As Mike looked up, the hum of the engine stepped up a level and a shudder travelled the length of the train. Jenny felt the floor sway and braced herself with one hand on the wall as the platform started to move slowly away outside.

Eleven hours to go.

50

The lounge car host, an older woman in the standard white shirt and dark-green waistcoat, took Jenny's order as they sat down at one of the tables: a gin and tonic for her, a beer for Mike. The lounge car was of a piece with the rest of the train: carpeting reaching up the walls, 80s vintage fixtures, even free-standing chairs and tables.

The train was up to full speed now, charging north. The outer suburbs of London flashed by them in a blur. The windows of the buildings in darkness, the rain-drenched streets almost empty.

'Never done this before,' Mike said, looking out at the night.

'The sleeper?'

He nodded, looking back at her. 'I didn't realise they still ran it until one of the guys in the station mentioned it a couple of weeks into the job. Seems like something from a bygone age, like ...'

'Fax machines?'

'Nicer than that. Hansom cabs, maybe.'

The host emerged from the galley kitchen and placed their drinks in front of them on paper coasters embossed with the Caledonian Sleeper logo, a stylised stag's head.

'They're bringing in fancy new carriages next year, you

know,' Jenny said. 'En suites, showers, all mod-cons.'

'Shame. I kind of like it like this.'

Mike took a sip of the cold beer and closed his eyes in appreciation. Jenny gratefully drank some of her G&T.

She looked around the lounge car. It seemed more attractive by night, somehow. The wear and tear wasn't as evident as she remembered from the dull morning light of a week ago. That was true of the rooms and the corridors as well. The train was like an ageing theatre actor, still able to put on its best face for the evening audience.

They didn't have much company. A few people staring at their phones, or reading on the couches at the front of the car, only two of the other dining tables occupied. A lone woman with a glass of wine eating dinner, and two men in shirts and ties conversing over glasses of whisky. They looked like they could be MPs, maybe heading back to their constituencies.

'Why did you move to London?' Mike said.

'I always wanted to live there,' she said. 'I moved down after uni, did some interning, some part-time stuff, fell into a career.'

'Always good to have a plan,' Mike said.

She shrugged. 'In software development they call it agile methodology.'

'That sounds a lot like making it up as you go.'

'Not quite. You have a plan, but it's flexible.'

The carriage swayed as the track curved. Crockery rattled in the small galley kitchen at the far end of the car. A station lit by yellow sodium flashed by, too quickly to read the name on the sign.

'I can't believe he's gone,' she said quietly, trying to blot out the image in her mind of Eric's body.

'It wasn't your fault,' Mike said again.

'Of course it was my fault,' Jenny said. 'If I hadn't got involved ...'

'No. There was no way you could have predicted any of this.'

She said nothing. It might be true, but it didn't mean it was helpful. She had started this, with her refusal to let things lie. Now it was up to her to finish it.

'How did you meet him?' Mike said after a minute.

'Through work, at some drinks reception. He was very charming, we hit it off, and a year later we were married.'

'What went wrong?'

'Lots of things, over a long while. But mainly, him sleeping with someone else. It's like that Hemingway quote about how you go broke – gradually, and then all at once. That's how it works with marriage too. Well, with mine, anyway.'

They finished their drinks and continued talking. They had spoken a lot since the day they had met, of course. Over the phone and then in the time they had spent together today. But this was different, somehow. It wasn't business, it wasn't planning. It was just two people with some time to kill, comfortable in each other's company. Jenny told herself to ignore the way she was feeling closer to Mike.

It was a classic workplace attraction – two people thrown together by circumstance, forced to collaborate on a high-stress project. And Eric's death muddied the waters too, of course. Fair or not, it made her feel a lot worse about it.

They reached a pause in conversation and Mike caught the eye of the host, ordering another drink. Coffee this time. They would need clear heads in the morning. Jenny declined. They both turned to stare out of the window, not feeling the need to fill the silence. A bright shopping centre flashed by, the arc lights of a giant Tesco burning through the night, and then it was past and they were in a stretch of countryside; the dark fields indistinguishable from the sky. In the reflection of the window, Jenny saw the two men in ties get up and make their way to the next carriage.

They were alone in the lounge car now, apart from the two staff busying themselves in the kitchen. It felt like they were the last two people at a very sedate party.

She studied Mike's face in the reflection. The dark brown, slightly tousled hair. The green eyes. The faint stubble on the angle of his jaw. Just a workplace attraction, not something real. And then his eyes moved and she knew he was staring back at her in the reflection. Jenny looked down, embarrassed.

'Why are you doing this?' she said, to fill the silence, but also because she wanted to know. 'Really. I mean, you had no more reason to believe me than any of the others.'

He was still staring out of the window at the dark countryside rushing past. He was silent for so long that Jenny started to wonder if he was ever going to answer. Just when she was about to tell him to forget it, he spoke.

'It was the last week of my second tour, early 2010. Sangin. Our platoon was on patrol with the Afghan army. We stopped off at a schoolhouse inside a compound to drop off supplies. Hearts and minds stuff, handing out books and pencils, that kind of thing. School was over for the day but there was a schoolteacher, and a handful of kids playing in the yard, waiting for their fathers to pick them up. There was one girl with a bright blue ribbon in her hair, maybe nine or ten years old.'

He took a sip of his coffee, his eyes not meeting Jenny's. She had a queasy feeling in her stomach that was nothing to do with the here and now.

'We were almost done when the section outside at the east perimeter came under attack. I don't know if the Taliban had been tipped off about our movements or it was just bad luck.

'RPG hit out of nowhere, then they started closing in. I don't know how many of them there were. It was mayhem. Two of our guys outside the walls were killed right away, Peters and McCain. Hodgson, my CO, was hit bad. The civilians scattered.

253

We returned fire, got Hodgson back inside the compound. We held them back until the air support got there. We had three dead and four injured. The teacher and one of the kids were wounded too.

'When the MERT got there…' He stopped as he saw the question in Jenny's expression. 'The medics. When they arrived, one of the kids comes over to me and starts talking. Hard to understand. My Dari isn't great at the best of times, but it's more that he's upset, which is understandable. He's saying something about a girl. He's pointing at his head.'

'The girl with the blue ribbon,' Jenny said after a moment.

He nodded. 'She got separated from us during the firefight. When the gate in the wall was open to bring in the casualties. She can't have been hit, because we would have seen the body. She must have got lost, or been too scared to come out of hiding. We didn't realise until it was …' He tailed off and looked back at Jenny. Only he wasn't looking at her. He seemed to be staring at something a thousand miles away.

He cleared his throat and looked down at the dregs of the coffee in his cup. 'Anyway. I saw a lot of bad things over there. I lost good friends. But the girl with the blue ribbon … I think about her every day.'

Jenny looked down and saw he was toying with the fabric bracelet on his left wrist again. The faded blue-grey fabric that she knew must have been a vivid blue when he had bought it. A memento.

She put her hand over his wrist, gave it a squeeze.

'Can I get you anything else? We serve drinks all night, but the kitchen's about to close.'

Both of them looked up with a start to see the host, who had appeared silently beside them.

Mike looked at Jenny before answering. She shook her head. 'No, thank you. We have a long day tomorrow.'

They walked back to their carriage and Mike said he would knock on the door between their rooms ten minutes before they reached the stopping place. They said goodnight, and Mike looked like he wanted to say something else, but then he just nodded and pushed his door open.

She stepped inside her own room, closed the door, and backed against it, letting out a quiet sigh. She thought she knew what he was about to say: that it was too dangerous, that he should go alone. He had thought better of it, or maybe he was just postponing that argument until the morning.

Her pyjamas were back at the hotel in Russell Square along with everything else, so she just stripped down to her underwear and stuffed the clothes she had been wearing into her small backpack, laying out the new outdoor clothes and the walking boots beside the sink. As she reached into the bag, she felt an unfamiliar shape: small and thin and cylindrical and cold. She withdrew her hand and saw that she had absent-mindedly taken Eric's pen the other night. She weighed it in her hand. He either hadn't noticed, or had been too polite to ask for it back. Or perhaps he had thought of it as a parting gift. Neither of them had known how permanent the parting would be.

She slipped the pen into her jeans pocket, stuffed them in the bag and tried to put Eric out of her mind. She quickly brushed her teeth at the tiny sink and splashed cold water on her face before turning to examine herself in the mirror. She had dark hollows under her eyes. She reached out and touched the surface of the mirror, thinking about the other Alice from her childhood books, passing through the looking-glass.

She climbed under the covers. She heard nothing from the adjoining room. She wondered if Mike would be in bed. If he was lying there, thinking about her.

And then she reminded herself why they were here, where

they were going in the morning. She felt a chill as she remembered how close the man in the black coat had come to her on the Tube. And then later, on the street. The way he seemed to appear like a ghost.

She got out of bed and tried the lock on the door to the corridor to reassure herself, then reminded herself that no one knew where they were. Besides, Mike was in the next room, with the gun. That thought reassured her a little. Whatever happened tomorrow, she knew there was someone who had her back. Whatever happened they would face it together.

She yawned and listened to the sound of the wheels on the track, the wind blowing by outside, changing in pitch whenever they passed a row of buildings, or the country widened out into open fields. They were on their way. All she had to do was close her eyes.

Perhaps the ride was smoother tonight, or perhaps her body was beginning to adjust to the motion of the train. Before long, she began to drift off.

She closed her eyes and in time she found herself in a long, windowless corridor lined with doors. Dim spotlights were recessed into the ceiling at regular intervals. She saw Alice at the far end of the corridor.

The little girl turned and walked away, and Jenny realised she was not at the end of the corridor, it extended beyond that point, but the lights were dimmed further along.

Alice slipped under the last spotlight, the illumination glinting off her hair. Then her blue dress vanished into the shadows. Jenny followed.

51

The sleeper thundered north through the night. The sound of the wheels on the tracks seemed to call out a nursery rhyme. *On the way, on the way.*

Klenmore sat on the edge of the bottom bunk and thought about how often his targets made his job easy, by repeating themselves, covering the same tracks.

The laptop he had taken from Eric Bowen's flat had answered a lot of his questions, but it hadn't immediately got him any closer to finding his target. Using the password Bowen had eventually relinquished, he was able to access Jennifer Bowen's email.

From reading through her inbox for the previous week, he was able to put together a timeline of her actions since the previous Friday. It answered almost all of the questions he had about this irritating, persistent woman. She had been contacting various agencies, asking questions about the woman she had seen on the train. He was grudgingly impressed at her tenacity. Scanning through some of the older emails gave him a clue about that: perhaps this was a kind of displacement activity, to distract her from what was going on in her personal life. Divorce, bereavement. A house to sell.

It was unfortunate that she had boarded at that precise

moment, when the Dawson woman had the door open for a second and the girl could be seen. If the child hadn't dropped her rabbit she might never have seen her.

He tried to anticipate what her next move would be. She hadn't returned to the hotel in Russell Square. The porter he had paid off had checked in at the agreed intervals, and there was no sign of her.

He was working on the assumption that she was still in London, which was a positive and a negative. Positive because she was a long way from what she was looking for. Negative because she was asking far too many questions. Sooner or later, she would have to return to Scotland, to the house that was mentioned in some of the emails. It might be easier to take care of her there. Pills and whisky in bed; or perhaps a razor blade and a hot bath. After her last few months, no one would suspect anything but suicide.

The PDF that arrived in the inbox just after eight o'clock was unexpected, and it changed everything.

The sender was a Meryl Martin. The attachment was a scanned copy of a property deed. The deed for Blacklaw House. He had called in this new development immediately. He didn't know how they had stumbled upon the house, but this could be a major problem. The reply came back almost instantly. The instruction was not a surprise.

It would be easy enough to head them off now he knew their destination, though it would be useful to know their likely time of arrival. He was about to check in with the transportation department to see if Bowen had booked a flight when a notification had popped up in the bottom right-hand corner of the laptop screen.

It had taken him a second to realise what it was. Some kind of online banking notification.

BALANCE BELOW £50: TIME TO TOP UP

He expanded the popup and saw that it showed him the most recent transaction.

ATM: £300 / EUSTON STATION

Of course.

Whoever Bowen's companion was, he had evidently known better than to fly. If they were travelling north from Euston tonight, there were very limited options. The last regular Glasgow and Edinburgh trains of the evening had left already. Besides, they would want to get as close as possible to Blacklaw. They were taking the sleeper.

He made his way to Euston, bought a ticket with cash, and boarded on platform 1. From his previous trip, he knew the front six carriages would form the Highlander service. When the host checked him in, he asked if he could check the spelling of his name on the booking. There was no Bowen on the list, but he memorised which bookings listed a male and female couple.

When the train was underway, he got confirmation. He approached the lounge car and got just close enough to see in. The two of them were sitting at one of the tables, deep in conversation. A quiet break before the task ahead.

He would wait until morning. The stopping place again. The woman had been asking a lot of questions about what had happened that night. It all came back to what she had seen on the sleeper. This was an opportunity to tie everything up neatly. Two people caught up in a paranoid fantasy; a folie à deux. A double suicide. Or perhaps a murder-suicide. He liked the symmetry.

He lay back on the bed and knotted his fingers behind his head, staring out of the window as the sleeping country flashed by and the rain streaked across the glass.

The train gathered speed, and the wheels and the tracks changed the words of their duet.

Nearly there. Nearly there.

Saturday, 1st December

52

Jenny woke with a start.

She had been sleeping deeply, now all of a sudden she was wide awake. It was still dark outside the window. The train was racing along at a steady speed. The storm seemed to have abated. From somewhere ahead, she heard the soft wail of the horn as the engine passed beneath a bridge. Was it time to wake up already? Had it been Mike's knock on the door that had awakened her?

She sat up in bed and waited for another knock. Nothing. She thought about calling out, and decided against it. Her phone was charging in the USB port in the panel above the window. Silhouetted against the window, she could see it swinging gently from the cable like a pendulum.

She got out of bed, shivering in the cold, and unplugged it.

She opened maps and waited for the geolocation to zero in on her position. Gradually, the contours around the blue dot at the centre of the screen took shape. A rail line surrounded by green; not so different from what she had been looking at last night. She widened it out. There was minimal mobile web access, so it took a while to focus in but eventually managed it. They were close to the stopping place.

She was still looking at the screen when she heard a faint noise from behind her.

Her head snapped around and she saw the handle of the door to the corridor move a quarter of an inch, and then stop as it met the resistance of the lock.

Somebody was trying the door. Somebody who did not want to wake her up.

She held her breath and watched the handle, a hundred possibilities running through her mind. Could it be Mike? No, Mike would knock. He wouldn't carefully test the handle to see if it was unlocked. Her phone was still in her hand. She dialled his number, hoping that she would hear an answering buzz from outside the door.

She could hear the soft ringing from her own phone's speaker, but nothing else. She put a thumb over the speaker in case the sound travelled. And then she heard another noise. A scraping sound at the lock.

Fear stabbed into her like a blade of ice, and she was suddenly certain of the identity of the person outside. He had found them. Somehow he had found them.

Wake up! she screamed inside her head, staring at the phone screen as though she could psychically will Mike awake.

She looked around her, frantically searching for ... for what? There was nothing. She was trapped in a six-by-five-foot box. The only conceivable place to hide was under the bed, and that would take an intruder no time at all to check. A weapon, then. The heaviest thing she had in her bag was her laptop. She reached in and slid it out. It felt pathetically light in her hand, and she wished she had kept her old HP brick, rather than the sleek hybrid.

She heard a click as the lock disengaged and steeled herself, gripping hard on the edge of the laptop. The handle began to move again.

And then she heard another sound. From further away. The handle stopped at a quarter turn, and then slowly moved back into position. The sound became more distinct. Conversation. Getting louder.

Before she could make out distinct words, she knew it was members of the train staff. They sounded fully awake, chatting in the way people do when they're engaged in normal every-day routine. She felt a surge of hope and moved towards the door. She could tell them someone had tried to get in.

And then the voices faded away. They had turned round, headed back the way they had come.

Shit. She looked around for something to brace against the door. Nothing. She caught her own reflection in the mirror by the door, desperation in her eyes. She looked behind her at the window. It might be possible to pull it down far enough to squeeze out, but she remembered the squeal it had made the other night. And it would take time to manoeuvre herself through, even if the train were at a standstill, not pushing north at sixty or seventy miles an hour. She was trapped in a box, in her underwear, with no way out.

And then she remembered there was a way out. Or if not out, exactly, then to somewhere else. Not quite through the looking-glass, but not far from it.

Cursing herself for not thinking of it before now, she yanked her coat from the hanger on the adjoining door, uncovering the handle. It stuck, and then travelled the full way. The door swung open into the adjacent room. She had time to grab her backpack and push it through before she heard the sound of the handle on the main door beginning to turn again. She pushed through into Mike's room and forced herself to close the door softly.

Holding her breath, she heard the slight squeak of her own main door opening, muffled through the thin wall.

He was in her room. Standing where she had stood a moment before. She turned and with relief, saw Mike's figure under the covers, rolled over facing the wall. She didn't dare make a sound, instead she reached out and felt her hand contact his shoulder. She shook him. He didn't respond.

She risked whispering his name, shook him again harder. She gave his shoulder a yank towards her and he rolled over at last. Something was wrong. He hadn't woken up, hadn't said anything. Jenny felt something warm and sticky on her hand and the full realisation of what had happened hit her like a kick to the stomach.

The phone was still in her left hand. She brought it up, waking the screen. Light glinted off the blood on her other hand.

Mike's green eyes were staring up at her. His throat had been cut from ear to ear. Blood coated the sheets. She staggered forward and her right foot stepped in a pool of it on the floor.

Jenny suppressed the scream down to a soft whimper. She brought the hand holding the phone up to her mouth and bit down on her knuckles, hard.

Forcing herself to move, she reached beneath the bed, certain that Mike's killer would have taken his bag and the gun. But it was there. She reached inside, felt her hand close around the hard plastic of the grip. She dropped her phone into her own backpack, kept hold of the gun. She put the bag down on the hatch on the sink and held the gun in both hands. She could feel the safety catch with her thumb. Was it click down to fire, or for safe? She couldn't remember, but clicked down anyway, reasoning that Mike would have stored it with the safety on.

The killer was still next door. Perhaps he had decided she had gone to the bathroom, and was waiting for her to return. Maybe he had even crawled under the bed. The clothes she had laid out for the morning were still in the room, after all, folded and stacked on the shelf next to the sink. Her toilet bag was there, her new outdoor coat and boots, too. Would he realise where she had gone?

Now there was something wet on her face as well as on the soles of her feet. With a feeling of disconnect, she realised that it was tears.

She felt as though she was rooted to the spot. Could she just open the door and slip into the corridor? What if he happened to be coming out at the same time? Wait and hope he moved on? Surely at some point he would check the adjoining door, and she hadn't had time to lock it. Not that locks were any barrier to the man in the next cabin. Use the element of surprise and go on the offensive? She forced herself to think about it. Could she get the door open before he reacted? Unlikely. And then she would have one chance to get a shot off before he closed the distance. She had never even fired a handgun. Hadn't fired anything since her dad's air rifle when she was a teenager. What if she was wrong about the safety catch? What if Mike had taken the bullets out?

And then the decision was taken out of her hands.

The train slowed for a bend and then swayed to one side. Her backpack tipped over from where she had rested it and dropped to the floor with a thud.

53

Immediately, she heard movement from the room next door. She grabbed the bag as she saw the handle of the adjoining door twist down. Reached out and yanked the handle down on the main door. Tumbled into the corridor as she saw a gloved hand stretch out of the darkness towards her.

She didn't look back, just ran. When she reached the end of the carriage she saw the emergency stop and yanked the chain. She was already on the move again as she heard the wheels screech on the rails and felt the lurch as the train slowed. She used the momentum, kept her balance and raced onwards.

She made it to the end of the next carriage. The train was still slowing, maybe down to ten miles an hour now. She tried the handle, then yanked the sliding window of the door down, feeling the cold air bite into her. It created a gap of about two feet square.

The train was almost at a standstill now. She put the gun inside the bag and threw it out of the window. She braced both hands on the wall to the right of the window, then her feet against the other, before moving her legs through the gap.

She heard footsteps from the corridor behind her. The layout of the carriages meant she would be out of his line of sight until he reached the corner, so he wouldn't know she hadn't gone straight into the next carriage. If she could just squeeze through in time . . .

Her legs were all the way out, now, the rain cold on her bare shins. She felt the metal runner on the top of the window pane scrape the small of her back as she twisted and manoeuvred herself onto her front, bringing her hands round to guide herself the rest of the way out.

And then she ran out of time.

He appeared from round the corner, filling the space. He had a knife in his right hand, streaked with red. Jenny screamed and wriggled backwards as he dropped the knife and reached out for her with both gloved hands.

She felt herself squeeze loose and begin to drop, and a split second later his hand closed around her wrist.

She felt fingers bite into the bones of her wrist like the teeth of a steel trap. It felt as though he was trying to rip her hand off. Her feet dangled in the air. She kicked, trying to get leverage on the outside of the door. Her bare feet slid on the rain-wet metal of the train, skidding and slipping on the bodywork.

He planted his feet and started to pull. She felt her body move back through the gap. His face was inches away from hers. His features were knotted in exertion, but the look in his eyes was as dead and as blank as it had been the night she first saw him.

Looking into those eyes, she knew he was going to drag her all the way back in, and he was going to gut her, and he was going to wait until she bled out, and all the while, those eyes would not register a flicker of emotion.

She screamed out again and kicked her legs and this time, the sole of her right foot found purchase on the door. A different texture from the wet steel; maybe a decal or some sort of patch. She pushed back, hard.

The man adjusted his grip, but this time he had grabbed hold of her other wrist, the one slick with Mike's blood. She felt the leather begin to slip, and pushed off her right foot harder.

The tall man tried to grab her other wrist again, but it was too late. The slide of the gloved fingers on the blood continued until it was slipping over her hand, then her fingers, and then she was falling backwards.

Jenny dropped to the ground with a yell that was half startled, half triumphant. She landed in a heap on the gravel at the side of the tracks and looked up at him. He had one shoulder out of the window, his gloved hand grasping at thin air like one of those rip-off fairground machines where you try to pick up a stuffed Dalmatian from the glass box.

He brought his arm back in and she could see him trying to force the handle of the door. It shook but it held.

Realising she was wasting time staring at him, she glanced around for her bag. The train had come to a full stop now, and she could see her backpack lying on the embankment about twenty yards away. She got to her feet and ran back towards it. The gravel dug into her feet, but she barely noticed, only hopping onto the grass because she knew it would allow her to move faster.

Her mind was working away, trying to estimate how long it would take him to find a way off the train. She didn't have long, she was betting. No point thinking about it. She bent low and grabbed the strap of the pack without breaking stride and then made for the top of the low embankment.

Mostly open moor. She saw a stand of trees a hundred yards away and thanked God. Cover. She could hear the soft, muffled drumming of raindrops on the ground all around her, but she barely registered it drenching her. She risked a glance back at the train, the line of carriages stalled on the tracks, light shining from the alternate carriages where the corridor was on this side.

She couldn't pinpoint the window she had crawled out of, and she couldn't see any sign of the man in the black coat. He would be trying to find a way out, and it wouldn't take him long.

She turned and started to run for the trees. The sky was beginning to lighten in the east. She needed to lose herself in the woods before she ran out of darkness.

54

There was just enough light from the horizon for her to avoid turning her ankle on the uneven ground. She didn't dare stop, kept running, feeling the rough ground and the wet grass beneath her bare feet. She stumbled once or twice, but by a miracle, managed to avoid falling.

Her lungs were burning by the time she reached the tree line. The ground underfoot changed from grass to earth and moss and leaves. As she reached the first of the trees, her foot hit a hidden divot in the ground and she lost her balance and fell headlong to the ground.

On her hands and knees, she risked glancing behind her.

He was there, a hundred yards back, running across the open ground towards her. As she watched, he quickened his pace.

She scrambled to her feet and ran into the woods, zigzagging beneath the trees, avoiding going in a straight line. She trod on something sharp and felt a stab of pain in her right foot. She ignored it and kept going. Before long, she had lost all her bearings. Which way had she come from?

Her breathing was loud, her heart beating frantically. It felt like the freezing air had shrunk her lungs. The thought made her realise just how cold it was out here, how cold *she* was. She heard the sound of movement, not far from her position.

There was a huge fallen tree ahead of her, the hulking roots and earth at what had been its base shrouded in moss like some 1950s movie monster. She crawled on top of the trunk and saw a slope down to a stream, the banks lined thickly with tall ferns. She pushed herself over the edge of the trunk and down the slope headfirst, dragging herself beneath the ferns. Then she pulled herself into a ball and listened.

She breathed through her nose, trying to calm her breathing and her heartbeat. She gritted her teeth together to stop them from chattering. There was a small gap through which she could see the slope and the fallen tree at the top. She kept her eyes on it and tried to will her body to stop shivering, her lungs to stop breathing, her heart to stop beating.

She heard a scuffing noise and the tall man appeared at the top of the hill, his upper body visible behind the tree trunk. As quietly as she could, she drew the zip on her backpack back, reached in and took out the gun. The safety was still in the down position.

He just stood there, staring. It seemed like he was staring right at her. She held completely still, didn't dare to blink. Her breathing was slower now, more regular, but could he hear her somehow? Had she left some kind of trail? She held her breath and watched.

Maybe all she had to do was wait. Someone on the train would find Mike's body and call the police. They might search the woods. She knew that was a long shot. Even assuming they found Mike's body right away, it would be a long time before they pieced together what had happened.

Jenny tensed as the tall man placed his gloved left hand on the tree trunk, preparing to climb over it. This was it, when he got to the bottom of the slope, there was no way he wouldn't see her in the ferns. She bit down on her lip and gripped Mike's gun, her finger on the trigger. What if she shot and missed? What if it jammed?

And then, just as he was putting his weight down on the hand, he stopped. His head snapped around, as if he had heard something from that direction. He paused and then set off away from the tree trunk. Away from her.

She let out a long, slow breath. She counted. Ten seconds. Twenty. Thirty. A minute. There was no sound.

All of a sudden it was as though a switch had been flicked and she could feel the cold biting into her skin. Pain from the soles of her feet, too. She sat back and reached down for one foot and then the other, examining the damage. Both were dirty and cut in several places. There was a deep gash on her right foot, from whatever she had stepped on as she entered the woods.

She waited a few more minutes to be sure he wasn't coming back, and then she crawled out from under the ferns and crept to the top of the slope. She peered over the tree trunk and scanned the trees. There was no sign of him. She had been sure he knew where she was hiding, but now she realised he had been banking on her giving herself away. From somewhere distant she heard the sound of a startled bird taking flight. Perhaps the same frightened animal that had saved her by attracting his attention.

She made herself wait, holding perfectly still. She heard no other noises. Was he gone? Or was he waiting her out? Eventually the cold forced her to make a move. She stood up and tensed, waiting for him to come charging out of the undergrowth.

Nothing happened. No sound, other than the soft trickle of the stream below her. She cast a last glance in the direction she had seen him go and then picked her way back down the slope to the stream, putting her weight on the balls of her feet, where there were fewer cuts. She stood at the edge of the water, shaking in the cold air. It looked freezing. Putting any part of her in there was the very last thing she wanted to do. But she was worried about the big cut becoming infected, so she sat down on a moss-covered boulder on the bank, gritted her teeth, and plunged her feet into the running water.

It was so cold that she felt only a numbness that erased the pain from her feet. She rubbed at the skin gently, wincing as her thumb passed over the big gash in her foot and woke the pain up again. She withdrew her feet from the water and examined them. They were clean, at least, though the wound had started to weep blood already. The sight of it made her think of the gaping slash in Mike's throat, illuminated in the white light of her phone screen. She shut her eyes. She couldn't process that now, couldn't think about Mike. Or Eric. Or how much death had been caused because of her. No, because of *them*. She became conscious of a staccato rattle and realised it was her teeth chattering. If she didn't find a way to warm up soon, she would be in trouble.

She was shaking uncontrollably now. She retreated back to the shelter of the ferns and unzipped her backpack again, grateful that she had had the presence of mind to grab it. She hadn't really thought consciously about it at the time, but now she recognised that it might make the difference between life and death, and she wasn't thinking about the gun this time.

She pulled out her clothes from the day before: black jeans, a grey jersey top, a pair of socks and – hallelujah – her purple Converse trainers, flattened out at the bottom of the bag. She pulled the jersey over her head, tugging it down over the damp and bloody white vest top. It didn't seem to make much immediate difference to how cold she felt. She dried her legs off and blotted the blood from her right foot with a pack of tissues and pulled the socks on, seeing the blood darken the grey cotton almost immediately.

She pulled the jeans on and then the shoes, lacing them up tight. She hoped it would help to staunch the bleeding.

Now that she was fully dressed, she wasn't shaking quite as badly. Her head felt a little clearer, too. She realised she hadn't looked back up the hill for several minutes and jerked her head up, half expecting to see him looming above her.

How long would he look for her? At some point, he would give up.

Shit.

Now she had time to think, the full impact of the last hour or so hit her. Mike was dead. She had come within seconds of being killed too. She reached into the bag and had a moment of panic when she thought her phone had dropped out somewhere in her flight from the train. But then she felt it at the bottom of the bag and her fingers closed around the familiar rectangle shape.

The *No Service* message at the top left of the screen did not come as much of a shock.

She came out from beneath the ferns again and, quietly, carefully, climbed the slope. At some point while she was hiding, the rain had stopped. Somehow the air seemed even colder now. As she reached the tree trunk, the *No Service* disappeared and was replaced by *Emergency calls only*. She hoped it would be enough.

She dialled 999 and held the phone to her ear as she crouched behind the tree trunk, her eyes scanning the woods. As she did so, she started to wonder what she would say. She had no real idea of where she was, specifically.

'Emergency, which service do you require?'

A calm female voice in her ear, though the line was poor. It sounded like the words were coming from another continent. She opened her mouth to say 'Police.'

Then she took the phone from her ear and cancelled the call.

Calling the police was worse than pointless, it was stupid.

She forced herself to think about the last half hour or so since she had awoken in the dark. The train staff would need to find out why someone had pulled the emergency chain. They would find her bloody footprints leading from Mike's room. They would find his body.

What would the police find when they got to the train? A dead off-duty police officer, and the room next door empty, but with evidence of occupation: the bed slept in, her new hiking clothes and boots neatly laid out. One corpse, one fellow traveller, missing. Who would they be looking for? She looked down at her hands. Mike's blood was washed away, but she could see traces of it under her fingernails. It was all over her vest, and would have transferred to the inside of her clothes. If she had touched her hair, there would be blood there too. No doubt there would be other traces invisible to the naked eye. She thought about her footprints again. She realised now why the killer hadn't used the interior door – he wanted to avoid stepping in the pool of blood.

She hadn't killed Mike. In time, she might be able to persuade the police of that, even if the tall man had once again managed to kill and leave no trace of himself. But there was no question that she would be the prime suspect for the moment. Mike's colleagues would put two and two together, when they heard the circumstances. She would have been recorded on CCTV boarding the train at Euston with Mike. The lady in the lounge car would remember serving them drinks. They had used fake names for the booking, but there were other ways to identify a person. If she called the police now, told them everything, the best she could hope for would be spending days in custody.

And in the meantime, she would lose any chance she still had of finding out what had happened to Alice. The killer would report back to his masters, tell them that Mike was dead and that she had fled into the woods. Devlin's people would have time to cover their tracks, if there were any tracks to cover. They would realise where she and Mike had been going; that they had made the connection with Blacklaw House. If Alice was still there, she would quickly be moved.

She looked down at the blank screen of the phone, wishing it could give her an easier way out. There was none. She was all in.

She opened maps, knowing it would be useless. The blue dot representing her location appeared, but the country around it remained stubbornly indistinct. That dot looked tiny, insignificant. She put the phone back in her pocket and reminded herself she had to keep going. For Mike. For Alice.

She tried to recall the lay of the land from her brief glance at it, back on the train. They had been a little south of the stopping place, which was roughly two miles due east of Blacklaw House. The railway tracks had run roughly parallel with the edge of the woods, meaning she would have to head northwest. It had been a long time since Girl Guides, but she remembered a little about orienteering.

She moved through the woods, trying to retrace her steps, keeping her eyes peeled for movement. The camouflage of the woods was unnerving; like anything could be in here with her. The shapes, the constantly changing light patterns, the sounds of birds and animals moving around. The runoff from the rain still dripping its way down through the branches. Her own footsteps.

The trees were mostly pine, blotting out the sky, but she could still tell it was getting lighter. After stumbling through the undergrowth for a few minutes, she was lost. The last familiar landmark she had seen had been the fallen tree near the stream, and she wasn't entirely confident she could retrace her steps to that. And then she saw a glint of light through the trees. She moved position and saw that the forest was beginning to thin out, and the dawn sun was piercing through the overcast sky.

That was all she needed. She knew which way was east, at least, which meant if she could keep the dim glow of the morning sun in view, she could keep going in the right direction.

She kept the gun in her right hand and started heading northwest.

55

Klenmore didn't like loose ends.

The woman was out there somewhere. Scared, barely clothed, with the temperature just above freezing. He hadn't expected her to get away from him. That hadn't been the plan. But in life, things frequently didn't go to plan. That was what adaptability was for.

Even though she had managed to get far enough ahead to conceal herself for now, her options were extremely limited. She couldn't stay out here forever. Klenmore was confident he had left no trace of himself on the train. The woman, however, was covered with her friend's blood. She could try to explain, of course, but her explanation would be suspect in the extreme. She had left enough of a trail over the past week, irritated enough of the authorities, that it would not be difficult to ensure that the narrative that took hold was that she was a deranged fantasist, as well as a murderer.

But to be on the safe side, they had to assume Blacklaw was compromised, and act accordingly. He could waste hours looking for her out here. The best course of action was to make sure whatever she could tell the authorities would be impossible to prove. That way, even if she survived, any information she had would be useless.

He took his phone out to confirm it had no signal, as expected, and switched on his radio instead. He raised the guard at the gatehouse and told him he was on his way in.

He walked cross country until he reached the road. A little further east, beyond the crest of the next hill, he knew the railway track ran by. He stepped off the rough grass and onto the welcoming smoothness of the tarmac and turned left, away from the rails. In ten minutes, he reached the gatehouse.

It was an original part of the estate. On either side, a high stone wall extended. Klenmore knew that there were subtle anti-climbing barbs ranged along the top of the wall. The road passed beneath the central arch of the gatehouse. The gates themselves weren't a period feature. The original iron had been scavenged during the Second World War, to be melted down to make Spitfires. The new gates were steel frames painted black, with just a touch of era-sensitive ornate detail. They would stand up to a van ramming them at full speed.

As Klenmore approached, the door opened in the gatehouse and a guard stepped out. Klenmore recognised him from his last visit. He was a little overweight with ruddy cheeks and a receding hairline hidden by his uniform cap. His jacket hung open, exposing his paunch. Klenmore knew his employer wouldn't like that. Or perhaps standards were looser, this far out on the frontier.

The guard gave a half-hearted salute as he approached and stood across the gate. Klenmore could see he was hoping he wouldn't have to actually ask to see Klenmore's identification, because then he might have to follow through with the pretence that he could effectively stand in his way in the absence of said identification.

Klenmore did him a favour and produced the card unasked. With visible relief, the guard took it and waved a small black device over it until it bleeped softly and a green light appeared.

'Do you need me to call ahead for a car?'

56

As Jenny walked, feeling the rough forest floor through the thin rubber soles of her shoes, she began to realise that her absolute terror of the man in the black coat had subsided a little.

Back there under the bushes, cold and alone, with him less than twenty feet from her, she had thought it was all over. Even with the gun, she had been almost resigned to it. A strange fatalism had gripped her; made her certain that she would miss, or something else would go wrong, and he would win again.

She didn't feel like that any longer. Since being able to clean herself and put on dry clothes, and even more so since finding her way out of the forest, she had begun to feel a new confidence. It wasn't as though the odds against her had improved much, but it felt like she had taken control of her own destiny. And more than that. For the first time, she had won a round against the seemingly invincible adversary who had lurked at the edges of her life for the last few days. She had given him the slip, forced him to give up on finding her for the moment. And now she had the element of surprise. As far as her pursuer knew, she was still wandering the woods in freezing temperatures, almost naked, defenceless. Perhaps he would conclude she was as good as dead.

She was still cold, but the shivering had subsided to a level that no longer alarmed her. Her breathing was regular, each breath escaping her lips and travelling up towards the treetops as a little cloud.

Up until now, she hadn't been altogether sure why she had persevered with this ... mission? Calling? Sure, she had had unanswered questions after the sleeper, but it would have been easy to rationalise them; to accept the verdict of others that she had imagined the little girl in the blue dress. After she got to London and discovered the link to Devlin, it had been almost like a game for a while. She hadn't wanted to quit. And suddenly it was too late to quit. Things had escalated and it was as though she had begun descending a steep hill and found herself able only to run, or to fall. So she had kept running.

Since the train, things were different. She still wanted to find out what had happened to Alice, of course, and she prayed she was safe. But ever since finding Mike dead, only hours after Eric had been killed, she wanted something else. She wanted payback. She felt like she wanted to take Blacklaw House down brick by brick, until her questions were answered and someone paid for what she had lost.

She reached the edge of the woods in twenty minutes, the patches of dull sky becoming more frequent until there were no more trees and her field of view expanded out to a sweeping stretch of moorland. She stopped at the treeline, resting a hand on the last pine, suddenly feeling a strong reluctance to leave the shelter of the forest. The ground dropped away gradually from this position, her view of the terrain ahead almost unobstructed. There were mountains in the distance. A road curving around the edge of a loch five miles or so to her west. She remembered the loch from the satellite image. It meant Blacklaw was about two miles straight ahead, roughly in the direction of the tallest peak of the distant range.

It took her a second to orient these landmarks, because what

283

first drew her attention was the sky. It had still been dark when she had entered the woods. Although she had since seen patches of daylight overhead and in the distance between trees, she hadn't noticed there was something off about the quality of light. Even though the sun was fully over the horizon by now, it was still burning dimly behind thick clouds. The sky wasn't just overcast, it was a dirty yellow colour. It was something like the way she imagined the sky might look after a nuclear war.

There had been something on the weather report about sand from the Sahara being brought over by the storm, but this was unlike anything she had ever seen. Together with the vast, deserted landscape, it was as though she had been transported to an alien world. Thinking about the unreality of the last few hours, perhaps that was not too far from the mark.

There was nothing else in her world now. Just her, and the path ahead, and Blacklaw House at the end of it.

She took out her phone again, knowing it was useless now. *No Service*. No maps, either. Not that a map would be much use anyway, this far from the nearest road. She just had to hope she could trust her memory of where the house lay. She looked out at the moor before her, and the quote she had read the other day came back to her: *A wearier-looking desert man never saw*.

She took a deep breath and started walking again.

57

Each time he came here, Klenmore remembered how much he hated all the blind windows watching him. Blacklaw House stood at the end of the long road through the woods, a sprawling red hulk holding its own against the scale of the mountains beyond. It seemed almost to draw light into itself, as though it sat in its own shadow even when the glass and sandstone should have looked bright against the weird reverse-twilight of the morning. He passed the huge oak tree and the two matching Lexuses in the driveway, his heels crunching on the coarse gravel that matched the sandstone walls. He climbed the main steps and stepped through the front door. In contrast to the security at the gatehouse, the door was not locked. But then, he was expected, and besides, the wall and the guard at the gatehouse was all that was really needed.

He stood in the hall. He had been here before, but familiarity didn't make it any less impressive. The black-and-white tiled floor extended fifty feet from the doorway, its path broken only by the twin grand staircases stretching up to the next level. He looked up there, to see if anyone was staring down on him from the stone arches that lined the next floor.

'Hello?' he called out, a bite of irritation in his voice. They knew he was coming, why had no one been here to greet him?

He moved towards the staircase and started to climb. The deep scratch on his face the man he had killed had given him was still smarting. He had made sure to take the broken toothbrush that had inflicted the wound. He reached the first floor and looked around. The house was entirely silent. Could they have cleared out already? That would save him a difficult conversation. He glanced up at the great oval skylight, saw that it was misted with condensation. Last night's rain evaporating in the dim sunlight.

'One body has been found on the sleeper, Mr Klenmore.'

His head jerked round in the direction of the voice. As the faint echo died away, he saw a hint of movement in the darkness on the other side of the staircase. He stepped out of the light and squinted his eyes to try and make them adjust faster.

'I took care of it,' he said. 'As instructed.'

'*One* body,' came the reply. 'Did you perhaps forget how to count?'

Klenmore took his time responding. His employer did not value obsequiousness as a virtue, which was a good thing, because he didn't have it in him. 'Unavoidable complications.'

'Fixable complications?'

He took his time answering again.

'Oh yes.'

58

It was starting to feel like the next line of trees was gradually retreating from Jenny, the more she walked towards them.

What had looked like a brisk twenty-minute walk across the moor was turning out to be more like an hour. At first, she spent time thinking about what was ahead of her. The house. The man from the sleeper. Then she thought about what was behind her. The police would be looking for Mike's killer by now. How many traces had she left? Her fingerprints all over both rooms, of course. Her mobile number would be in Mike's recent calls. Likely, she was a person of interest already. With that in mind, knowing that no one else in the world knew precisely where she was felt almost reassuring. And then she remembered why that might turn out to be a bad thing, as well.

As she kept walking, she stopped thinking about anything. Her mind fell into the rhythm, one foot after another, keeping the weak glow of the sun at her back and the tallest mountain on the horizon in the centre of her view.

The clock on her otherwise useless phone told her it was just after ten when she reached the next patch of forest. If she was right, Blacklaw was on the far side, before the foothills of the mountain she could see rising above in the distance.

At first, she was able to make her way through the second

forest more quickly. The ground was more even, the under-growth less tangled than in the previous stretch. The pain in her right foot hadn't gone away, but it had settled into a dull numbness rather than the sharp pain from earlier.

She was less than ten paces from the boundary wall by the time she saw it. Eight feet high, sandstone, blending in with the woods beneath a curtain of weeds and ivy. She walked along the boundary for a couple of minutes until she found a tree with a branch that reached close to the top of the wall. She scrambled up onto the branch and saw that there were sharp barbs lining the top of the wall, six inches apart. Carefully, she maneuvered herself onto the wall and dropped down on the other side, landing on John Devlin's land for the first time.

She took a second to check the position of the sun and started walking again. Though she knew it covered less ground, she thought the trees were denser in this forest than in the other one, and for a while she worried she was losing her bearings. A minute later she saw a strip of tarmacked road and knew she was close to her goal: the main approach road to the house. She moved back from it, knowing she couldn't approach the house front-on.

A few seconds after changing course, she came into view of a tree formation that looked a little out of place. The wood was darker, the trunks seemed to curve in a way that defied nature. And then she realised what she was looking at. A stone arch, covered with moss and ivy. The old priory.

Perhaps half of the original structure remained, almost sub-sumed into the forest. Two of the walls were still standing, the others lay in hunks of scattered rubble, covered in old moss. She stepped through the archway and looked around. There was part of a tower at the far corner, the roof long caved in and the stone spiral staircase exposed.

She saw a glassless window ahead facing in the way she had

been going, and decided to climb through it to rejoin the path.

She knew she had no time to waste, and yet she couldn't help lingering. She stepped carefully onto the first two steps up to the ruined tower and looked up to the platform above. It might be possible to jump the gap and access the room. She stepped down and headed towards the other side of the wall. She was paying careful attention to her footing, and it was a good thing too, because there was a concealed hole in the ground.

The hole was about three feet wide, and looked down into some kind of sub-level. A cellar, or even a crypt. Either way, it was pitch black, and she couldn't see how far down it went. Leaning closer, she could smell musty damp. She turned away and moved to the western wall. There was a glassless window, and a drop of around ten feet onto uneven ground. She retraced her steps and went around the exterior of the ruin.

When she had taken a dozen paces, she stopped and looked back at the old priory, wondering how long it had lain here undisturbed in the woods.

The trees closed in again and she lost sight of the slightly brighter spot in the sky where the sun was. She walked for another five minutes, hoping she was going in the right direction. And then there began to be slightly more space between the trees and the yellow sky began to show itself again. Unknowingly, she had been staring straight at her goal for a while before it registered.

She stopped dead when the shapes in between the trees suddenly resolved themselves into a familiar form. The house. She had never been able to see the picture in those Magic Eye posters that had been so popular when she was a teenager, but she could only imagine this was the same kind of effect.

She moved closer to the edge of the woods and stopped to take in her destination.

Blacklaw House was bigger and grander than she had expected

from either of the pictures she had seen. It looked much more like it had in the primitive black-and-white Victorian photograph, not the version from the more recent image where the house had been overgrown and weather-beaten. Devlin had obviously spent a lot of money on it. It was red sandstone, something that hadn't been obvious in either picture. The windows had all been replaced, most of them slate grey in the morning gloom. A couple of windows on the first floor were lit up. The roof of the north wing had been repaired, as she had guessed from the satellite images. The jungle-like gardens at the front had been brought back into submission. The grass looked as though it had been trimmed square five minutes ago. She could see the sweeping gravel driveway, and the towering oak tree, and two black cars parked beneath its branches near the main door.

The house and its gardens were surrounded by the woods on all sides. She felt a catch in her breath when she contemplated approaching over the two hundred yards of open ground. There would be nowhere to hide.

She crouched behind the trees, surveying the house for a few minutes. There were no signs of life beyond the few lights in the downstairs window. The cars outside were the only suggestion that anyone was home.

She sat back against the tree and rubbed the side of her head. What the hell to do now? Mike would have known. Or maybe he would have been as conflicted as she was. Either way, it would be better in every way to have him with her.

She realised that Mike's killing had hit her far worse than Eric's, the man she had been married to for years. Perhaps because her relationship with him was in the past, while Mike might have been a part of her future. She thought about the frayed blue wristband, the memory of another little girl that had kept him awake nights. If only she hadn't looked inside that particular room at that particular moment, none of this would have happened. It was her fault Mike was dead, Eric too.

She knew exactly what Mike would say to that if he could hear her, of course. If she hadn't been there, then nobody would know about Alice. She had to find her now. It wouldn't bring Mike or Eric back, of course, but at least something good would have come out of this.

The tree cover seemed to encroach closer to the house on the north side. There was perhaps only a hundred yards of open ground there, rather than two hundred. Perhaps there would be fewer windows on that side. She might be able to get in closer without being seen. Agile methodology. Completely different from making it up as you go, honest.

She picked up her backpack and checked the gun was still there, feeling the weight of it in her hands. She thought about how she had frozen back beneath the bushes. She still wondered if she would be able to use it, if the need arose.

She moved round the edge of the woods, keeping her eyes on the house all the while.

There was a thicket of rhododendron bushes directly opposite the northern edge of the house. She walked in a wide clockwise circle, keeping at least twenty feet of tree cover between herself and the open ground at all times. She saw no sign of life from the house. She wasn't sure what she was expecting. Armed guards and pit bulls, perhaps. But if they were there, they were doing a good job of keeping a low profile. The absence of overt signs of security gave her no reassurance, however. She remembered how she had been so very nearly imprisoned in the shining tower on the South Bank.

She reached the rhododendrons and crouched down to crawl beneath them. The road from the main entrance curved round here, skirting the large ornamental pond. She had been right: the edge of the bushes was at most a hundred yards from the house. The north side was less ornately decorated than the front of the house. Almost as wide, but with fewer windows; none of them lit. Extending from the rear of the building and visible side-on from her position, was a large glass conservatory. It looked grand, and of the same period as the house. A winter garden. She could see what looked like exotic blooms and tropical trees through the misted panes of glass.

She laid the backpack down and moved as close as she dared to the edge of cover. Looking back at the main body of the house, she saw something promising. A railing, suggesting there was a drop behind it, and just visible above ground level, the lintel over a doorway. A cellar door? There was a small area near the wall fenced off by six-foot high planks – it looked like a refuse area.

She lingered a minute longer, wondering if she was just waiting for an excuse not to move. There were no signs of life. No movement at any of the windows.

She flinched as she heard the sound of a door opening. As she watched, a man's head appeared at the railings, then a white shirt, then dark trousers. He was ascending the stairs, clutching a tied up black bin bag. Not the man from the sleeper; someone much less imposing. She could see the door was open behind him. He walked across to the small fenced-off area and stopped at a padlocked gate in the side, reaching in his pocket with his free hand.

The cellar door was open.

She hesitated. It wouldn't take him long to dump the bag. Could she possibly cover the ground in time? She doubted it. And then she saw that the man had stopped digging in his pocket. His head was up, he was looking in the direction of the front of the house. And then she heard it, too. Wheels on gravel. Someone arriving. The man laid the bin bag down and started forward to see who was there.

As soon as he rounded the corner, Jenny took a deep breath, braced on the ground like a runner on the blocks, and took off across the open ground.

She had almost reached the edge of the flagstone path running along the north wall by the time she realised she had left her backpack in the bushes.

Her backpack, and the gun inside.

59

It could not have taken more than fifteen seconds to cover the stretch of neatly mown grass between the bushes and the house, but to Jenny it felt like an hour. She kept her eyes on the windows as she ran, thankful that the approach was across firm grass rather than gravel or paving.

She reached the railings and saw they guarded a narrow flight of stone steps, leading down to a cellar door. Without pausing, she used the edge of the railing to swing herself around and down the steps, crouching as soon as she reached the bottom.

She turned round and slowly ascended two of the steps so her eyes were back at ground level. She watched the grounds for signs of life. Then she turned and looked up at the windows, what she could see of them from this angle. No movement. Not a sound, other than the distant call of some bird of prey on the moor. She looked back at the rhododendron bushes where she had left her bag and wondered if she had time to go back to retrieve it.

The sound of a car door closing at the front of the house persuaded her she did not. She breathed out softly and descended again.

The door was ajar. It was a heavy oak slab. If it was not an original feature then it certainly looked the part. There was a bronze knob above a keyhole. The man in the white shirt had left it open, so she knew he would likely be coming back this way, and soon.

It was dark inside. Blessedly warm after the bitter cold outside. She could make out a stone floor and some gardening tools arranged against one wall. She took her phone out and tapped on the flashlight app. She swung the beam around to get a feel for the dimensions of the space, and more importantly, to make sure she was alone. She saw bare brick walls, more gardening tools, an old bicycle, wooden furniture stacked against another wall. There was a door, six feet high, set into the wall with a rainbow-shaped lintel. As she moved towards it, she heard the sound of footsteps on the stone steps outside.

Without having time to think, she ran for the pile of furniture and crawled beneath a stack of chairs. She held her breath as she saw the man from outside. Or, to be exact, saw his lower legs and shoes as he closed the door behind him and turned the key in the lock. He walked briskly across the space and went through the interior door. Footsteps ascending, then another door opening and closing. A couple of seconds later, the fainter noise of a third door closing.

She counted to twenty. When she was sure he wasn't coming back, she slid out from under the stack of chairs and went back to the exterior door. The key was still in the lock. She unlocked it again, opened it, and then closed it over. Sensible to have a way to get out of the house in a hurry, if she needed to.

She crossed over to the interior door and tried the handle. This one was unlocked. It opened onto a steep flight of stone steps. She shone the beam of her torch upwards. There were a dozen or more steps leading up, and the beam reached just far enough for her to see there was another door at the top. It was almost totally silent inside the stairway. The occasional gusts of wind from outside seemed a long way away.

She climbed the stairs, taking her time, directing the beam of light down at her feet. When she reached the top of the stairs she stopped and put her ear against the door. Hearing nothing, she grasped the handle, still not sure if she wanted to open it. She held her breath and turned it.

The door opened onto a kitchen. She let out a relieved sigh as she saw it was empty.

She let the door swing the rest of the way open and let her eyes roam over the space, taking her time now she knew she was alone.

It was a huge room, and for the first time she had confirmation that the interior of the house had received as much TLC as the exterior. Long granite worktops lined two of the walls. There was a huge breakfast island on her right-hand side, also topped with granite. The island looked bigger than the entire galley kitchen in Jenny and Eric's flat in Highbury. Everything was the highest spec. Polished chrome fixtures, beautifully carved cupboard doors.

There was something wrong about the kitchen, though, and it took her a few moments to realise what it was. There was no clutter whatsoever. Not just clean and tidy, but antiseptic. No pots on the hob, no shoes arranged in a corner, no important letters stuck to the gigantic American fridge.

She remembered what Mike had said about Devlin when they started looking into him. Properties across the world, homes on every continent. He probably didn't spend enough time here for any clutter to accumulate. And yet, it didn't feel deserted, exactly. There was no dust, no cobwebs. The room felt frozen in time.

She wondered if they had been wrong about this place. Perhaps the sleeper stopping near one of Devlin's properties had been a coincidence. Perhaps it was impossible to pick a spot anywhere in Britain that was more than a couple of miles from something he owned. Or perhaps she and Mike had been right: Alice *had* been brought here, but then taken somewhere else.

It didn't matter. She had come too far to turn back now.

She opened a couple of the drawers and tried some of the cupboards, not sure exactly why she was doing it. She didn't intend searching every room in the house thoroughly, not least because it would take her weeks. She felt almost comforted when she saw there were utensils and cutlery in the drawers, canned food and pasta and cereal boxes in the cupboards. Kellogg's Cornflakes, Lucky Charms. She opened the freezer: it was stocked with large cuts of meat from a Highland butcher. It was as though the house was on standby. It was clean and stocked and could be made fully operational at short notice.

She opened the kitchen door onto a wide hallway. The floor was tiled in black and white, like a chess board. There were other doors along the wall, all in a uniform dark mahogany, all closed tightly. She shut the kitchen door behind her quietly and looked up and down the hall, her breath catching when she saw a figure across the hall from her. A woman. The woman flinched, she looked terrified.

It took her a second to realise that the woman was her, reflected in a grand ornate mirror, at least fifteen feet high. She swallowed and glanced around. The front door was at one end. At the other was a grand staircase that swept up from the centre before forking to reach opposite sides of the mezzanine level overlooking the hall. On the next floor were stone arches, like theatre boxes. She didn't like the analogy, it put her on centre stage.

She was moving towards the stairs when she heard a sound for the first time since entering the house.

Voices.

60

Jenny backed against the wall, fumbling behind her for the handle of the kitchen door. And then she realised the voices were staying put, coming from somewhere above her. She felt very exposed in the grand hall. A blue dot in the centre of unknown country. For the hundredth time, she wished Mike was with her.

She stepped out and looked up at the floor above. In between the stone arches, she could see doors leading off the landing. One of them was open, watery daylight spilling out. The voices were coming from within. She couldn't make out distinct words, just that one of the voices was male, one female.

She moved across to the staircase, which was carpeted. As she climbed the stairs, the voices resolved themselves into a conversation.

'. . . would advise caution, that's all I'm saying.'

'I know you would, that's what I pay you for.'

There was a silence. The unmistakeable silence of a subordinate biting their tongue. There was something about the female voice. Something familiar.

Jenny reached the first level and looked around. There was a wide landing, and a smaller staircase leading up to the second floor. Above her was a huge oval skylight, the stained glass dull and lifeless beneath the yellow clouds. The open door, the one the voices were coming from, was one of eight. She moved to the closest door and tried the handle. It was locked. She looked up as one of the voices spoke after a long silence.

'I'll let you know when your car arrives.'

Two realisations hit Jenny at once. The first: the voice sounded familiar because she had heard it recently. It belonged to Lucine Rinzler, the woman from the London office. Jenny didn't have time to dwell on that, because the second realisation was infinitely more pressing: she was coming out of the room, heading in Jenny's direction.

Jenny lunged for the next door, knowing she would not have time to try a third time. This one was unlocked. She turned the handle and fell into the space beyond, not having time to worry about whether there was anyone behind this one. She closed it after her, hearing footsteps on the carpet outside. They paused as they passed the door, and Jenny was certain Rinzler had heard her, or spotted the door closing.

She stood motionless, holding her breath. And then she heard the footsteps again, retracing their steps. Voices again. Perhaps Rinzler had forgotten something. With the door closed, they were too muffled to hear. Who was she speaking to?

Jenny looked around the room she was in. It was large, like everything else in this house, but it was sparsely furnished. Neutrally papered walls in an off-white colour. A recessed bookcase with bound volumes that looked as though they had been chosen by an interior decorator, rather than a reader. A bay window that looked out on the rear gardens and the mountains, and across from that another huge mirror that gave the illusion there were two identical gardens and two mountain ranges. There was a suite of chairs, a couch and a coffee table set up near the window.

Jenny crossed to the door on the opposite side of the room

and opened it. She found herself facing a long corridor. This one was narrow and dark, and it took her a second to realise why she hesitated before entering. It reminded her of the corridor in her dreams last night.

It was almost as narrow as the corridor on the sleeper, and it led past a series of doors. Seemingly endless doors. This was more like a hotel than a house. If Alice really was in this house, how could Jenny hope to find her?

At the far end of the corridor was another door, which gave onto a narrow stone spiral staircase. She guessed this was the tower on the north wing. She tried to picture it, and thought she could recall windows on four levels. If she was on the first floor, then there were two tower rooms above her. She hesitated again. Climbing the stairs would mean knowingly walking into a dead end.

And then she heard something. Not a voice, this time. A rhythmic rattling sound from behind her. Like someone carrying crockery. She spun round to see the door at the far end of the corridor opening. She pushed through into the spiral staircase.

But this time, she was a second too late.

61

She heard a surprised yell from the corridor as the door swung shut behind her, followed by a louder rattling. No choice now, she had to go down.

As she started down the steps, she heard running footsteps on the other side of the door. She tumbled down the staircase, almost losing her footing on the tight, winding stairs. She pushed through the door on the ground floor, ignoring the rest of the stairs leading down beneath the house.

A small hallway with no windows and two doors. She chose the nearest and found herself in a large drawing room. Two huge antique couches, rugs, a giant fireplace. There was another door on the opposite side. If she could find her way back to the main entrance hall, she could leave the way she had come in. As she ran to the adjoining door, she glanced at the windows, trying to orient herself by the view outside. Was this the front or the rear of the house? There was no time to stop and think. Whoever was behind her would know she had come this way.

A snap decision, she let the door swing open and then retreated back into the room, crouching behind the couch farthest from the centre of the room.

She heard running footsteps. Kept her head down as someone passed by her without stopping. As the footsteps died away into the room beyond the next one, she stood up. Finally, a positive thing about the scale of this place: it was easy to find a hiding place when you needed to.

She went back to the previous room and tried the other door. More stairs, climbing up to the first floor. The place was like a bloody Escher painting. Every way out turned into another staircase or a dead end. She closed the door behind her and climbed to the next level. The stairs led to a small landing with two doors. One was a small cupboard with a window that was jammed shut when she tried it. The second was a much larger room. It was a library.

The library room was two storeys tall, with a narrow metal catwalk platform and railing running all the way round the upper half of the room. Every wall was lined with bookcases. On the upper level, the shelves were behind elegant mesh cabinet doors. The floor was polished wood, with a giant Oriental rug spreading out to cover it, leaving a margin of wood floor three feet wide on all sides. In the centre of the ceiling was another ornate skylight, even bigger than the one in the entrance hall, and Jenny realised that this was the circular skylight she had seen from the satellite images. She was in the heart of the house.

There was no time to admire the decor. There was another set of double wooden doors at the far end. If she remembered the outline of the house from the satellite view correctly, it would lead into the front of the building. Perhaps she could get out that way. Even as she thought about it, she knew it all depended on the number of staff in the house. If they only had two or three people, she might be lucky. If they had more people to spare, they would certainly station guards at all the exits.

But it turned out to be academic. She reached the double doors and tugged on the handle. It stayed securely locked. She tried it again, not wanting to rattle the door too much, in case there was anybody on the other side.

She hurried back to the doors she had entered by. When she was at the edge of the carpet, her hand already stretching out, she heard a sound that she felt in her solar plexus: the hard click of a lock engaging.

62

Jenny was trapped in the centre of the maze.

She fell back into the middle of the room, scanning the walls for another exit. It was harder than she expected to rule this out. The thousands of spines, the clean vertical and horizontal lines, created a kind of camouflage, where each square foot required careful study. But after a few moments she was certain that there were no other exits on the ground level. A metal spiral staircase in the corner led up to the catwalk, and she could see that there was another door up there. She wanted to get back to the ground floor, though, not go higher up.

She glanced around again. Books, books, as far as the eye could see. The only window the giant, inaccessible glass circle thirty feet above her head.

She felt the rush of panic return, overcoming the numbness that had allowed her to keep functioning this long.

No, she was down to one option. With the uncomfortable feeling that she was being herded, she ran for the spiral staircase. She grabbed the banister and started to run up the stairs, feeling the antique structure creak even under her slim nine stone.

And then she heard another loud click, from directly above her.

Jenny froze, one hand on the guardrail, halfway up the spiral. For a moment, she heard nothing, other than her own short breaths and the thudding of her heart. A creak as the door on the upper floor swung open.

A man stepped out onto the mezzanine and put his hand on the banister, peering down at Jenny. He wore a grey linen suit over a white open-necked shirt. He had grey hair so shiny it looked as though it had been buffed and waxed, and his brown eyes regarded her from behind the lenses of a pair of wire-rimmed spectacles. She hadn't noticed how brown his eyes were in the photographs. She had only ever seen eyes that dark once before.

'Good morning,' John Devlin said with the scrupulously polite air of a maître d' at a restaurant Jenny couldn't afford. 'I don't believe we've met.'

63

Jenny didn't say anything. She just gripped the handrail with her right hand as she looked up at Devlin, wishing for the hundredth time she had not laid down her bag and the gun.

Devlin opened his mouth again, presumably to prompt a reply, but before he could speak Jenny heard the click as the doors below her were unlocked. She looked down and saw Rinzler standing in the doorway, a hand on each of the twin door handles, as though expecting Jenny to make a break for it from her current position. She glared up at Jenny, almost daring her to.

'It's fine, Lucine. I'll call you if I need anything.'

Rinzler looked from Jenny to Devlin, then back to Jenny again. Devlin leaned forward a little and raised his eyebrows. In response, Rinzler retreated from the room, closing the doors as she went.

'Are you going to stay halfway up those stairs all day?' Devlin said once the doors had clicked shut.

Without waiting any longer for a reply, he turned and walked back through the doorway, leaving it open. After a moment's consideration, Jenny climbed the remainder of the stairs.

When she reached the top, she hesitated a second, and then entered the room.

It was much smaller than the other rooms she had passed through, with a sloping ceiling on one wall with a skylight built in. The only adornment to the walls was a framed painting. It showed sailors clinging to a small sailboat as it was buffeted by giant waves beneath a threatening sky.

'Rembrandt. It's real,' Devlin remarked. 'Although I'd be grateful if you kept its whereabouts to yourself.'

Now that he said it, it was familiar. She assumed his words meant that it was stolen. She turned round, unable to work up much interest in the fact that Devlin acquired Old Masters of dubious provenance, as well as everything else. There was a small table with three chairs in the corner beneath the skylight. Devlin pouring tea from a pot into two china cups. She noticed his hands shook very slightly.

'How do you take it?'

Jenny lingered in the doorway, unsure of what to do or say. The situation was surreal. She had been fleeing for her life, now she was being asked, 'One lump or two?'

'I'm not thirsty,' she said.

If Devlin noticed the slight tremor in her voice, he didn't let on. He took the closest cup, ignoring the sugar bowl and the milk jug and sipped, looking at Jenny over the rim of the cup. Jenny took the seat opposite him.

'I don't suppose you'd like to explain why you've broken into my house.'

She shook her head. 'You know exactly why I'm here.'

She was expecting some sort of reaction to that. A shake of the head, or a wry smile, perhaps. Devlin's expression didn't change at all. He seemed to consider what she had said.

'Assume I know nothing,' he said. 'Enlighten me.'

'You had your daughter kidnapped,' Jenny said. 'This morning, your man killed my friend, and he tried to kill me too.'

307

'That's . . .' He paused, as though looking for the right word. 'That's quite a theory.'

'It isn't a theory. We know it all. Alice. Your daughter. You tried to get her through the courts, and when that didn't work, you got what you wanted by other means.'

'Other means?'

'You had the mother killed in a car accident and, when you found Emma Dawson, she was made to look like an overdose.'

He said nothing, just held her gaze. Waiting for her to speak again.

'Where is Alice?'

Devlin put his hands on the table in front of him and knitted his fingers together. She noticed he left a pause of several seconds before replying to anything she had said. His expression hadn't changed since she entered the room. His eyes hadn't wavered from hers. He would make a hell of a poker player, Jenny thought. Probably something innate, part of what made him so successful in business.

'You've wasted your time, I'm afraid.'

'I don't think so. I think you know exactly where she is.'

He cleared his throat. 'Can you explain to me why I shouldn't call the police and have you arrested? You come out here to my house, you insert yourself into my life with no reason. It could be construed as stalking. It's certainly trespassing.'

'You won't call the police.'

'Won't I?'

She shook her head. 'I can tell them what you've done. All of it.'

'What exactly have I done?'

'Kidnap. Murder. You had Hazel Parry and Emma Dawson killed. My husband, Eric Bowen, and Mike Fletcher as well.' Her voice trembled slightly when she said Mike's name. She cleared her throat and was pleased when the words came out clear and deliberate. 'Do you even know what your pet thug did this morning? He murdered a police officer. I'm betting they'll want to catch the person who did that.'

Devlin's lips widened a little, and it took Jenny a second to realise that it was a smile. The bastard was actually smiling.

'Let's speak plainly, shall we? I don't mind doing you the courtesy of being candid, since it's just the two of us. After you contacted my London office, I asked my employee to keep an eye on you because you were an unknown quantity. At first I thought you might be related somehow to Emma Dawson. That you were planning to blackmail me. My employee followed you onto the sleeper last night. He had an altercation with your travelling companion and, regrettably, was forced to defend himself.' He stopped to consider. 'I'm surprised to discover that he was a police officer. Was he aiding you in an official capacity?'

Jenny didn't answer. She had an idea Devlin knew the answer to that question.

'An unfortunate development, certainly, but hardly the fault of my man.'

'Bullshit. He broke into his room and murdered him in his bed, and he would have killed me too.'

'I can assure you that you are mistaken.'

'We'll see what the police think when I tell them.'

'You can tell them nothing. All you have is an outlandish story. At best, they'll assume you're delusional.'

'You seem very sure of that. You think the police will just leave an unsolved murder on the books? One of their own? He didn't make this one look like an accident.'

'I didn't say they'll ignore it. They'll look at the evidence. I know my employee will have been careful. Do you think there are other traces, left by another person, Ms Bowen? Who might that trail lead to, I wonder?'

Jenny couldn't stop her eyes wandering to her hands, resting on the table. The fingers that had left prints all over both rooms. The blood beneath her fingernails.

Devlin sat back in his chair like he was concluding a presentation to the board. When he spoke, his voice was utterly certain of his conclusion.

'You won't tell the police anything. It is simply not in your interests.'

Jenny felt a surge of anger. She had been prepared for anything but this dispassionate dismissal. She stood up and, before she knew what she was doing, swiped the full teacup from the table, spilling some of the hot tea on her hand. The cup smashed against the wall. Devlin didn't flinch, didn't look away from her. She registered the heat of the liquid where it had spilled on her hand, but on an almost abstract level. She knew it was painful, but she didn't really *feel* it.

'What have you done with her?' she yelled.

For the first time, Devlin dropped his gaze. He waited for another few seconds before he spoke. And just like on that first morning on the sleeper, Jenny heard the next words in her head a moment before they were spoken.

'Alice is dead,' he said quietly.

64

It took a moment for the words to hit home. 'What?' The word sounded dull and distant, like it was being spoken by someone else, in another room. It had all been for nothing.

'She died the night you saw her,' Devlin said. 'On the sleeper.'

Jenny shook her head. Not believing it. Or perhaps just not wanting to believe it.

'You're lying.'

'I only wish I were.'

'No. Someone took her. Your man, he killed Emma Dawson and he took Alice, he brought her here, didn't he?' Unbidden, a note of uncertainty crept into her voice.

Devlin shook his head. 'Dawson had kidnapped her. She wasn't taking her to safety, she was taking her to an individual who specialised in these types of activities. She was ransoming her. My employee was supposed to make the payment. Dawson didn't care about Alice, she only cared about getting enough money to keep filling her arm indefinitely.'

'You're lying.'

'How much do you know about Emma Dawson really? She was an addict. A criminal. Hazel had met her while volunteering for a charity. For whatever reason, she took her in, gave

311

her a chance. She helped with housework, childcare, I'm told. After Hazel's death in the accident, she took Alice and went into hiding. I think she believed Alice was her winning lottery ticket.'

Jenny was thinking about what Monica had said, back in the café. *She had her problems.*

'She was mentally ill,' Devlin continued. 'Who knows why she did what she did? At any rate, she boarded that train and at some point she decided to kill herself and Alice. She injected both herself and Alice with a lethal dose.'

Jenny felt lightheaded. Devlin leaned forward, it felt uncomfortably like he was a doctor, evaluating her.

'Are you all right? You look ill.'

'It isn't true, I don't believe you.'

'It is true. I understand how you're feeling. You thought you were helping, but I'm afraid it was too late before you ever got involved.'

'Why wasn't she found with Emma Dawson, in that case? Where did she ... where did her ...'

'My employee removed her from the train,' Devlin said. 'You were right about that much.' He stood up, abruptly. 'Come with me.'

Devlin led her out of the house via the winter garden at the rear of the building. There was a wide expanse of neat lawn, which gave way to a stretch of longer grass, like the fairway into the rough on a golf course. Beyond that was the lake, with the island in the middle, and beyond that was another stretch of woods. There was a wooden jetty extending thirty yards out over the water. Devlin stepped onto the boards and paused with his hand on the railing.

'Her grave is out there,' he said.

Jenny looked out at the island, a bump jutting out of the

centre of the lake like a pregnant belly. It was roughly the length of a football pitch, dotted with pine trees.

'The dinghy is in storage for the winter now, but if you'd like to swim ...'

Jenny looked back at him; wondering how he could be so flippant when discussing the final resting place of his only child. His face was as impassive as it had been back in the house. His eyes dry behind the lenses of his glasses.

'How could you be so ...?'

Devlin said nothing for a moment, and then looked down. 'I've accomplished a lot in my life. The one thing I had almost resigned myself to never accomplishing was having a family.'

Jenny watched him. So they had been right. No children from the first two marriages, and it wasn't a choice. Devlin was infertile. Or as close to as made no difference.

'Almost no problem in this world is insoluble,' he said, glancing back at Blacklaw House. 'Take this place. It was condemned. There was no hope. I spent twenty million on it, and voilà. Problem solved. Almost any problem can be fixed with money. Except one.

'I spent a lot of money on that problem too. A great deal more money, in fact. I went through a lot of specialists. Eventually, one of them was brave enough to tell me that there was nothing more they could do. Oh, of course I could have explored other options, but ... it wouldn't have been the same. I became resigned to it, in time. The desire didn't go away, but I came to terms with it. I occupied myself with dalliances. I didn't see the point in marriage after my second divorce. Hazel Parry was one of those dalliances. I had forgotten all about her, to tell the truth.

'And then, at the start of this year, one of my employees ran into her in London. Her and her daughter. She put two and two together, and ...'

313

He seemed to remember who he was speaking to, and stopped talking. To elaborate further, presumably, would be to test the plausibility of his claim that the trail of dead bodies was an unintended development.

'Anyway, for a few brief months, I was a father. And now, things are as they were.'

Jenny turned away from him, looked back across the grounds to the house. She had come all this way for nothing. And now there was only one question that needed an answer.

'What are you going to do with me?'

65

When Devlin didn't answer, Jenny looked back at him. He looked puzzled by her question.

'I don't follow.'

Jenny felt an incredulous smile break out on her face. 'What? You're going to let me just walk out of here?'

'Of course. Why would I have any say whatsoever in what you do?'

'But I'll just go to the police and tell them everything. About your man killing Mike, for starters.'

'No evidence, even if they believe you. And whom exactly are you going to accuse?'

Jenny opened her mouth to object and then realised he had a point. She didn't have a name. All she had was a description. She might be able to point him out from the CCTV footage on the platform at Pimlico yesterday, but if he wasn't on the police radar, that wouldn't do a whole lot of good. Even if she could persuade the police to come here, it would be too late. They would leave this place, and take care of the evidence. Was Alice's body really out there on the island? Was her grave marked?

'So, if I understand you correctly, you propose to go to the police, explain that you were travelling with the victim, claim you had nothing to do with his death, and point the finger of blame at an unidentified person no one saw get on the train.'

'The CCTV. I knew he had a way of gaming it. That's why there was no trace of Alice getting on the train.'

She wasn't looking directly at Devlin, and perhaps he thought she was too preoccupied, but his mask slipped just a little there. She saw the hint of a smile out of the corner of her eye.

'I told you all of this because I wanted you to understand, and perhaps because I thought you deserved an explanation after going to all this trouble. But it's all deniable. I've made sure of that. It's the first rule of business: if you have to break some rules, don't get caught.'

Jenny saw a movement beyond Devlin's shoulder now. A figure had appeared at the door of the house. With a shiver, she realised who it was. He was too far away to make out his features, but Jenny knew those emotionless grey eyes would be staring right at her.

She shifted her focus to the rhododendron bush where her backpack was. It was roughly equidistant between her and the house, on the eastern point of a triangle formed by their relative positions. It was impossible to see if the bag was still there. Had they found it since she was in the house? If she made a break for it now, could she reach it before he did?

'You're right,' Devlin said. 'I would prefer you didn't speak to the police about any of this.' He saw Jenny's gaze was elsewhere and looked round, seeing his employee. He held up a single gloved finger to tell him to wait a moment, and then looked back at Jenny. 'But that's the problem, it's going to be very difficult to avoid you speaking to them whether you want to or not, isn't it?'

Jenny felt her mouth go dry again. Should she make a break for it now? Hope that the element of surprise was on her side?

'You said they'd be looking for me anyway,' Jenny said. 'Don't you think they'll look here? When they find out what Mike was doing?'

'It's a possibility,' he agreed. 'As I said, a potential inconvenience for me. The consequences for you seem far graver. But perhaps we can come to a compromise.'

A compromise? What the hell could this mean? Much as she hated to admit it, Devlin was right. It was unlikely the police would buy her story without evidence, and even with evidence, he could afford the best lawyers in the world to throw the suspicion right back on her.

'As you guessed, my operative was able to make sure there was no footage from the platform that night. He has already done the same for last night's footage too. Less elegantly, perhaps. You and the officer boarded the train together, so there is no tidy image of Sergeant Fletcher boarding alone. Another software glitch has led to the footage being irretrievably lost. You are still on the booking system but as Mrs Thornhill, I believe.'

'Well done,' she said, not bothering to hide the heavy sarcasm.

'Unless there is anything else tying you to the train, the police have no way to prove you were Sergeant Fletcher's travelling companion.'

'My fingerprints are all over the rooms on the train.'

'Irrelevant, if they're not able to show good cause to take your fingerprints.'

Was he right? Couldn't they compel her to give samples or something like that? 'What are you suggesting?' she went on, playing for time but also interested. 'That I keep quiet and hope they go away?'

Devlin reached into his jacket and took out a business card. He held it out and Jenny reluctantly took it from him. The card was heavy stock, with an expensive grain. The letters were subtly raised above the card.

Wolfe, Hodge & Pryce

There was a phone number printed below the names, nothing else.

'I already have a lawyer,' she said, holding the card back out.

'Not like these ones, I assure you.'

Devlin made no move to accept the card. After a second, Jenny opened her fingers and let it fall to the ground.

'They'll contact you,' Devlin said airily. 'All you have to do is say you have no knowledge of where Mr Fletcher might have gone after you met him in London. The police will have one opportunity to ask you questions, with counsel present of course, and that will be it.'

'You expect me to go along with this?'

'I don't think you have much choice, other than spending a significant amount of time in jail, or ...' He tailed off, with the merest nod back at the man who waited at the side of the house like a hangman by the gallows.

'A regrettable few days for us both,' he said. 'You can't make this situation any better, you can't bring back the dead. All you can do is ensure your own freedom. With a small contribution in recognition of your inconvenience, of course.'

'Contribution?'

'Five hundred thousand pounds,' Devlin said with the casual air of someone estimating the bill at a restaurant. 'This is not a jumping-off point for negotiation, and it is not the first in a series of payments. It is a one-off. This is how much avoiding this inconvenience is worth to me.'

'Take it or leave it?' Jenny said, shaking her head at his audacity.

Devlin nodded.

This bastard was making this problem go away the same way he made every other problem go away, with money. Only, that wasn't quite true, was it? There were other ways of making a problem go away. The man from the sleeper waited, two hundred yards from them. Waiting for another signal from Devlin, no doubt. Between her and the gun.

An all-or-nothing gamble with no guarantee of success, or a deal with the devil. Not much of a choice. She thought about Alice. Not the picture Rinzler had showed her, or the mental picture sketched for her by Monica at the refuge, but the one time she had actually laid eyes on her, on the sleeper. Holding her grey rabbit and looking back at Jenny with her deep brown eyes, eyes so brown they were almost black.

Jenny took a deep breath and met Devlin's eyes again. She didn't really have a choice, did she? All of this had been for nothing.

'I'll take it.'

66

Devlin nodded approvingly and gave the tall man a wave.

Immediately, the man walked to the nearest door, opened it, and vanished inside the house. Jenny wondered what the signal would have been had she answered Devlin's question differently. Perhaps he would simply have walked away, leaving his employee to do his work.

'Come,' Devlin said, turning and walking across the grass back towards the house, without a backwards glance. The third time he had done that. A man so used to being obeyed that it wouldn't even occur to him to ask politely.

Another business transaction. Another potential threat bought off. Jenny wasn't thinking about the money. Would Devlin follow through on the offer? She had agreed to be bought only to buy herself time, because the only certainty was the consequence of her refusal.

She wasn't even convinced she had bought herself that. What if Devlin was just toying with her? What if he called her bluff, handed her over to his fixer? Try as she might to stop her mind going there, she counted off the ways this man had brought death to innocent people. A high-speed car crash, a heroin overdose, a hanging, a simple blade. How would he deal with her?

She thought about those large, leather-gloved hands. She thought about the facts of her situation: in the middle of nowhere, with no witnesses, at least none who would ever talk. She knew he would need nothing more than those hands.

She didn't buy Devlin's explanations for those deaths, which he had offered in the manner of someone who did not care if he was believed. People had got in his way, and they had been removed. An accident, an overdose and a self-defence killing. Plus Eric's apparent suicide, of course, even if that could be connected. One of these might be plausible. Four was not. So did that mean she didn't have to believe him about Alice, either? Nothing would make her happier than for that to be a lie.

But it was plausible. Emma Dawson had a history of problems. A shady past, a criminal record. She had sensed that Kate at the refuge had never quite trusted her. What if she really had done what Devlin accused her of?

Devlin stopped when he reached the path round the house and allowed her time to come abreast of him. He led her round to the front of the house.

Perhaps he was on the level then, about a deal for her silence, if not the rest of it. It felt like if he was going to have her killed, it would have been back there, by the lake. Why risk keeping her alive any longer?

Lucine Rinzler was waiting for them at the front of the house, standing beside one of the twin black Lexuses that were parked on the sweeping circle round the oak tree at the top of the gravel drive.

As they approached, Rinzler opened the rear door, never once taking her eyes from Jenny's face. Jenny glanced inside. The interior of the car was generously proportioned, the seats upholstered in beige leather.

Devlin stopped beside the open door.

'The money will be delivered to your address in Bridge of Dean. In cash. It should arrive before you do. My legal team will be there to arrange the interview as soon as the police make contact. As long as you keep to your side of the bargain and say only what you are instructed to say, this will all go away and your life will continue as normal.' A smile flickered across his lips. 'Well, perhaps a little more comfortably than before.'

'You seem very sure you'll be able to get me ... get *us* out of this,' Jenny said.

He nodded with approval at the use of the word 'us'. They were accomplices now. 'I'm certain I can. It wouldn't be the first time.'

He paused and his eyes took on a faraway look.

'I am very sorry it has come to this,' he said. 'I hoped things could be different. Not least for little Alice. But God has a plan for us all.' He raised his eyes to meet hers and held out his hand to shake. Jenny ignored it, fixing him with her hardest stare. After a moment he let the hand drop.

'Goodbye, Ms Bowen. Have a peaceful life.'

Jenny got into the car and sat back on the leather seat. Rinzler got in the driver's side and started the engine.

67

Klenmore watched as the brake lights of the Lexus flashed briefly as Rinzler slowed for the corner, and then it vanished out of sight along the winding road.

He turned to Devlin. 'You think she believed you? That you'd just let her walk out of here?'

Devlin shrugged. 'Who cares?'

He shot his cuffs and examined the face of his platinum Maîtres du Temps watch. 'Give her ten minutes, then take the other car to meet them. Tell Lucine I'll need a lift to the airfield this afternoon. I'm afraid she's quite the chauffeur today.'

Klenmore watched as his employer walked back towards the house. When he had gone four steps, he stopped and turned around again. 'Oh, and Klenmore, make sure the body is easily found.'

68

'You're very fortunate,' Rinzler said as she turned in the drive and circled the tree, heading for the main gate.

'You'll have to excuse me if it doesn't feel that way.'

'I'm taking you to your house in Bridge of Dean. Mr Devlin's legal team will meet us there, they'll be ready to make arrangements.'

Jenny looked back at the house, receding from view in the rear window. Devlin had already disappeared back inside the house.

She sighed. Maybe it was finally time to take the line of least resistance. All she had to do was sit back, shut up, and let the rich man's machine work. If Devlin was telling the truth, there had never been a chance for her to save Alice. Alice had been lost all along.

That was the most terrible thing, wasn't it? He hadn't been too bothered about convincing her the deaths of Hazel Parry, or Emma Dawson, or Eric, or even Mike were accidental, but when he had talked about Alice, she had thought he had really meant it. In any case, he couldn't have hidden Alice indefinitely. If she had still been alive, he would have had to hide her for ever after.

The car was circling round past the rhododendron bushes,

and she remembered what she had left there. Idly, Jenny wondered when her bag would be found. She wondered what she would have done even if she had had the gun back in the house. Shot Devlin or one of his men? Perhaps, if she had been cornered. Maybe it was for the best she hadn't had the option.

And then she was thinking about Devlin's words again. What if he hadn't sounded convincing because it was the truth, but because it was the one part of his story he needed to convince Jenny about? And then she was thinking about the Old Master hidden in the little room above the library, and about something else she had seen in the house as well.

'I'm going to be sick!' she yelled.

Rinzler slammed on the brakes and turned round. 'What?'

Jenny was tugging at the door, which was locked. She had expected that, which was why she had yelled out before trying it. She puffed her cheeks out, like she was barely containing the urge to vomit.

Rinzler let out a muttered curse and got out, opening Jenny's door from the outside.

'Keep it out of the car,' she warned, and Jenny knew that she had guessed right, the job of cleaning vomit off the upholstery would fall to Rinzler. It had got her to open the door. Jenny stepped out and turned her back to Rinzler, bending over and making a retching noise as her eyes scanned the bushes.

Where the hell was the bag? Had she got mixed up, picked the wrong stand of bushes? Had it been discovered?

She stumbled closer to the bushes, spitting and retching. There. She saw the blue canvas of one of the straps protruding. It was still there.

'Hey!' Rinzler said, and Jenny could tell she knew she was faking. 'That's enough, come here ...'

As Rinzler put a hand on her shoulder, Jenny ducked out of her grasp and ran for the bushes. She ignored Rinzler's calls as she dived for the strap and grabbed the bag. She yanked the zip open and fumbled inside as she heard the sound of Rinzler's footsteps closing in on her.

At the last second, her hand wrapped around the butt of the gun and her finger slipped through the trigger guard as she turned round.

Rinzler was almost upon her. She froze in place, an expression of disbelief on her face. Her lips formed into a circle, but no sound came out. Jenny guessed she was trying to pick a question from the many competing options.

In the end, she decided on one. The most important one. 'Is that real?'

Jenny nodded. 'And I won't fucking hesitate. Like your boss said, no one knows I'm here. I could turn you off like a switch and drive away.'

Could she? She wasn't altogether sure, but she was pleasantly surprised that her voice betrayed no equivocation.

It seemed good enough for Lucine Rinzler, who raised her hands slowly.

'What are you going to do?'

Jenny kept the gun trained in the middle of Rinzler's stomach, remembering Mike's direction, and put her left hand on the grass to steady herself before getting to her feet.

She jerked her head in the direction of the Lexus, which was idling twenty feet away, its engine purring expensively.

'Open the boot.'

69

Rainbow Cheerios. Rainbow Cheerios.

The two-word phrase repeated in Jenny's mind like a nursery rhyme as she ran through the woods, circling the grounds of the house back to the position opposite the cellar door. The rhythm matched her stride as she covered the ground, keeping her eyes on the house all the while.

How long did she have? She hoped long enough. She assumed Rinzler would be expected to check in when they reached their destination, but Bridge of Dean was at least two hours' drive from here. Rinzler's phone was in Jenny's hip pocket. No signal on her network either, which was another reason to be optimistic about her window of opportunity. Now, the only question was whether she could get back into the house and find Alice.

Thinking back to her conversation with Devlin, now she was free, she realised it had been a little like being hypnotised. He had persuaded her of what he was saying, that Emma Dawson had killed Alice that night on the sleeper. He had used the little shard of doubt she had been unconsciously ignoring for days. The fear that something exactly like this had happened. He had honed it, sharpened it into a weapon. She had been taken in. But even as she started to give up hope, she knew that something was not quite right.

Jenny reached the bushes across from the cellar door and hunched down, feeling the gun in her hands. She didn't think twice about her ability to use it. She didn't know if she would have been able to shoot Rinzler in cold blood, had she called her bluff and refused to get in the boot. It would be different if the man from the sleeper came at her.

It's funny how you can hear something without really hearing it, then see something without really seeing it, and only realise the significance later.

Rainbow Cheerios.

Monica at the refuge had said Alice had liked 'Rainbow Cheerios'. Just a throwaway comment as she talked about a little girl she had known briefly and liked. Jenny had barely registered the comment at the time, but now she realised she was talking about a breakfast cereal. Only there was no such cereal as Rainbow Cheerios. It must have been Alice's name for Lucky Charms. Same thing as Cheerios, essentially, but with lots of disgusting Day-Glo marshmallow pieces mixed in, like little rainbows.

Lucky Charms was an American cereal brand. You could get them over here, but it was unusual to see them outside of big supermarkets, in cities. She doubted you would be able to find them within a couple of hundred miles of Blacklaw House. Yet there had been an open box of Lucky Charms in the kitchen at Blacklaw, and the man in the shirt had been carrying a tray of crockery.

Alice was there, and she thought she knew exactly where.

She tensed as she heard footsteps on the gravel and kept her eyes in the direction of the sound. The tall man walked outside and stood beside the lone black Lexus, smoking a cigarette. Jenny kept her eyes on him, not daring to breathe, though he was at least a couple of hundred yards away. For a moment, he seemed to be looking right at her. She tightened her grip on the gun and held still.

And then he dropped the cigarette and ground it underfoot. He bent to pick up the end and opened the door of the Lexus.

Jenny took a deep breath and broke cover, running for the set of stairs at the side of the house, praying no one had worked out how she got in the first time. Her feet thudded on the firm grass. Rainbow Cheerios, Rainbow Cheerios.

She reached the door. She had made her mind up now, if they had locked it, she would just walk up to the front door and order them to take her to Alice. But it was still slightly open, the way she had left it.

She retraced her route up the stairs to the kitchen, moving quickly, more confidently this time. She opened the kitchen door a crack and listened. Hearing nothing, she opened it a couple more inches. The hallway was clear. She counted off the people she knew were still in the house. Rinzler was accounted for, and the tall man was outside, so that left the man in shirt sleeves and Devlin himself. She closed the kitchen door behind her and moved quickly to the big staircase, stepping lightly on the deep carpet.

70

A minute later, she was back in the long, dark corridor. This was where she had been discovered the first time. Again, with time to reflect, she had heard and seen things here that were important, too. The rattling noise just after the man spotted her. The sound of a tray of crockery being set down, perhaps? Breakfast, being brought to someone who could be reached by traversing this corridor. Jenny had gone down the stairs last time, which meant there was only one other option.

She reached the door at the far end and opened it onto the stone spiral staircase. It was cold in the stairwell, almost as cold here as it was outside.

She climbed upwards, circling round and round. The door on the second floor was wide open, the room empty, as though this part of the house was never used. She kept going, up to the top floor of the tower. Only now did the doubt begin to creep in again. What if she was wrong? What if she was simply backing herself into a dead end again?

There was another door at the top of the stairs, a full-length mirror hung on it. One last looking-glass. She took a deep breath and turned the handle.

As the door swung open and she felt a current of warm air

on her face, she knew that she had been right. She had been right all along.

But the tower attic room was empty. It smelled faintly of fresh paint and new wood. It had been redecorated recently. The walls were a very pale pink. There was a stained-glass window on the east wall, and a break in the clouds cast an elongated coloured rectangle of morning sunlight over the deep beige carpet.

Something made her grip the edge of the door as it swung closed behind her on a spring-loaded return. She was glad she had.

There was no handle on the inside of the door. Not even a keyhole.

Jenny realised with a shudder that if she had let it swing shut, she would have been locked in here. She glanced around for something to use as a doorstop, and saw a huge Hello Kitty bean bag on the floor. Keeping the door open with her heel, she grabbed it and jammed it in the gap, propping the door open. When she was confident it wouldn't close all the way, she turned and took in the rest of the room.

There was a television screen fixed to another wall, the screen dark but the little red light indicating it was on standby. There was some kind of elaborate wooden play set on the floor. A light-blue doll's house. It took Jenny a second to realise why it looked familiar. It was a scale model of Blacklaw House, but made over as a fairy-tale castle. Around the castle were laid out various dolls with flowing hair, and items of furniture, and a drawing pad with a tub of crayons. And something familiar.

A stuffed grey rabbit.

Jenny tucked the gun into the back of her waistband and crossed the room to the castle. She bent down on one knee and picked up the rabbit, turning it over as it sagged in her grasp. She saw the loose stitching on the side, just as she remembered from the sleeper.

331

A toilet flushing brought her back into the moment and she turned to see the door at the far side of the room open. An en suite bathroom for the occupant of the room. For the prisoner.

The door opened and the girl stood in the doorway.

She didn't gasp or scream, just looked at Jenny as though she was merely an interesting new development. She was exactly as Jenny remembered. Long brown hair running down her back, dark brown eyes that didn't waver from her own.

'Alice,' Jenny said.

71

'What are you doing with Bye Bunny?' Alice said, after coolly regarding her unexpected visitor for a moment.

'What?' Jenny asked, not understanding at first, then she looked down at the stuffed rabbit. 'Oh, I'm sorry.' She held the grey rabbit out towards Alice. 'He looked like he needed some company.'

Alice seemed to consider, and then stepped forward and took the rabbit from Jenny. She didn't clutch it to her chest, just examined it briefly to confirm the strange grown-up hadn't damaged it, and then dropped her hand to hold it loosely by her side.

'Who are you?'

Jenny didn't know how to answer that at first. She hadn't really considered what she would do if she got this far. She had been so focused on following the trail, proving herself right. But it was a good question. Who was she?

'My name is Jenny.' She smiled. 'We met each other really briefly before, on the train.'

'The night train,' Alice said, and her expression turned more solemn.

'That's right. Do you remember me?'

'You're the lady who found Bye Bunny.'

'That's right. Do you ... do you remember what happened?'

She immediately regretted asking the question. It was like turning on a tap. Tears streamed down Alice's cheeks and she brought Bye Bunny up to grip tight in both hands. Jenny didn't think about it. She rushed forward and took Alice in her arms, hugging her close.

'Oh honey, I'm sorry. It's all right.'

Alice's voice was flat. No sobbing, just silent tears. 'The man came in in the dark. He came through the secret door. Emma shouted at him, and then he made Emma go to sleep. I said I didn't want to go but ... but ...'

Jenny squeezed her tighter, patting her back. 'Don't think about that now, everything is going to be okay.'

Alice wriggled free and Jenny loosened her grip. The little girl took a step back and seemed to compose herself. She wiped the tears away with the back of her hand and spoke in halting words.

'John says I have to stay here. He says I can't leave for a while. But I don't want to stay here. I miss Emma.'

'You don't have to stay here. I'm here to take you h ...' She stopped herself before she said it, because this little girl didn't have a home, not any more. 'Take you away, if you want.'

Alice seemed to consider it, and then nodded.

Jenny's mind was working overtime. They could take the stone spiral staircase all the way to the bottom, try to find another way out. She could force the lock on the door at the back of the winter garden if necessary. From there? As long as she got to the car, they could dump Rinzler and get away.

'Do you have a coat? Something warm to wear?'

Alice nodded again. 'It's in the room beside the big hallway, we can get it on the way out.'

Jenny shook her head. 'I don't think we're going to go that way. I think ... John might be angry if he knew we were leaving.' She lowered her voice to a conspiratorial whisper. 'I'm not supposed to take you away yet.'

'Okay. Is it cold outside?'

'It is quite cold, yes. Do you have any other clothes?'

Alice directed her to the pink dresser. Jenny noticed there was a blue suitcase tucked neatly under it: the missing case from the sleeper. A minute later they had added a long-sleeved t-shirt with a unicorn design and a hooded green zip top to Alice's ensemble. It would have to do.

'We have to be very quiet,' Jenny said as she opened the door to the spiral staircase again, kicking the bean bag out of the way.

'John doesn't know you're taking me, does he?'

Jenny considered lying, but then shook her head. 'No, no he doesn't.'

'He isn't nice. He's trying to pretend to be.'

'That's right. You're a smart kid, Alice.'

'How do you know my name?'

'It took me a while to find out. But listen, we can talk about all this later. We need to go now.'

Alice said nothing, but reached her hand out. Jenny took it and they started down the spiral staircase.

'We're going to have to be really quiet while we find a way out.'

'We could go out into the playground, but the wall is quite high.'

'Playground?'

'Mr Colquin takes me out in the afternoons. There's not much to do out there. You go all the way down, through the corridor, and then the big door.'

'Can you show me?'

Alice considered for a long moment, then nodded.

72

Alice led the way through the maze of the house. They went all the way to the bottom and then along a corridor. There was a door which led out to a small courtyard with an eight-foot-high wall around it. It would be difficult but not impossible to scale.

Jenny looked around the space. It was a rectangle about thirty feet long by fifteen wide, bounded on one side by the house itself and on the other three by the walls. There was a locked iron gate in the centre of the wall, and she could see the gardens beyond. She tried tugging on the gate to see if there was any give in the lock, but there was none. Jenny felt rage swelling up inside her as she thought about what Devlin had done to take possession of his daughter. She was a prisoner in a locked room, complete with an hour in the exercise yard, if she was good.

She looked around for any furniture, boxes, anything to stand on, but there was nothing cluttering up the even flag-stones of the courtyard.

'Does Mr ...' She tried to remember. 'Collins?'

'Mr Colquin.'

'Colquin. Does he use the gate? Is there a key around here anywhere?' She glanced around again, hoping there would be a plant pot or an ornamental rock that might secrete a key, even though she had seen nothing on her first inspection.

'He has the key in his pocket. Sometimes I'm allowed to go out and look at the flowers.'

'Very generous,' Jenny muttered under her breath as she surveyed the wall again. It was sandstone with a curved top. At least there wasn't any barbed wire up there. Be thankful for small mercies.

Just as she was thinking through the logistics, she heard a sound that chilled her blood. The creak of the door on the second floor opening and then closing.

Someone was in the stairwell.

'Shit,' Jenny hissed, earning a reproving look from Alice. She looked up at the exterior of the tower and saw a figure pass by one of the windows on the way up to the attic room. They didn't have much time. Less than a minute before whoever was up there reached Alice's room.

'How are you at holding on tight to things? If I lift you up there, can you hold on to the top of the wall really tightly?'

Alice nodded.

Without further ado, Jenny picked her up around the waist and lifted her up. She was light. She braced Alice against the wall and waited until she had got a grip on the top edge.

'I'm going to push you up, and I want you to go over the top, and then hang on really tight, okay?' Jenny whispered. 'Don't let go, there's a bit of a drop.'

She got a hand underneath Alice's left foot and gently guided her up as Alice pulled herself up and over. A second later Jenny could see only her little hands gripping on.

'You okay?'

'Yes.' Calm and composed. Jenny wished she could feel that composed.

'Just give me a second and I'll—'

Just then, Jenny heard the inevitable sound of the door on

the top floor banging closed. She backed up against the wall as she heard the sounds of rushing footsteps on the stone stairs.

'Jenny?' Alice's voice sounded a little less sure of herself now.

'I'm just coming, sweetheart.'

Jenny took a run at the wall, jumped and just managed to grab the top. She kicked and scrabbled at the wall, pushing herself up, up.

The door to the stairwell opened and she heard a yell behind her. She didn't try to look round, just focused on hauling herself up and over. She felt a hand grab at her right leg as she pulled it up, the fingers wrapping around her ankle. But it was a loose grip, and Jenny had momentum on her side. She pushed down hard on her arms and went over the edge, glancing off Alice as she dropped. She felt a sharp pain as she landed on the gash in her foot. She looked up in time to see Alice fall backwards from her perch with a surprised squeal, and caught her.

'Get back here!'

Jenny looked up to see the man in the white shirt at the gate, one arm stretching through as though he could grab them and drag them through the bars. He pulled his arms back in and rattled the gate, as ineffectively as Jenny had done a couple of minutes before.

She glanced down at Alice to check she was okay and helped her to her feet. She took a step and winced at the pain in her foot. She ignored it and took Alice's hand and they started to move towards the trees. Behind her, she could hear the man shouting into his radio.

All thoughts of a quiet escape and then a straight run to freedom were gone. Their cover was blown.

73

Klenmore was considering how to handle the woman as he drove the black Lexus through the interior gates and turned right at the fork, driving on to the place he would be meeting Rinzler.

Killing her would not be difficult. Doing it without leaving a mark on her would be. He had underestimated her before. She was a fighter. The course of action he had recommended to Devlin was detailed and specific. The woman was to be found within easy distance of where she had fled the sleeper train. Unless she had got rid of her undergarments, Klenmore knew she would still be covered with the policeman's blood. In any case, traces would certainly remain.

She was to be found hanging from a tree. The police would have a dead victim and a dead suspect. No one else who could talk. He detected a certain reluctance in Devlin's voice as he agreed. He did not doubt that his employer would indeed have resolved this with a financial settlement, had it been viable to do so.

As he approached, Rinzler would open the door and tell Bowen to get out. He almost regretted that he wouldn't have another chance to pursue her. She had been a wily prey.

He rounded the corner before the clearing and knew

something was wrong when he saw Rinzler's car was nowhere in sight.

Just then, his radio crackled on the seat.

'Klenmore, are you there?'

He hit the button. 'I'm at the clearing, no sign of—'

'Get back to the house, now!'

74

'They're going to hurt you, aren't they?'

Jenny looked back at Alice as she spoke. They had reached the tree cover, Jenny practically dragging Alice behind her by her hand the whole way, and were running through the woods in what Jenny hoped was the general direction of the road where she had left the Lexus.

'Don't worry, we're going to get out of here.'

'They'll catch us,' Alice said. Her voice betrayed no emotion, she spoke matter-of-factly, as though from experience.

'Not if I have anything to do with it,' Jenny said through gritted teeth. She stopped to try and get her bearings. The main road ran due east from the house. The quickest route would have been straight out of the main gate, of course, but that wasn't an option. She had to hope they could circle round and come out roughly at the right spot on the road, before Devlin or his men managed to locate them.

Behind them she could hear male voices raised in anger from the direction of the house. How many of them were there? Had they worked out what had happened yet?

'Is there someone coming to get us?'

Jenny looked down into Alice's dark brown eyes. She shook

her head. 'No, no one's coming. We're just going to have to get out of here ourselves. Okay?'

Alice thought about it and seemed to accept the proposition.

They moved through the trees quickly. When they had gone a reasonable distance straight ahead, Jenny made a sharp turn to the left in what she hoped would be the direction of the main road. She shot frequent glances above, but between the overcast yellow sky and the thick pines, it was impossible to use the sun to orient herself now. Behind them, they could hear bushes crash and branches crack as men moved through the forest without trying to conceal their movements. Where the hell was the road? They should have reached it by now.

And then she saw it: the spire of the old priory. Which meant they were near the road. They covered the ground quickly, and soon the long black bonnet of the Lexus came into view, parked at the side of the road where she had left it. A relieved grin breaking out on her face, she gripped Alice's hand and took a step forward. And then froze.

She saw Rinzler first, facing in the opposite direction. She ducked back into cover, shooting a glance at Alice and putting a finger over her lips. Someone had freed her already. As she watched, she heard footsteps on the road and Rinzler turned. A second later, the one Alice had called Colquin appeared.

Damn it. They had worked out what had happened and cut off the escape route. She risked moving forward a little and peering through the leaves. Rinzler was massaging her left shoulder with her right hand, sore after being stuffed into the boot. Both of them were scanning the trees, looking for movement.

'We need to go back that way,' she whispered to Alice, keeping her voice so low that her lips barely moved. They moved back down the steep hill, taking care on the incline. Jenny kept glancing over her shoulder to reassure herself that no one was coming, looking back to check their footing.

Too late, she saw Alice put her left foot on a loose rock. She tightened her grip on her hand and pulled her back as the rock turned and Alice lost her balance. She stopped her from falling, but the rock tumbled free of its position and clattered down the slope noisily before crashing into the bushes at the bottom.

She heard the sounds of movement from behind them. They were coming. There was no way the two of them could outrun them this time.

Jenny saw the spire of the old priory up ahead and an idea occurred to her.

Maybe it was time to stop running.

75

Alice screwed her face up in discomfort as she wedged herself in the crevice, getting mud and moss all over her clothes, but she didn't complain. She crouched down in the space and pulled her arms and legs in, making herself as small as possible.

'Stay here, and keep really quiet until I come back for you,' Jenny whispered.

Alice nodded and Jenny took a step back, pleased that you couldn't see she was there even from a couple of paces away. It was a good hiding spot. She only hoped she would be able to fulfil the promise she had just made.

She moved to the edge of the big glassless window of the ruined priory, keeping her eyes on the overgrown path through the woods below. They would have to be coming this way. She could still hear their movements. They would check the ruins. She took a deep breath, wondering exactly how she should act if she managed to get the drop on them. Make them walk back to the house? How would she know they had really gone? What if they called her bluff?

There was a louder rustle, close this time, and she saw the branches of the bushes move. Colquin emerged onto the path. Jenny cursed under her breath. He was carrying a shotgun at waist height. A bloody country estate, of course they had guns. But where were the other two?

When she heard the whisper of movement from behind her, it was too late.

Gloved hands clamped over her own, squeezing, wresting the gun up and away from her. As the gun slipped loose from her hands, he ripped it away from her body with his left hand while pushing hard on her chest with his right. She fell down heavily on her backside and started to scramble to her feet, stopping when he pointed the gun square at her chest.

Without taking his eyes off her, without moving the muzzle of the gun an inch, he yelled out, 'Up here! I've got her.'

76

'You didn't trust me, I see,' Devlin remarked, looking down at Jenny where she still sat in the dirt. After disarming her, the man from the sleeper had dragged her out of the ruins of the priory, and marched her a hundred yards away to a clearing where they were gathered now.

'Thank you, Mr Klenmore,' Devlin said, addressing the tall man. She had a name for her nightmare at last. Devlin turned back to her. 'I can't say I blame you. Tell me where Alice is now and save me some time.'

'Why would I want to save you anything?'

'Because if you don't, I'll simply kill you and wait for her to get cold and hungry enough to show herself.'

Jenny had no answer to that. She looked up at the three men. The tall man – Klenmore – was cradling his shotgun like a pro. Devlin held his a little less confidently, like he was accustomed to going after clay pigeons or grouse, but a human target was a new experience. Colquin looked even less comfortable. He was sweating fiercely, and blinking so often that Jenny worried he would discharge his gun by mistake.

Jenny looked over at Klenmore. 'You mean you'll get him to do it. You don't like getting your hands dirty.'

Devlin didn't rise to the bait, he simply nodded, conceding the point.

'How many?' she asked.

He looked puzzled by the question. 'How many what?'

'How many people have you had killed? How many people have you had Klenmore here, or people like him, get out of the way quietly, so you could get what you want?'

Devlin smiled. 'Probably fewer than you would assume. Money is a far more agreeable way of solving problems than bloodshed. It's a shame you didn't agree.'

'You were always going to kill me, no matter what.'

He held her unblinking stare for a while. 'Yes. But it can be quick. Or ...' His eyes moved away from her and towards Klenmore. 'He has other skills, too.'

Klenmore's eyes seemed to shine slightly at the suggestion in Devlin's words. Jenny felt a knot of equal parts fear and repulsion in her stomach.

'I would still prefer that this could be handled as painlessly as possible,' Devlin said, giving Klenmore a wary glance. Jenny thought she caught a note of distaste in Devlin's voice. He knelt down in front of her. 'I won't harm her. You know she'll be safe here with me.'

'Safe as what? As a prisoner?'

'Not forever. When the time is right we will go elsewhere. Somewhere warmer. Until then, she will have everything she needs. From her sole blood relative.'

'You made sure of that, didn't you?'

'You don't have children, do you, Ms Bowen?'

She didn't indulge him by responding.

'Then you couldn't possibly understand.' He looked in the direction of Blacklaw House. 'This is one of my favourite houses. Robert McAlpine built it in the 1820s, as a wedding present for his daughter. It's important to keep your children close.' He looked back at her and shook his head. 'I didn't believe in miracles, but she is a miracle. A million to one chance. And that's worth killing for, don't you think?'

Jenny was thinking about the magazine article. Devlin flattering himself, talking about leaving legacies for future generations. Alice was his legacy; a miracle child for a man who had thought he could never have children. Hazel Parry wouldn't give him what he wanted, so he took it. Perhaps, in the end, Alice was just one more possession, like the priceless paintings he kept locked away from the world.

He leaned in closer, lowering his voice as though he didn't want his henchman to overhear. 'Please. It doesn't have to be painful.'

Jenny closed her eyes took a deep breath. 'All right. I'll tell you where she is if you answer one question.'

Devlin motioned for her to continue.

'How did you do it? Get Alice on the train without it showing on the cameras?'

'You could say it was overcautious, since we didn't think anyone would see or remember Alice, but Mr Klenmore likes to be very careful indeed. It's one of the reasons I've kept him on my personal staff so long.'

'So what, did you doctor the footage somehow?'

Devlin shook his head. 'Nothing so technical. The contract for the camera operator team is run by one of my subsidiaries. One of my employees was in contact with Emma Dawson.'

'Kelly.'

He looked surprised, almost pleasantly surprised. 'Indeed. We gained her trust and told her that it would be better if Alice wasn't seen getting on the train. She was instructed to take Alice aboard while the staff were in another carriage, and then go back and check in as a single passenger. That meant there was footage of her boarding the train alone. Alice's boarding was timed to coincide with the cameras going offline. It worked perfectly.'

'Jesus. She helped cover up her own murder.'

'I suppose you could say so. Only she couldn't even do that right. Because she let someone see Alice, didn't she? And that's how you came to find yourself in this situation. Unfortunate for all of us.'

Jenny thought back to the look on Emma Dawson's face that night. She had put it down to ordinary travel stress, but she knew now it was something else. Fear that she had screwed up, jeopardised herself and Alice. She couldn't know that she had already walked into the lion's den.

'Now,' Devlin said, straightening up again. Jenny noticed his right hand was shaking slightly on the gun. 'Tell me where she is.'

Jenny waited a long time before answering. 'All right.'

77

Jenny lowered her eyes, as though giving up all resistance. She pointed in the direction of the old priory. 'She's back that way. You can get up into the tower, if you're careful. It's quite high up.'

Devlin looked down at her for a long moment. She didn't blink.

'Shall I . . .?' Colquin began.

'No,' Devlin said, an irritated expression on his face. He considered. 'Go and get her,' he said to Klenmore finally. 'And be very careful. Don't scare her.'

Jenny felt a strange compulsion to laugh at that. Instead she kept her eyes down, listening as Klenmore's footsteps fell away.

'She's better off,' Devlin said. 'I can give her everything. A life you couldn't dream of. And one day, she'll inherit all of this.'

Jenny let him talk. She was counting the seconds in her head, waiting for the optimum moment. The moment when Klenmore had got as far away as possible, and just before he discovered she had lied.

A gamble. Devlin might have sent Colquin, or gone himself, leaving the exponentially more deadly Mr Klenmore guarding her. She wouldn't have fancied her chances; he wouldn't need a gun to kill her. But an old man with shaky hands? Maybe the odds still weren't great, but she liked them a whole lot better.

She shifted position so that her right side was hidden, and started working something out of her pocket. Colquin had wandered a little along the path Klenmore had taken, peering into the woods with interest.

Devlin took a step forward, perhaps wondering why she wasn't looking at him, or responding. She felt the firm metal of Eric's stainless steel pen slip into her palm and gripped it tightly. She glanced at Colquin who had turned to move closer towards the priory, in the direction Klenmore had gone. He was fifteen yards away now. It was now or never.

'It won't be painful, I promise,' Devlin said.

'Wish I could say the same,' Jenny said, and jammed the pen into the side of Devlin's thigh, just above the knee. He screamed out and she was already moving, grabbing the shotgun and twisting it. The gun went off with a deafening bang and a jolt that travelled all the way from Jenny's hands and up her arms.

The sounds around them disappeared to be replaced with a dull ringing as she grappled with Devlin, their gritted teeth inches apart. The old man was stronger than he looked, he was holding on. She was conscious that Klenmore would be running back to them; equally conscious that she wouldn't hear his footsteps. She had to get that gun away from him.

She adjusted her grip and swung her knee up into his crotch, finally managing to wrest the gun from him before staggering backwards. For a moment the two of them froze in position, and then Devlin, his face red and his eyes blazing, launched himself at her.

It was difficult to parse what happened next. In the moment, it was like some kind of choreographed magic trick.

Instinctively, she flinched backwards as Devlin lunged forward. In the same instant, something strange happened to his arm. One second it was stretched out towards her, the next it seemed to disappear.

She felt something wet spatter her face, then saw Devlin pitch forward, blood spurting from where his forearm had been, as the dull sound of another gunshot penetrated the ringing from the previous one.

Her head snapped round to see Colquin standing with his mouth agape, his gun still raised. Without thinking about it, she knew what had happened. He had arrived to see her grappling with Devlin, and her fall back with the gun, giving him a clean shot and a strong incentive to take it. But then his boss had got in the way.

A second later, Klenmore appeared as well, momentarily frozen as he processed what had happened. He quickly snapped out of the daze and brought his shotgun to bear on her, just as she fell backwards behind a thick tree. Another blast spattered the moist bark on the trunk, but missed her.

'Help me!'

Devlin was on the ground, clutching his ruined arm into his chest as blood pulsed out. Colquin had dropped his own gun and was standing with his palms outstretched in some sort of bizarre pantomime of an apology.

She took the chance and ran for it, weaving between the trees. She knew Klenmore would have to choose: run her down, or try to stop his employer bleeding out in the dirt. When she made it ten paces without being shot, she knew Klenmore had made his choice.

78

Klenmore cast a final glance in the direction the woman had fled and dropped the gun, unbuckling his belt and whipping it loose from the loops. Without conscious thought, he began to count the seconds in his head.

Colquin was stammering. 'She got in the way ... I didn't mean ... I didn't mean ...'

'Shut up,' Klenmore barked, not looking up at the idiot.

Devlin was lying on his side, his good arm clutching the shot arm beneath him. Klenmore knew from once glance it was hopeless, but he did what he could anyway.

The woman had a ten second start now. The old man's face was white as a blank page, his eyes straining to focus. Blood-flecked spittle at the corners of his mouth. He tried to resist Klenmore's movements as he prised his hands away from his arm. Blood spouted from the stump. Klenmore wrapped the belt around it and cinched it tight, cutting off the flow.

Twenty seconds.

He started to move Devlin onto his side, in a position that would keep weight on the wound.

Thirty-five.

'Breathe shallow,' he said. 'Help's coming.'

As he said the words, he knew it was useless. Devlin's eyes

were wide open, but unresponsive. He bent and listened at his mouth. Removed his glove and felt for a pulse.

Fifty seconds. He forced himself to focus. He had to be sure.

'Is he ...?'

He ignored Colquin.

Nothing.

Nothing to do now but take care of the woman.

Klenmore stood up and raised his shotgun. Colquin had time to get out the start of the word 'No,' before he pulled the trigger and blew a hole in his chest. He turned and ran in the direction Bowen had gone.

She had a sixty second head start. It wouldn't be enough.

79

Jenny ran between the trees, her pulse thudding in her temples and her lungs burning as she pushed herself to go faster, to run for her life. She flinched at the sound of another gunshot, taking a small measure of relief that this one came from a distance.

She reached the old priory and made straight for the hole in the ground she had almost fallen into earlier. Her breath caught in her throat.

Alice wasn't there.

She got down on her knees and stuck her arms into the hole, reaching blindly. She called Alice's name. She heard a muffled gasp and whirled round. Alice was there, a hand held to her mouth. 'You're hurt.'

Jenny looked down at herself and saw she was covered in Devlin's blood. She touched a hand to her face and felt it smear under her fingers.

'It's okay, it's not my blood.' She wiped her hand on her jeans and held it out. 'We have to go.'

They circled back round and this time approached the Lexus from the opposite side. Lucine Rinzler was standing by the door staring into the woods with a concerned look on her face. She had to have heard the shots. Jenny didn't waste any time on threats this time. She crept as close as she could and then rushed her, swinging a tree branch for Rinzler's head as she turned round. The woman went down like a felled tree.

Jenny looked in the driver's side of the rear Lexus to see if there were keys in the ignition, thinking it would be a good idea to toss them, but no such luck. Instead she dug the keys for the front car out of her pocket and pushed Alice into the passenger side, before rushing round to her side. Rinzler was holding her head and moaning. Still conscious, but she didn't look like she'd be getting up anytime soon.

As Jenny opened the door, she heard the sound of a large body crashing through the undergrowth.

Shit. Either Klenmore had got the bleeding under control, or Devlin was dead. Either way, he was coming.

She got behind the wheel and twisted the key in the ignition, starting the engine. No time to strap Alice in.

'Keep your head down,' she said, trying to keep the panic out of her voice as she hit the accelerator and pulled out onto the road.

The rear passenger window exploded in a snow storm of shattered safety glass a split second later. She heard Alice scream and ducked her head, gripping the wheel and pushing the pedal to the floor as the road straightened out.

She risked a glance over at Alice, who was still crouching in the seat. She looked terrified, but otherwise unharmed.

'Do you think you can pull the seatbelt on?' she asked, shifting her eyes to the road, then to the rear-view, then back to the road.

In the corner of her eye she saw Alice reach up for the belt.

In the mirror, she saw the other Lexus appear. Klenmore had made up the ground faster than she expected, and he knew the road.

He had to catch them now. If he let them get to safety, there would be no covering this up.

356

And there was something else, Jenny realised as she heard the click of Alice's seatbelt sliding home. Until this moment she had had one advantage that had allowed her to survive by the skin of her teeth. But if John Devlin was dead, Klenmore would no longer have an interest in making sure no harm came to Alice.

80

Jenny kept the car on the winding road with an effort. She had hoped to put more distance between them and Klenmore before he had been able to start after her, but it was no good.

The black twin of her own car was gaining in the mirror. At least Klenmore couldn't shoot and drive at the same time, but that would be academic if he could catch up and force their car off the road. And he would. It was only a matter of time. He knew the road well. Jenny was driving much faster than she felt comfortable with, sometimes taking blind corners so wide that she would have no chance if something was coming the other way.

She slowed for a tight corner and Klenmore's car closed the last few yards, shunting into the back of her. She felt the wheel jerk in her hands but kept the car on the road with an effort, using the shunt to keep her moving ahead.

It was short-lived. Klenmore was bearing down on her again, so close she could see his blank eyes staring straight at her in the mirror. This time he yanked the wheel to the right and came up on her flank. She looked over and saw him staring back at her. If the way he was driving hadn't convinced her, the look in his eyes did. He wasn't looking to bargain or negotiate, he was trying to destroy them.

Alice wasn't speaking, just staring past Jenny at Klenmore in the other car. She felt Alice's hand on her leg and wanted to reach down and comfort her. She forced herself to keep both hands on the wheel.

Klenmore slammed his car into her once, twice. With an effort, she managed to keep the car on the road. His car started to pull ahead and she knew it was over. The other Lexus cut across her and she was forced to steer into the side of the road. The ground dropped away on the passenger side and she felt the car start to tip over. The car rolled and the world outside the windscreen flipped upside down.

With a shattering crash, the car came to rest on its roof.

Jenny felt stabbing pain in her right arm. Probably broken. She looked up to see Alice, suspended upside down by her seatbelt. She was uninjured, just crying as she looked down at Jenny, her brown eyes wide open.

Jenny angled round so she could look back at the road, crying out as the movement put pressure on the broken arm. She could see the road out of the shattered driver's window. She could see the other Lexus had stopped and was reversing back.

She closed her eyes. 'I'm sorry, Alice.'

The Lexus stopped parallel with their upturned car. The engine still running. She heard the door open and Klenmore's boots step one after another onto the road.

This was it. End of the road.

81

She knew it was useless, but she had to try.

Jenny reached up with her left hand and pushed the button to release Alice's belt. She slipped down and Jenny hugged her as she watched Klenmore's boots start down the grass verge.

'Can you get out?' she asked, gripping Alice tight with her left arm, not caring about the pain in her right.

Alice shook her head. Not in answer to the question, just telling her she didn't want to leave her. The passenger-side window was smashed, but there were frosted fragments sticking out from the window edges. Jenny let Alice go and opened the glove box. She found the leather-bound owner's manual and used it to clear the glass from the edges.

'Go. Run.'

Alice hesitated, but did as she was told, pulling away. Jenny turned to look the other way. Watching Klenmore's boots approaching. He took his time. He had all the time in the world.

But then the boots stopped mid-stride. He turned, looking back towards the road. Like he had heard something. And then he was moving, running back towards the car.

She heard the engine of the other Lexus growl to life and it took off, wheels spinning. And then they were left alone in the upturned car, with only the sound of the wind to keep them company.

'Is he gone?' Alice whispered. She had stopped halfway out of the window.

'Keep going.'

Alice crawled the rest of the way out.

And then the sound of an engine, getting closer.

'Hurry,' she said. 'When you get out, don't wait for me, just run for those trees and hide. Just like you did before, okay?'

'You're coming next?' Alice asked.

'That's right, but just wait for me, don't come out.'

Alice crawled out and, good as her word, ran for the trees without looking back.

Jenny shifted forward, unable to stifle a cry as the pain in her arm sang out. The car was getting closer. She had got halfway through the window when the car pulled to a stop. She wasn't going to make it. She kept pulling herself forward with her left hand, gritting her teeth against the pain and waiting for the sound of the door opening and closing and Klenmore's boots on the road surface.

But instead, she heard something else. Shouts. More than one voice. Male and female. Someone was telling her to stay where she was. She ignored it, pulling herself forward, almost clear of the window now.

And then felt a hand on her shoulder and someone knelt down next to her. She raised her head and saw a female police officer, her blue eyes narrowed in concern.

A soft voice. 'Are you all right, ma'am?'

Jenny wanted to laugh at the form of address. From condemned prisoner to royalty. 'Ma'am like jam,' she said to herself. The words made her rescuer look even more worried.

'Are you hurt?' The police woman was examining her eyes, looking for signs of head trauma.

Jenny ignored the question and pointed over in the direction of the woods. 'Over there,' she said. 'Alice! Alice, you can come out. It's okay, it's the police.'

'Try not to move,' the officer said. 'Help's on the way, you're going to be fine.'

Jenny considered that and realised it might not be true. None of them might be fine, if Klenmore was coming back. 'The man in the other car ...'

'He did this? Don't worry, we'll catch him.'

The police officer looked up and her expression changed from concern to a curious smile. Her voice switched up in tone. 'Who's this?'

Jenny saw Alice's red shoes approach and raised her head to see her. Alice sat down on the ground, cross-legged beside Jenny and took her hand. 'My name is Alice,' she answered. 'I was trapped in the tower, but Jenny saved me.'

The officer looked back at Alice, then down at Jenny, puzzled.

'Actually,' Jenny said. 'It was a team effort.'

Three Weeks Later

82

A heavy snow had fallen in the night, dropping six inches on Bridge of Dean. The garden was a perfect blanket of white, the pine trees at the bottom frosted with snow as though they had been dusted with icing sugar.

Jenny stood at the kitchen window of her mother and father's house, sipping a mug of coffee and feeling cosy in her dressing gown. She had got quite accustomed to the sling and plaster cast on her right arm now, and to doing everything with her left.

The work on the house was almost complete now. It would be going on the market in the New Year, in time for the fresh batch of divorces and resolutions. The walls were all freshly painted, new carpets laid. The garden had been tamed, not that you could see it at the moment. The house was a blank slate, waiting for a new life to begin.

Things had moved quickly after she had been moved to the hospital at Fort William. She and Alice had been kept in overnight as a precaution, even though none of their physical injuries were serious. The police had interviewed her in the ward. She had told them everything. The trip to London, putting together the fact that there really was a missing girl, and who she was related to. What had happened to Mike on the sleeper.

The police had found Mike's notes about Blacklaw House on his body and had been coming to question the owner when they saw the black Lexus being driven in the opposite direction at speed. They blocked the road and Klenmore had fled the scene into the woods, incapacitating two of his pursuers before being cornered and restrained. He had denied everything, but the police expected Jenny's testimony would be enough to put him away for good. Even if they didn't manage to tie him to the murder of Emma Dawson or Eric, he had killed a police officer, and that was more than enough. Needless to say, the Emma Dawson investigation was being reopened in light of developments. An internal investigation was taking place into why the case had been closed so quickly even when Jenny had raised questions. Porter would be lucky to get out of it with his pension.

John Devlin himself had escaped justice, although Jenny didn't think it would have come as much of a comfort to him. The police found him along with Rinzler. Dazed, she had wandered into the woods after Klenmore left her at the side of the road and found her boss already dead, Colquin just as dead a few feet away. Klenmore had applied a tourniquet with his belt, but the wound was too grievous for a man of Devlin's years. He had bled out in the woods.

Rinzler had agreed to cooperate, and in exchange for a reduced sentence, she would testify about everything she knew about Devlin and the plot to kidnap Alice. Between her and Jenny, Klenmore wouldn't see daylight for a long time.

After they had been discharged from the hospital, both she and Alice had spoken to counsellors from the family unit. The experts said Alice was coping remarkably well, but then children often did at that age. She suffered from bad dreams, but they expected that would fade in time. Jenny wondered if her own bad dreams would fade as quickly. Every night she had the same nightmare. That she was lying on the bottom bunk of the sleeper, knowing what was above her. As the train rocked on the tracks, she saw blood seep down from the bunk above her, and then the adjoining door started to open. That was when she always managed to wake herself up.

The funerals had been hard. The arrangements had been awkward at Eric's, but the well-attended service at the crematorium had passed without incident, and she opted out of the gathering afterwards. Mike's, a few days later, had been tougher. This one was a burial, in a small graveyard near where he lived. A smaller crowd, fewer people left behind. She had come back in the evening when the grave had been filled in. She left lilies, no card, tied with a blue ribbon.

The final funeral of a year that had seen too many. The week since then had been spent in contemplation of everything she had lost. She realised that when the house sold, she would be bidding farewell to the last vestige of her old life.

Her phone buzzed on the counter with a message from Meryl.

30 mins, you ready?

She finished her coffee and got dressed.

It was more like three quarters of an hour by the time Meryl pulled up outside in her Land Rover Discovery. Jenny locked the door and pulled her suitcase down the path through the snow. She would take the rest of her things when she came back with a van in a couple of weeks.

Meryl helped her put the case into the boot and Jenny got into the passenger side as Meryl got back behind the wheel.

'We'll make good time once we get south of Perth, they've barely had any of the snow in the central belt.'

'Will there be cassowaries at the zoo?'

Jenny looked behind her to the back seat, from where the bright voice had come.

Alice was strapped in on her booster seat. She wore jeans

and mini Doc Martens and a red velvet coat with a matching bobble hat. Bye Bunny sat propped up on the seat beside her, the rip in the seam now repaired.

'What's a cassowary?' Jenny said.

'It's like an ostrich, but sometimes they attack people. I like cassowaries.'

Jenny exchanged an amused glance with Meryl. 'We'll have to wait and see. I'm sure there will be ostriches, if not.'

Caroline, the lady from the fostering agency beside her, was the other occupant of the back seat. She wore her usual placid expression. They were still in the early stages, and Alice's visits were supervised. But Caroline had confided in Jenny that she didn't think there would be a problem once the induction period was complete. Aside from being single, Jenny ticked all of the boxes in terms of income, stability and so on. The only concern was the recent traumatic experience she had undergone, but because Alice had been involved in that too, it played to their advantage.

Alice considered what Jenny had said for a moment, the way she always did, and then she nodded. 'Good.'

Meryl started the engine and they pulled out onto the road.

'Roads are a bit of a nightmare,' she said as they turned onto the main road out of town, 'but don't worry, we'll get there.'

Jenny looked up at the rear-view mirror, where she could see Alice reflected. Both of them had lost so much. But they had gained something, too.

'We'll get there,' she agreed.

She smiled, and Alice smiled back at her.

Acknowledgements

The biggest thanks are due to Laura, Ava, Scarlett and the boy with two names for putting up with me while I make stuff up for a living and go gallivanting off to far-flung events.

Thanks as always to Luigi and Alison Bonomi for their unwavering support and brilliant feedback, which was particularly appreciated on this new direction. Thanks to Francesca Pathak for her usual amazing job of editing and making annoyingly good suggestions I hadn't thought of. Thanks also to Bethan Jones, Lauren Woosey, Emad Akhtar and everyone at Orion for the great job they've done and continue to do on my books.

I ended up doing more research than normal for this one, but knowledgeable people will have guessed that I tend not to let the facts get in the way of a good story. For anything that I got right, you can thank the following people: Kim, Derek, Tom and everyone at Caledonian Sleeper for giving me a tour of the train, answering all of my questions, and not minding when I changed stuff to make the story work. Thanks again to my military expert, Craig Williamson. Thanks also to Naomi at UK Missing Persons, and to the First Contact team at British Transport Police.

Writing would be a lonely profession without my friends in

the book community, so a big shout out to all of the authors, readers, bloggers, publishers, booksellers, librarians, festival organisers and volunteers who make the crime fiction scene such a groovy place to be.

And as always, thank you for reading. Without people who read, buy, sell, loan, review and talk about books, there wouldn't be much point in us writing them. Thanks for keeping us in business.

Enjoyed *What She Saw Last Night*?

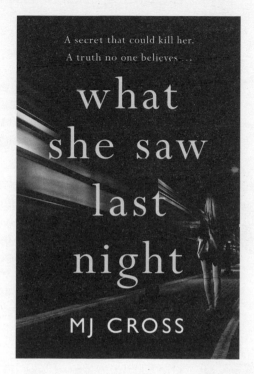

Keep up to date with all M.J. Cross's latest news at

Twitter: @MasonCrossBooks

Facebook: facebook/MrMasonCross

Find your next read from M.J. Cross . . .

THE CARTER BLAKE SERIES

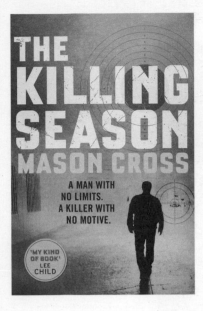

The Killing Season – Case One

A man with no limits.
A killer with no motive.

When Caleb Wardell, the infamous 'Chicago Sniper', escapes from death row two weeks before his execution, the FBI calls on the services of Carter Blake, whose skills lie in finding those who don't want to be found.

Blake must track Wardell down as he cuts a swathe across America, apparently killing at random. But as he desperately tries to second guess a man who kills purely for the thrill of it, he uncovers a hornets nest of lies and corruption. Now Blake must break the rules and go head to head with the FBI if he is to stop Wardell and expose a deadly conspiracy that will rock the country.

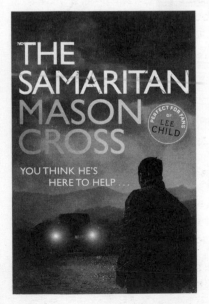

The Samaritan – Case Two

You think he's here to help . . .

When the mutilated body of a young woman is discovered, LAPD Detective Jessica Allen knows she's seen this MO before.

A sadistic serial killer has been operating undetected for a decade, preying on lone female drivers who have broken down. The press dub the killer 'the Samaritan', but with no leads, the police investigation quickly grinds to a halt.

When Carter Blake shows up to volunteer his services - sharing some uncomfortable similarities to the man Allen and her team are tracking – he must find a way to stop the killer . . . even if it means bringing his own past crashing down on top of him.

The Time to Kill – Case Three

**They taught him to kill.
Now they want him dead.**

It's been five years since Carter Blake parted ways with top-secret government operation Winterlong. They brokered a deal at the time: he'd keep quiet about what they were doing, and in return he'd be left alone.

But news that one of Blake's old allies, a man who agreed the same deal, is dead means only one thing – something has changed and Winterlong is coming for him . . .

It's time for Carter Blake to up his game.

Don't Look For Me – Case Four

But Carter Blake never did follow the rules . . .

It was a simple instruction. And for six long years Carter Blake kept his word and didn't search for the woman he once loved. But now someone else is looking for her.

Trenton Gage is a hitman with a talent for finding people – dead or alive. His next job is to track down a woman who's on the run, who is harbouring a secret many will kill for.

Both men are hunting the same person. The question is, who will find her first?

Presumed Dead – Case Five

So why are they convinced she's still alive?

Fifteen years ago, an unidentified killer terrorised northern Georgia, killing hikers in the vicinity of Blood Mountain. The killer was never brought to justice.

Returning home after a long time away, Carter Blake is reminded of a girl from school who vanished without a trace. The girl's mother mentions a case in Georgia, where someone is convinced their relative is still alive, fifteen years on.

Adeline Connor was the Blood Mountain Killer's last suspected victim. She vanished without a trace. So why is her brother so convinced she's still alive?